"I sense there are some hard feelings between us…"

"I mean, I don't remember it, but you seem… uncomfortable with me."

"It's fine," Angelina said.

"What did I do?" Ben asked. "Because I'm looking at you and I see a beautiful, successful woman I'd be proud to be with. So…what happened with us?"

Her green gaze flicked over to meet his. "Your family happened."

What had his father said? *And perhaps expect some jealousy toward our family.*

"What did they do?" he asked.

"They hated me." She said it so matter-of-factly, with no emotion behind it.

"I find that hard to believe…" He smiled. "For what?"

"For being beneath the quality standard they set for you," she said. "They wanted you to marry someone who came from a family equally well situated. I'm just a regular woman."

"Not so regular…"

She'd achieved an awful lot, and she drew every eye in a room…

Dear Reader,

This miniseries has been such a joy to write, and getting to Angelina's happily-ever-after is a really special feeling for me. If you haven't read the other three books in this miniseries, I hope you'll pick them up and join the other women in this dinner club as they find love again.

If you'd like to connect with me, come by my website at patriciajohnsromance.com. You can also find me on Twitter, BookBub and Facebook, where I hold continual giveaways with other fantastic authors you'll want to discover. Definitely come by and join the fun. I love to hear from my readers!

Patricia Johns

HEARTWARMING

Snowbound with Her Mountain Cowboy

———

Patricia Johns

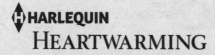

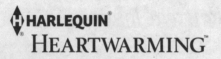

HARLEQUIN®
HEARTWARMING™

ISBN-13: 978-1-335-42650-5

Recycling programs for this product may not exist in your area.

Snowbound with Her Mountain Cowboy

Harlequin Enterprises ULC
22 Adelaide St. West, 40th Floor
Toronto, Ontario M5H 4E3, Canada
www.Harlequin.com

Printed in U.S.A.

Patricia Johns is a *Publishers Weekly* bestselling author who writes from Alberta, Canada. She has her Hon. BA in English literature and currently writes for Harlequin's Love Inspired and Heartwarming lines. She also writes Amish romance for Kensington Books. You can find her at patriciajohnsromance.com.

Books by Patricia Johns

Harlequin Heartwarming

The Second Chance Club

Their Mountain Reunion
Mountain Mistletoe Christmas
Rocky Mountain Baby
Snowbound with Her Mountain Cowboy

Home to Eagle's Rest

Her Lawman Protector
Falling for the Cowboy Dad
The Lawman's Baby
Her Triplets' Mistletoe Dad

Love Inspired

Redemption's Amish Legacies

The Nanny's Amish Family
A Precious Christmas Gift
Wife on His Doorstep
Snowbound with the Amish Bachelor

Montana Twins

Her Cowboy's Twin Blessings
Her Twins' Cowboy Dad
A Rancher to Remember

Visit the Author Profile page at Harlequin.com for more titles.

To my husband, who makes these cold winters warm for me. I love you!

CHAPTER ONE

A THUD SHOOK the front door of Mountain Springs Resort. Then another one—the pounding of a fist on the other side. The lodge was closed to new visitors for the next few days. Had someone made it through the storm? Angelina Cunningham hurried across the chilly foyer and flicked the lock, then pulled it open. The heavy door blew inward with a rush of frigid wind and swirling snowflakes, but it was the man standing in the snow who made her breath catch. Blood trickled down one side of his face and matted a section of his mahogany hair, and he stared at her blearily. He was tall and broad, and he swayed slightly as if the wind might push him over. Why was he looking at her so vacantly?

Angelina reached for him, catching the sleeve of his lambskin coat, and tugged him inside. It took all of her strength to shove the door shut against the howling wind. The news was calling it the storm of the century, and it had only begun.

"What happened to you?" she breathed. "Oh my God!"

His cowboy hat was clutched in one hand, and he dabbed at the wound on his head with his free hand, wiping the blood from his eye. His blue jeans were smeared with a streak of blood, and there were a couple of drops across the toes of his scuffed cowboy boots.

"I—I was in an accident," he said. "And I think I belong here?" It was a question. He peered at her hopefully. "Do you know me?"

Angelina looked past him, out the narrow window that flanked the heavy doors, her gaze moving over the snow. His footsteps were still visible out there, along with a trail of crimson dots. Her heart hammered in her chest.

"This is not funny, Ben!" she said. "What happened? Where's your truck?"

"Is that me? Am I Ben?" he asked hesitantly. "So you do know me?"

Angelina's breath seeped out of her, and for a moment she struggled to take another. Ben King was staring at her, his expression perplexed. Was he being serious?

"You don't know who I am?" she breathed. "Ben, look at me. You don't know me?"

"I don't remember… I… I don't remember anything," he said. "But this is familiar—" He looked around the foyer.

Mountain Springs Lodge should be familiar to him, but then again, so should she!

"Snap out of it!" She grabbed the front of his coat. "Hey! Look at me. Seriously, Ben!"

He just blinked at her. "Do I belong here?"

"No," she said, releasing his coat. "You don't."

"Oh…" He licked his lips, and Angelina grabbed a cloth dinner napkin from a pile on the counter waiting to be put away. She dabbed at the gash on his head, then clamped the cloth over top of it and applied some pressure. He didn't know her…

"Your name is Ben King," she said, lifting the cloth to look at the wound before covering it again firmly. "And you're my ex-husband."

"Huh…" The information didn't seem to be landing.

"Come on. Hold this to your head—" Angelina took him by the arm and tugged him toward her office. "Let's get you cleaned up. You need a doctor. Where's your truck?"

"In a ditch—" He gestured behind him.

"Right. That's okay," she said. "Leave it."

One of the housekeeping staff who had volunteered to stay at work during this storm looked at them in surprise.

"Tammy," Angelina said to her, "can you go find Dr. Thomas? Maybe he could help me out here. And bring back a blanket, too, if you could."

"Right! I'll go see where he is," the young woman said, and she disappeared into the foyer.

Maybe having a couple of guests stick around during this blizzard wasn't the worst thing in the world—especially since one of them was a doctor. Most people had wisely left for Denver to avoid the mountain storm, but a few had held out against better advice, along with a handful of staff who were willing to work the extra hours.

Angelina guided Ben down the hallway and into her spacious office. Ben sank into a silk upholstered wingback chair in her trademark pink. She gingerly lifted the napkin, and looked down at the cut. He could probably use stitches, but the memory issue was more worrying than the blood.

She idly wished she had a towel in here to protect the chair.

"Where were you going in this weather?" she asked.

"I don't know. Here, maybe?" He looked up hopefully.

Ben's coat was already undone, and she reached to tug it off his shoulders. He allowed her to remove it. He wore a starched white dress shirt underneath with a bolo tie, and gold horseshoe cuff links glittered at his wrists. That was Ben—his shirts were always immaculate, and it was the balance between wealthy city boy and rancher that he never quite got right. She tossed his heavy coat over another matching chair.

"I doubt you were headed here." She sighed. "I'm not your favorite person."

"Really?" He smiled faintly. "How come?"

"We got divorced, for one," she replied. "And you were engaged up until recently."

"Not anymore?" he asked.

So he didn't remember Hilaria Bell, either. It had been quite the drama, that breakup, and Ben had come here to tell her he was about to do it only a few weeks ago. He hadn't updated her after the fact, although she did hear some rumors.

"You two broke up," she replied. "The wedding was called off. I don't know the details."

Ben raised his eyebrows, but that was all the reaction she got out of him. At a tap on the door, Angelina turned to see her guest, Dr. Thomas, standing there with Tammy at his side. She carried a folded blanket in her arms.

"Thanks for coming," Angelina said. "This is Ben King, and he said he was in an accident. Ben, this is Dr. Thomas."

"You can call me Warren," the older man said, and he came inside. "Can I take a look?" He gently peeked under the napkin, then nodded toward Tammy. "Can you bring us a first aid kit, please?"

"And a few towels, if you could, Tammy," Angelina added, accepting the blanket from her.

Tammy nodded and disappeared out the door again. The doctor took Ben's hand and brought it back up to his head to get him to hold the napkin in place, then he perched on a chair in front of him.

"His memory seems to be gone," Angelina said. "I know this man—very well. He has no idea who I am, or who he is."

Warren met her gaze. "This is… Benjamin King?"

So Warren knew the name. It shouldn't surprise her. Anyone in Colorado had heard of the King family.

"He is," she confirmed with a nod.

Warren turned to Ben and asked, "Do you know what day it is today?"

Ben paused, then shook his head.

"Do you know what year it is?"

"Um…what year?" he repeated.

"Yes, what year is it?" Warren asked.

Ben shook his head again.

"Do you know how to scramble eggs?" Warren asked.

"Yeah." Ben brightened.

"Tell me."

"You crack a few eggs into a bowl, whisk them up, add some salt, a dash of milk…fry it."

Warren nodded. "Your address?"

Ben sighed. "I don't know."

"Phone number?" Warren pressed.

Ben shook his head. "Sorry. I don't know."

"Your name?" Warren pressed.

Ben didn't answer for a moment. "Well, you said it was Benjamin King, right? I don't actually remember that, though. I don't know the name."

"Right…" Warren sighed and crossed his

arms over his chest. "How do you drink your coffee?"

Ben's expression brightened slightly. "Cream and sugar."

Warren nodded. "Okay, I've seen this before. It's normally very temporary amnesia brought on by head trauma. It does pass. The brain just needs to rest and heal."

"He remembers some things, though," Angelina said. "He knows how to scramble eggs, and how he likes his coffee. I don't get it!"

Warren looked over at her, then lifted his shoulders. "It's just the nature of this kind of injury. Not everything is lost, and every case is different. It depends on which part of the brain has been bruised," the older man replied. "I'd recommend a CT scan, just to be on the safe side."

"The problem is getting him to the hospital."

Angelina paused, thinking. The King family wasn't exactly used to waiting in emergency rooms. They had private doctors who came to them…and when they went to the hospital, it was to a private room.

"His family has their own doctor. They call him in for everything," Angelina went on. "Ben, can I see your phone?"

He patted his pockets, and pulled out a cell phone. He looked mildly surprised to see it.

"Thumbprint—" she held it out for him, and Ben obliged.

She flicked through his contacts and stopped at Dr. Ballinger, then passed the phone over to Warren.

He pressed the call button and put the phone up to his ear. Angelina turned back to Ben, and he met her gaze uncertainly.

"You really don't know me?" she asked softly.

He shook his head. "I feel like I remember this lodge, though."

Of course. He wouldn't remember the wife he divorced, just the settlement. But Mountain Springs Lodge had been built in the early seventies, and this section of land beside the mountain lake had been in his family for longer than that. She glanced over her shoulder when Warren paused in his conversation.

"Do you have a penlight?" he asked her.

"No—my cell phone has a flashlight. Would that do?"

"It might actually." He toggled the light and shone it in to Ben's pupils a couple of times, and then put his fingers against his neck. He gave Ben a reassuring pat on the shoulder and then returned to his phone call.

"Yep… Agreed… Yep… Okay, hold on. I'm going to put you on video and let you talk to him." He turned the phone on to video then, and passed it over to Ben.

Dr. Ballinger asked Ben his birthdate, his hometown, how many eggs made a dozen… Ben could only answer the last question, but he did seem to be less bleary now. Warren took the phone back, and they continued talking, their conversation sprinkled with medical terms.

Tammy came into the room then with a first aid kit and towels, and Angelina accepted them with a smile of thanks. She put the towels over the armrests of her chairs, then opened the first aid kit and sorted through, looking at what they had to work with.

"Sure, hold on," Warren said, and he passed the phone to Angelina. She accepted it, and Warren settled himself in front of Ben again. "I'll patch him up. But Dr. Ballinger wants to speak with you."

Angelina stepped away, watching as Warren pulled the napkin from the wound and began to work with the contents of the first aid kit.

"Hi, I'm Angelina Cunningham," Angelina said, looking down at a mild-faced middle-aged man. He was dressed in a sweater vest and dress shirt open at the neck.

"Ms. Cunningham," Dr. Ballinger said briskly. "How does he seem to you?"

"He was confused, and kind of muddled," she replied. "But he seems a bit better now. With a few butterfly bandages, his head should be okay. Dr. Thomas mentioned a CT scan—"

"I doubt that is necessary," Dr. Ballinger said. "Dr. Thomas and I have both seen this before. With the storm really blowing, I think it's probably safer if he stays with you until the streets are clear. I'm going to call Karl King and speak with him. I'll tell him to call Ben's cell phone. You pick up and speak with him first, if you could."

She felt that familiar sinking sensation of discomfort at the mention of her former father-in-law. She hadn't spoken with him directly since just after the divorce, when she signed the nondisclosure agreement in exchange for this old lodge. The King family had been heartily glad to be rid of her, and they hadn't even tried to mask their happiness at the end of her marriage to Ben. She probably could have gotten a bigger settlement out of them if she'd wanted it, they'd been so eager to see the back of her.

Five minutes later, Angelina's cell phone rang, but it was Belle Villeneuve, one of Angelina's close friends.

"Hi, Belle," Angelina said, picking up. All eyes turned toward Angelina, and she angled away from them. She did have a whole life apart from her ex-husband, after all.

"I guess the Second Chance Dinner Club won't be meeting tonight," Belle said with a smile in her voice.

"No, I don't think we'll manage that," Angelina replied. "I've sent most of my guests down to Denver to miss the storm. But I'm kind of in the middle of something. Do you think I could give you a call back?"

"Of course!" Belle said. "You sound… stressed. You okay?"

"I am stressed," Angelina admitted. "I'll tell you what I can once I'm done dealing with this. Promise."

Ben's phone rang next, with an incoming video call.

"Hi, Angie." Karl King had silver hair and

the tanned face of a man who'd just come back from vacation. "Where is my son? What's going on?"

It was as if no time had passed. Angie. He didn't exactly have a right to use Ben's nickname for her, but Karl King wasn't a man who deferred or asked permission.

"Ben showed up with a bloodied head at my door," she said. "It seems he was in a car accident. He has no idea who he is."

"No memory at all?" Karl frowned.

"Not much of one."

"Doesn't he remember *you*?" He sounded incredulous there.

"No. Apparently our short marriage didn't make the cut. But he doesn't seem to remember Hilaria, either, if that makes you feel any better. I don't know what to tell you. He's here, though. Do you want to talk to him?"

"Yeah, fine," Karl said with a curt nod.

Angelina passed the phone over. The Kings would have to figure out a solution here. She was no longer part of the family, so it wasn't her place to make the call. In fact, she fully expected someone to come pick Ben up and get him safely out of her clutches.

Ben answered a few questions, then handed the phone back to Angelina.

"He wants to speak with you," he said.

"Yes?" she said.

"I have to say, I concur with Dr. Ballinger's opinion," Karl said. "This storm won't be kind to anyone, and it sounds like his memory will come back pretty quickly. I think the bigger risk is trying to get him down from the resort to town. If you're okay with it, I'd like him to stay with you."

"Are you sure?" she asked. Since when did they want Ben King with *her*?

"You have a doctor on-site," he said.

"A guest," she clarified.

"Dr. Ballinger seems convinced that he's competent," Karl replied. "We'll pay him for his time, and cover his room and board while he looks after Ben. We'll pay you for your trouble, too, of course."

"Feel free to compensate Dr. Thomas, but don't worry about paying me," she said with a sigh. Not everything came down to money—something Karl King might never grasp.

"It's the least we can do," Karl replied blithely. "You'll be compensated, too. We don't take advantage of people's kindness in this family. And I'm sure I don't need to remind you about the nondisclosure agreement you signed."

"No, I remember that just fine," she said.

"So if you could keep the fact that my son is there and without his memory as close to the vest as possible, I would take that as a personal favor."

"I can't exactly hide him," she said.

"Agreed, but you could keep him sheltered."

"I'll see what I can do, but I have a few guests here. I won't be announcing anything, but I can't control who Ben talks to, or who recognizes him."

"Fair enough. But no media."

"Mr. King, I don't have the time or the inclination to contact any journalists about this," she snapped. "I have a handful of guests to keep safe during the storm of the century, and my hands are going to be full with that. I have other responsibilities here, and it might surprise you to hear, an entire life of my own. I did sign a nondisclosure agreement at the divorce, but that was about the marriage and your family, not about your son landing on my doorstep. If the public finds out, it won't be from me. That's the best I can do."

Karl's eyes narrowed, and she felt the resistance through the phone. Karl had never liked her. "Fine. Can I talk to my son again?"

Angelina brought the phone over to Ben once more. Ben looked at his father's face on the video chat, and his gaze remained mildly curious.

"Step outside the room, son," Karl said. "I want to talk with you in private."

As Ben moved to the hallway, Angelina looked at Warren tiredly.

"Wow," she said.

"Yeah." Warren pursed his lips. "So Benjamin King is your ex-husband, is he?"

"He is," she said. "Of all the weekends…"

"Of all the gin joints, in all the towns, in all the world, he walks into yours," Warren said, and Angelina smiled at the reference.

"A little like that." She met the older man's gaze. "Mr. King is concerned about keeping this quiet. If you could use some discretion here—"

"It's fine," he replied with a shake of his head. "I can be discreet."

"So what does he need? What do I do to make sure he's okay?"

"His memory will come back," Warren replied. "There isn't much else to do. We should probably keep an eye on him to make sure it doesn't get worse, but other than that…"

Angelina nodded. "You're supposed to be

on vacation yourself, and I'm about to ask you to help me with an amnesiac."

"Glad to do it." Warren shot her a smile. "I kind of miss medicine. It's only been six months, but retirement itches."

"Thank you." She sucked in a deep breath and glanced toward the door. Ben probably shouldn't be left unsupervised too long.

BEN LOOKED AT the older man's face on the phone, searching inside of himself for some memory, some tickle of recognition, but there was nothing. This was just a man—older, tanned, gray-haired. Ben glanced over his shoulder toward the office. The woman…it wasn't that he remembered her exactly. But he felt like he should. If that counted.

"Son, you are Benjamin King," the man said soberly.

"Yeah, so they tell me," he replied.

"Listen to me," the man's voice firmed. "You *are* Benjamin King. I am Karl King, your father. You come from an incredibly wealthy family. You need to remember that, because people will try to take advantage of you. They'll say pretty much anything to get their hands on the kind of money we've got. You understand?"

"Not entirely," Ben replied. "I'm rich, and that's a problem?"

"*We're* rich, and that's a vulnerability," Karl replied. "You're there for a reason. It'll come back to you. In the meantime, just be careful, son."

"Careful how?" he asked.

"For example, don't sign anything. And perhaps expect some jealousy toward our family."

"Okay," Ben said, and he slowly nodded his head. "I guess I can't argue with that."

"Good, now—" The image on the phone froze, then disappeared when the phone beeped a warning. Ben checked the reception and saw there were no bars. The long, narrow windows that flanked the front doors to the lodge showed thick white snow.

Behind him he heard the woman's voice as she came out of the office.

"No service on my cell phone, either," she was saying. "It looks like a cell tower must have gone down, and the phone in my office is out—"

She swept past him to the reception desk and picked up the phone there, putting it to her ear.

"This phone is dead, too," she said, glancing back at the doctor. "The landlines are out."

Ben couldn't help but admire her. She was curvy, tall and immaculately put together, from her golden hair swept away from her face to her understated makeup. Letting his gaze move over her, he felt mildly intimidated. She was stunning. The woman's chest rose and fell with a sigh, and her gaze moved back to him. She regarded him thoughtfully, as if he were a problem to be solved. And he was—he could admit that.

"What's your name?" Ben asked. "Did someone call you Angie?"

A smile turned up her lips. "Angelina Cunningham."

"Angelina," he repeated her name. It sounded nice in his ears. "It's a distinct pleasure to meet you."

The smile faded from her lips. "You've said that before."

"When?" he asked.

"When you met me the first time," she replied. "It was on a cruise ship, actually. And you said it…just like that."

It had seemed like the polite thing to say—that was all. Ben wasn't sure how to respond. He couldn't remember a ship, or even this woman's face. As far as he knew, this was the first time he'd met her. And it *was* a pleasure. He reached up and touched the bandage on his head.

"Maybe it'll come back," he said.

"It will," the doctor interjected. "Don't worry over it. That will only make it take longer. The best thing you can do for your own recovery is to relax a little bit."

Easier said than done. His head ached, his feet were wet and cold, and he felt a shiver move through him.

"Ben, you're soaked through," Angelina said. "I have some clothes that have been left behind by guests over the years. I imagine we can pull together something for you to wear."

The damp from his jeans and socks was working its way through him.

"Thanks," he said. "I'll take you up on that."

"Come on up with me, then," Angelina said. "This way."

Angelina headed over to the reception counter again and picked up a stack of clean towels.

Ben followed her, and they made their way up the wide wooden staircase, his leather cowboy boots melting into its plush carpet. She led the way down one corridor flanked with doors with brass room numbers. At the very end, she pulled a key from her pocket, unlocked the door and opened it.

Inside, the room opened up into a much larger living area, and he followed her inside, glancing around at a small apartment. There was a kitchen, a living room with a TV, a fireplace, a balcony, a leather love seat and a plush chair angled toward the center. The floor was a polished hardwood, just like the rest of the lodge seemed to be underneath that carpeting, and when she flicked a switch, soft lights came on. She went over to a phone on a small table and picked it up, listened, then hung it back up with a sigh.

"Just checking," she said with a wan smile. "I told my friend I'd call her back. Doesn't look like I can make good on that now. Come on in."

"Is this where you live?" he asked.

She eyed him again, then shook her head. "Sorry, it's hard to get used to you like this."

"Like what?"

"A blank slate," she said. "Yes, I live here. I had my own place off-site for a while, but I decided to sell it and put the money toward retirement savings instead."

"So you…own this lodge?"

There was something about this place that tickled the back of his brain, but he couldn't quite get a grasp on it. She gave him another evaluating look.

"It's called Mountain Springs Resort," she said at last, "and it's a far sight more than the lodge. But yes, I own and operate it."

He nodded. "It's…impressive."

"Thank you," she said. "I've worked hard."

"You're concerned about retirement. How old are you?" he asked.

"Two years younger than you," she said. "And I'm a regular person. Regular people worry about those sorts of things."

"How old am I?" he asked.

"Forty-five," she replied. "Your birthday was last month. We're a week into November, now. Happy birthday."

"Thanks." He smiled faintly. "I wish I could remember that."

"I'm sure you celebrated in style," she said. Was that judgment in her tone?

Angelina disappeared into a bedroom, and then came back out with a pile of clothing in her arms. She held up a gray T-shirt, inspected it, then tossed it toward him. He caught it in one hand. She shook out two different pairs of pants until she settled on a pair of jeans and tossed those in his direction, too.

"They'll be a little loose, but they'll fit," she said.

"Thanks."

She held up a red woolen sweater emblazoned with the image of a skier. "It's warm," she said.

"Sure. I don't know what my taste in fashion is anyway." He looked down at the clothes he was wearing—blue jeans, a thick, glossy belt the color of dark caramel, a starched button-down shirt, cuff links.

"You can use my bedroom to change," she said, nodding in the direction she'd come from.

Ben went into the bedroom and looked around. It was lit with a bedside lamp. Her bedding was a mauve color, definitely soothing, and everything seemed to smell faintly of lavender. There were a few pictures on the bedside table, and he picked up the first one—a picture of a couple holding a fair-haired little girl. The second photo was a black-and-white portrait of a woman from what looked like the 1930s. He wasn't sure how he knew that.

What was Angelina like? She seemed

organized—the bedroom was tidy, and everything was attractively arranged. There was a little vanity, and he paused at it, his gaze moving down to a perfume decanter with an atomizer ball attached. It looked antique.

He swung the bedroom door shut and began to undress. His fingers seemed to know how to remove the cuff links and bolo tie without too much thought. And then he sat on the edge of the bed and pulled off his boots one at a time. His socks were wet, so he took those off, as well. The jeans weren't quite so loose as Angelina had predicted—maybe he was heavier now than he'd been when they were married. And the T-shirt and sweater cocooned him with warmth. He dropped the cuff links and tie into his jeans pocket, not sure what else to do with them.

"Just toss your clothes in the hamper," Angelina called from the other room. "I suspect that shirt is dry clean only, but we'll see what we can do. You're particular about your dry cleaning."

Was he? He wasn't sure. He looked down at the crisp white shirt he'd taken off—it was good quality. His gaze moved toward the perfume again, unsure of why he was drawn to it, but he didn't touch it. Instead he pulled open the bedroom door once more and headed back out into the living room.

Angelina shot him a smile.

"Well, you look downright approachable now," she said.

He fiddled with the cuff links in his pocket. "Am I not usually?"

"No, you aren't," she said with a wry smile.

"What do I do for living?" he asked her.

"You live on a ranch," she replied. "So you call yourself a rancher when you're trying to be all salt of the earth, but that's not the source of your main income. You're inheriting an investment property corporation."

"Ah. Yes, my father said that we were... well-off."

"Well-off is an understatement." She pursed her lips, looking unimpressed. "And I had no idea about your family's wealth when I married you, for the record. You made sure of that."

His gaze moved along some framed photos sitting on a side table. One picture showed a group of women sitting in a dining room in what appeared to be this lodge. They were all smiling, half-full glasses of wine in front of them, and Angelina at the center of them.

She was smiling, and light glittered off her necklace.

"Friends?" he asked.

"Good ones," Angelina said. "They got me through the aftermath of our divorce."

Their divorce. Those words sounded ugly, and the way she said it spoke of pain.

"Was I so terrible then?" he asked after a pause.

She eyed him for a moment. "Not as terrible as I originally thought. Other women went through worse."

"But you aren't with me anymore," he said. "Something happened."

"That was a long time ago, Ben," she said. "We don't have to do this."

"But I don't remember any of it," he said.

"That might be for the best," she replied. "Besides, how can I ask you to apologize for something you don't even remember doing? That's not fair of me. When your memory comes back, if you have anything to say, you can say it. Until then…"

"I'm at your mercy," he said with a small smile.

What was it his father had said—be careful and don't sign anything?

"You don't have anything to worry about

from me," she said, her tone softening. "You'll be fed and sheltered. I'm over it. Really."

He'd been joking. Mostly.

Angelina nodded toward the door. "Let's head down and get the fire started. It'll give people somewhere to warm up, boost a few spirits."

"Sure." As he followed her to the door, he glanced over his shoulder once more at that cozy, feminine space. It tugged at him, somehow.

But she shut the door firmly, locked it, and he felt the line drawn. That space was hers, and he didn't belong there.

CHAPTER TWO

ANGELINA GUIDED BEN down the corridor, glancing up at him as they went. It was strange having him here—he had no memory of anything that had passed between them... their whirlwind courtship, tumultuous marriage, her tears, his frustration, his family's disdain... When they'd signed the divorce papers, she'd cried, and his eyes had welled up. She still felt emotional at the memory of those tears glistening in his eyes as he passed the pen back to the lawyer.

And looking at him now, his head bandaged, his gaze polite, curious, gentle... He still tugged at her heart more than was strictly safe. And there was something between them when their eyes met—something that had always been there. Could they really have the same undeniable chemistry when the bitter memories were removed from the equation? For him, maybe. But she'd done this before, and no amount of King charm was going to change how a relationship between them ended.

She could hear some laughter filtering out from the rooms in the opposite wing where the young snowboarders who had decided to stay were lodging. It was nothing too raucous, but she did wonder if boredom would set in and she'd end up with a bunch of drunk twentysomethings.

Angelina and Ben went downstairs side by side, and she led the way toward the fireside room. It was a large space that combined rustic log walls and a dominating stone fireplace with more delicate touches like watercolor paintings in gilt frames and beveled-edged mirrors that cast light around the room. The artist who did the watercolors, Verity Blake, was known locally for painting historical scenes. She'd been working on a project about Camp Hale, a Colorado Rocky Mountain training site for soldiers located about forty miles from Blue Lake, and the artwork was evocative. Verity's work had appealed to Angelina on a very deep level. It was delicate but strong. It was resilient, and that was everything that Angelina had wanted for this fresh start. She had immediately bought some pieces from the artist for the fireside room.

Although built much later than the WWII mountain training camp, this lodge somehow seemed to hold some of that heart and courage within its walls. Something about that pristine mountain lake spoke of a determination to survive, and for good to overcome, no matter what the cost.

Outside the tall windows the snow was whisking past the glass horizontally, the wind moaning like a lost soul. A finger of cold worked its way down the chimney, and Angelina hitched her shoulders up against it.

Ben moved in a slow circle, looking around the room. There were couches and stuffed armchairs that sat facing the windows. In the center of the room hung a large chandelier, scattering prism rainbows across the walls. She wondered what he was thinking.

"Did you decorate this?" he asked.

She laughed softly. "Yes, this is all my touch."

"Wow…"

Was he really impressed? It was nothing compared to the kind of lavish lifestyle his family enjoyed.

"You gave me an old hunting lodge in our divorce settlement," she said.

"And this is the result." His dark gaze

moved over to meet hers, and her breath caught as he raised one eyebrow.

"This is the result," she replied. "This place had such good bones, and I wanted to make it beautiful. It worked."

But it was more than just good bones… this old place had a good spirit, too.

"How bad was it when you started?" he asked.

Her mind went back to those early days when she'd been the brand-new owner, much to the unease of the men who socialized and drank there. She'd been about as welcome as her new design scheme. Worse, she wasn't local, having originally come from California.

"It was full of hunting memorabilia from the seventies," she said. "There were lots of moose heads, stuffed fish, flannel-themed decor. The guys who came here for a beer and some hunting talk really liked it."

"Where do they go now?" he asked.

"A few come here for nice dinners with their wives," she replied. "But when they want that beer under the glassy stare of a moose's head, there's a pub a few miles down the road where they meet up. Don't worry about them. They're taken care of."

Ben chuckled. "I'm sure. This is beautiful. Did I...ever visit? See what you did?"

"Whenever you needed to find me," she said. "For example, a few years ago, we sat in the dining room together and shared a bottle of wine. Talked about old times. You told me about your new girlfriend, how the family approved of her, how she seemed to understand how your social circles worked."

"That sounds unnecessarily cruel," he said.

"I had a boyfriend at the time," she replied. "And in your defense, you did end up asking her to marry you. You came and told me about the engagement, too."

"That's the *canceled* engagement?" he clarified.

"That's it."

"What was I doing, rubbing it in?"

"No," she said. "I think you wanted my blessing, somehow."

"Did you give it?"

Angelina smiled faintly. He'd been completely oblivious to the pain it was causing her as he described this young heiress who'd captured both his heart and his family's.

"Yes," she said. "I did."

As much as it had hurt, it had been good for her—forced her to face the fact that Ben was destined for loftier things. It had been a good reality check.

"Is there still a boyfriend in the picture?" he asked.

She wished she could say yes—maybe just to save face. But it wouldn't be true.

"You don't want to know more about your ex-fiancée?" she asked instead with a teasing smile.

"I'll get there," he replied. "Right now, I'm asking about that boyfriend."

"We broke up," she replied.

"Why?" He moved closer, crossed his arms over his chest and a quizzical expression on his face.

"Because—" She looked up at him. He'd asked all these questions before… "Because we didn't have whatever spark it is that makes everything worth it. He was great. He was kind, smart, successful…but I didn't feel it the way I should."

She cleared her throat. She was saying too much.

"But you did feel it with me?" he asked.

"A very long time ago, Ben," she said with a rueful smile.

"All right." He shot her a grin. "Just checking."

He always had been a flirt, this man. With her at least. He'd never been the type to play the field, or let his eye roam. But with her, he'd been incorrigible…up until things went sour. This reminder of his charm wasn't helpful.

She moved toward the fireplace and picked up a box of kindling and some matches. She needed to get the fire started. It was chilly in here—the problem with having this many windows in a place was keeping the cold out.

"You want me to do that?" Ben's voice was low, by her ear, and goose bumps stood up on her arms.

"Uh—" She looked back at him, and he was so close that her heart skipped a beat. "Do you remember how?"

"Yeah. I mean, I have no idea who I am, but I'm pretty sure I can build a fire." A smile quirked up one side of his mouth.

"Sure, then." She handed him both the matches and kindling.

Ben knelt down at the hearth and started to arrange kindling, crumpling some old newspaper to go beneath it.

"It's kind of a relief to know I remember some things," Ben said, his attention on his work. "I wonder if I do this often."

"You live on a thousand-acre ranch that's run by three different managers. You have a cook, housekeeping staff and enough cowhands that you don't kindle your own fires. Trust me on that."

"Oh. This feels familiar, though."

"You and I used to go camping together," she said.

They would drive up to Mountain Springs for the pristine lake and the idyllic mountain town. Ben used to joke about how when he was a Boy Scout, he'd gotten a badge for these things. Every time he started the fire or warmed a pot of beans on the propane stove, he'd hold up three fingers and start reciting the pledge, making her laugh.

Ben put a match to the paper and a small tongue of flame leaped up toward the kindling.

"So I'm a relatively useful guy," he said, glancing up at her.

"Relatively." She smiled faintly.

He reached for a piece of wood and laid it on top of the kindling, then another. As the fire started, the smell of smoke wafted toward them, and she reached out and opened the flue.

"Thanks," he said, and he froze, a strange

look on his face. Was he remembering those summer nights when they'd sit together in front of the fire, a sleeping bag around them both, and his arms holding her close?

"Are you remembering something?" she asked hesitantly.

"I don't know…" He paused. "Something about the smell of the fire."

Her pulse sped up, and he rose, brushing his hands off.

"Scout's honor?" She raised three fingers.

"What's that?"

She put her hand down. Maybe he didn't remember. Maybe that was just her.

"Nothing," she said.

"I just—" Ben reached for another piece of wood and squatted down to add it to the growing blaze. "I remember a scent—"

"Campfire?" she asked. "Everyone loves the smell of a campfire."

"Something floral…maybe a bit of vanilla?"

Her breath hitched, and she swallowed. He was remembering the smell of her perfume… It was Chanel No. 5. She used to wear it all the time—it had been a connection to the grandmother she'd been named after who had also worn Chanel No. 5. And Ben had loved burrowing his nose into her neck, and pulling her close…

New scent, new beginnings. It had been for the best.

"I don't know," she lied, and she pasted a smile on her face. "It's funny how memories work, isn't it?"

If he was going to remember her, let him remember the whole person, not just a fragrance. Because she'd always been more complicated than he'd been willing to admit. She'd been more intelligent than he'd realized, too, and more capable than he'd ever given her credit for. She was willing to bet that the King family had never anticipated her creating a tourism hot spot with this old lodge when they let it go thirteen years ago.

"Come here," Ben said, his voice a low rumble. It held a note of command, like there was some part of him still used to being obeyed.

She eyed him for a moment, then walked closer. He leaned toward her, inhaling. Then he lifted her wrist to his face, so close that she could feel the tickle of his breath. She raised an eyebrow.

"That isn't the perfume I remember," he said.

No, it wasn't. She had been ready for a new

personal scent after the divorce. She was in her forties now—moving forward with the resort, with her friends, even with her personal life.

"Maybe I'm remembering someone else," he said, and he released her hand. "Sorry."

Angelina pulled her arm against her stomach. Someone else—like his ex-fiancée? Hilaria was the heiress of some logging fortune. She'd been the kind of woman the King family could accept and celebrate. They could show her off at parties and introduce her around without people getting that perplexed look, wondering who this Californian was, and how she made it past scrutiny. Angelina had been a little bit jealous of the other woman, if she had to be honest. Hilaria was going to get Ben to herself—there would be no more impromptu visits to the lodge once he was remarried, she was sure.

"I'm going to go check on the kitchen," Angelina said, taking a step back. "With so few guests and only a skeleton crew, I'm instituting meal hours where the kitchen will be open. I'll let you know when you can go order some lunch."

"Thanks."

He eyed her uncertainly as she turned and headed toward the exit. He was probably confused as to why she wasn't matching up to whatever memories were swimming under the surface, but that wasn't her problem. Either he was remembering Hilaria, or he was remembering a much younger version of herself. Angelina wasn't the same woman anymore. Whatever he might remember—she'd changed. She was stronger now, more sure of her own abilities, more confident in herself as a woman. Her divorce had crushed her, but she'd survived, and she was a better person for it. She now had some wisdom to pass on to other women who were going through similar heartbreak: there was life on the other side.

There was more than life—there was abundance and beauty. There was growth and laughter. The world was different post-divorce. *She* was different. And there were still good things waiting.

Ben King had been her weakness once upon a time, but not anymore. Some things, like moving on after heartbreak, had to start out as a choice until she grew into them. And she was choosing this—Ben couldn't be her weakness any longer.

BEN SANK INTO THE leather armchair he'd pulled a little closer to the fire. The heat from the blaze emanated comfortably against his shins, and he leaned back, stretching his bare feet toward it. The fireplace was made out of uncut stone and mortar, the effect both imposing and cozy at the same time. He felt safe here.

He didn't know why that mattered, especially with his father's warning still ringing in his mind about being careful.

"Here, I brought you these."

A pair of socks appeared over Ben's shoulders, and he looked up to see the doctor from earlier. The older man pulled up a chair next to him and settled into it with a sigh.

"Thanks," Ben said. They were thick outdoors socks, and Ben leaned over and pulled them on gratefully. "What's your name again?"

"Dr. Warren Thomas," he replied. "Call me Warren."

"Nice to meet you. I'm Ben."

The older man gave him a cordial nod. "You know, most people left when the weather prediction started to look dire."

"Yeah?" Ben looked over at him. "Not you, though."

"No, I figured I could write my memoirs here during a blizzard or in Denver in a different hotel room just the same. I didn't see the point in leaving."

"What's in your memoirs?" Ben asked.

"Oh…my life," Warren said. "Childhood stories, boyhood dreams…few years in the army, long years in medical school and growing a family. I don't suppose it sounds terribly interesting to a man your age, but it's my story and I wanted to write it down."

"I don't remember my life," Ben said. "So I suppose you've got a leg up on me there."

"Give it time," the older man said quietly. "I've seen this with some car accident victims, and I've read some research papers about the same condition with war injuries overseas. A good knock on the head can rattle things around more than you think. And unless there are some psychological reasons where you don't want to remember, you'll heal up just fine."

"Psychological?" Ben asked warily.

"PTSD," Warren said. "Shell shock. Sorry, it was a poor attempt at humor. I'm sure it doesn't apply."

Ben leaned his head against the back of the chair, and when his gaze moved from the crackling fire toward the window and the blowing snow outside, he struggled to remember as far back as he could. The first clear memory he had was of crawling out of his overturned truck into the snow—the icy slap of the wind, the ache in his head, the sticky warmth of blood on his face. His hat had been upside down in the snow, and he'd scooped it up...

Ben was grateful to be here—inside the lodge with a fire, fresh clothes, a sturdy roof over his head. But he couldn't shake the feeling he'd had when he saw the place looming ahead of him in the storm. He belonged here. He'd been certain of it. This was the place he needed to get to...

Where had that certainty come from?

"She's beautiful," Warren said after a moment of silence.

"Hmm?" Ben roused himself from his thoughts.

"The owner—Angelina. She's beautiful," Warren repeated.

"Yeah." Ben smiled faintly. "She is."

"And you were married to her?" Warren asked.

"So she says."

But then, the man on the phone—his father—

had told him to be wary of what people might do for the money he apparently had. So why hadn't his father warned him that he'd been married to this woman?

Warren looked over at him quizzically. "What's the matter?"

"I don't remember her," he said.

"Do you remember anyone?" Warren asked.

Ben shook his head. "But she seems like the kind of woman a man wouldn't forget, doesn't she?"

Warren laughed softly. "She's impressive."

"What do you know about her?" Ben asked.

"Not much. I'm only a guest. I know a bit about this resort, though."

"Yeah?" Ben turned toward the older man. "Because this place feels familiar to me."

"You know, rumor has it that Blue Lake was used in some Camp Hale training exercises," Warren said. "I'm a bit of a World War Two buff, and that's some trivia that not many people know about. Camp Hale was a training site for mountain terrain. It's about forty miles from here, so the soldiers marched out this way a couple of times."

Ben nodded. "That's interesting. So is that what brought you here?"

"It factored in," Warren said with a nod. "It's an inspiring location because of the lake, too. It's a place to commune with nature."

Ben was silent.

"Anyway, more recently, this used to be a hunting lodge," Warren went on, "and when Ms. Cunningham there bought it, she completely refurbished the entire place. She opened some hiking trails up the mountain, brought in canoes and kayaks for the lake, and almost overnight this place turned from a beautiful photographic secret into a tourism must-see. My wife talked about this place—"

Warren sighed, his voice trailing off.

"And?" Ben said.

"Oh…she was impressed by Ms. Cunningham's ability to create something beautiful. She visited this resort on her own a few years ago when it first opened."

"You didn't come with her?" Ben asked.

"I was busy at the hospital. I had patients to see, and hours to log, and…money to make, I suppose."

"I see." Ben leaned forward and picked up a metal poker. He jabbed at a log, pushing it farther into the flames.

Ben looked over at the man's left hand. There was no ring, but there was a dent in his left ring finger. A recent divorce, maybe? Warren seemed to notice Ben's scrutiny because he closed his hand into a fist and pulled it out of sight.

"Writing has a way of bringing a man's life into focus," Warren said. "It shows you the patterns, the direction, the ironies."

"Are you going to try and get it published?" Ben asked.

"Oh…" Warren sighed. "No one cares about your life unless you've endured something horrific, or done something amazing. I don't fall into either category. But I do think it might be of interest to my grandchildren one day. Maybe my great-grandchildren. Once I pass on, I'll stop being the boring old grandpa who lectures them about our family's tendency toward high blood pressure and diabetes, and I'll be an ancestor. It's much more mysterious to be an ancestor, trust me."

Ben chuckled. "I could see that."

"And maybe I want a hand in the way I'm remembered, or thought of, later on," Warren said. "It's handier to be able to tell your own story, instead of have stories told about you."

"What sorts of stories would they tell?" Ben asked.

Warren shrugged. "Depends on who does the telling, doesn't it?"

"Do you have enemies?" Ben asked.

"I have an ex-wife."

Ben smiled. "Right."

So did Ben, apparently. And his ex-wife was the one providing this roof over his head, the clothes on his back... What stories were told about Ben? He had no idea. Apparently, he was wealthy and divorced from a beautiful woman. But was he a well-liked man? Was he respected?

"Do you, um—" Ben hesitated. "Do you know anything about me, personally?"

"We've never met," Warren replied, but there was wariness in his tone.

"About my family, maybe?" he asked.

"Everyone in Colorado knows the King family," Warren replied.

"Oh..." He wasn't sure what to say to that.

"Your family has its proverbial fingers in a lot of pies," Warren went on. "There's the King Stadium, King Park—there are streets named after your family, and you own a property development firm, I think about two grocery store chains, and you're into a bunch of Wall Street trading. I think I read somewhere that you own majority shares in some meatpacking plants, too. You come from a family that does business, son."

"Okay." He nodded a couple of times.

The sound of voices in the foyer silenced them. Some other guests had come downstairs, talking noisily.

Ben rose from his seat and went over to the arched doorway just as Angelina came out of the dining room.

"Yes, the phones are down!" Angelina said, raising her voice in answer to one of the guests' questions. "But we do have electricity, television and we've started up a fire in the fireside room for your enjoyment. The dining room is open now to serve lunch. We have a limited menu, but most of our classic favorites are all available for you today."

"We should go outside!" a young woman said with a laugh.

"No, you shouldn't," Angelina said, her voice carrying. "Can I have everyone's attention, please? This storm is not to be toyed with. There are whiteout conditions and the temperatures are low enough to cause hypothermia. These mountains are not safe for sightseeing during any kind of storm. You could easily get lost out there, and none of us would be able to find you. I must insist that you stay inside the lodge until the storm has passed. This will not last forever. It's a few days at most."

"What are we supposed to do for days?" someone muttered.

Angelina's gaze turned flat, and Ben couldn't help but smother a smile.

"We have board games," Angelina said. "Cable TV, the beautiful sight of falling snow and a roaring fireplace. Read a book! We do have a small library stocked with everything from paperbacks to a few meaty classics should your taste go in that direction. You're here to experience the mountains, ladies and gentlemen, and part of that experience is respecting a storm." She paused, looking around the room, and her gaze landed on Ben. He smiled slightly. "The dining room is open! Enjoy!"

The younger guests moved into the dining room, and Angelina pulled a hand through her blond waves. She'd lost some of her earlier poise, and her exhaustion was peeking through.

"How much would you bet they'll want to try snowboarding before the storm is over?" Ben asked.

Angelina raised her tired gaze to meet his. "They'd better not."

He smiled ruefully, attempting to show her that he was joking, and she returned it.

"If you want to eat, I recommend you do it now," Angelina said. "I have some things to take care of."

Ben glanced over his shoulder toward Warren, who was staring moodily into the fire.

"You coming for lunch, Warren?" Ben asked.

The older man looked up, then slowly pushed himself to his feet.

"I guess I'd better," he said.

The rest of the day passed rather slowly. Ben flipped through a hunting magazine, then tried to read a paperback novel that didn't grab his attention. Outside the snow just kept falling, and the wind howled around the mountain peaks and swirled over the top of the partially frozen lake. In spots, the turquoise water could be seen in contrast to the bluish ice along the lakeshore.

A few hours later, Angelina showed him up to his suite—a generous room with a view of that icy lake, or what could be seen of it when the wind suddenly changed direction and visibility came back in a rush. There was a king-size bed in the center of the room, and heat poured from the register.

"I brought you a few more clothes that might fit," she said, putting a small pile of items on the table by the balcony door. "I also have some toiletries. And your hat—" She passed it over. Somehow, he felt better having it in his hands.

"Thanks." He flexed the hat in his palms.

"It's the least I can do," she replied, but she looked to the side, not quite meeting his gaze.

"Angelina," he said. "I sense there are some hard feelings between us. I mean, I don't remember it, but you seem...uncomfortable with me."

"It's fine," she said with a shake of her head.

"What did I do?" he asked. "Because I'm looking at you, and I see a beautiful, successful woman I'd be proud to be with. So...what happened with us?"

Her green gaze flicked over to meet his. "Your family happened."

What had his father said? *And perhaps expect some jealousy toward our family.*

"What did they do?" he asked.

"They hated me." She said it so matter-of-factly, with no emotion behind it.

"I find that hard to believe…" He smiled, hoping that she'd soften her stance there. "For what?"

"For being beneath the quality standard they set for you," she said. "They wanted you to marry someone who came from a family equally well situated. I'm just a regular woman."

"Not so regular…"

She'd achieved an awful lot to consider herself ordinary. And look at her! She drew every eye in a room.

"You'd be surprised." She didn't return his smile, and her gaze didn't waver. This wasn't a joke. He was inclined to believe her.

"So my family hated you, and we broke up?" he asked hesitantly.

"I got tired of trying to prove myself," she said. "And I think you got tired of fighting for us. A man's family is a part of him, Ben. Remember them or not, they formed you. They raised you. Their DNA flows through you. And I wasn't acceptable."

Ben felt her words spinning through his mind like that blinding snow outside. His family had been the cause of their divorce? Was that why his father had given him that warning—he saw Angelina as a threat?

"Why did I come here?" he asked.

Angelina shook her head. "I have no idea."

"We didn't have plans to…talk?" he asked. "Because I don't know why else I'd be driving this way. Do I know anyone else here or have any business to take care of?"

Angelina shrugged. "I wouldn't know. I'm not a part of your life."

"But you said we talked sometimes," he said.

"We did," she said.

"Maybe I wanted to talk again. You said we broke up? Maybe that was weighing on me."

"Maybe." She met his gaze. "I wouldn't know, would I?" She was silent for a moment. "We always have held on to some feelings for each other. I won't deny that. I think you regretted how things ended with us. But we aren't friends. You can't feel the way we did for each other, go through that kind of heartbreak and be friends afterward. It doesn't work."

No, he could see that. Knowing next to nothing about her, he'd felt drawn to this woman. And even now, knowing that nothing had worked between them, he still found himself wanting to keep her close.

"But I came *here*," he said. "With a storm

at my back, no less. That has to mean something. I feel absolutely certain that I was trying to reach...this place."

As she looked at him, he could see that her resistance was up. She didn't have his answers, and maybe he was asking too much of her to expect her to know why he'd come out here.

"Do you want me to have your clothes laundered tonight, or do you want to have them dry-cleaned?" she asked.

Right. She was backing away from the personal.

"I—" He shook his head. "I have no idea. Let's try and wash them, I guess."

She smiled faintly. "You were particular about your shirts. I should warn you."

He thought about it for a moment. "I'm not right now. I wouldn't mind having my own clothes back. Let's see how it goes."

"All right." She turned toward the door.

He wanted to stop her, ask her more questions, convince her to stay awhile, but he could sense that wouldn't be appropriate. Whatever they'd been, it was well in the past.

"Good night," he called after her.

"Good night, Ben." Her voice was soft, cutting off when the door shut behind her.

Standing in that room alone, he let out a sigh. Whoever he was, he was no one to Angelina. Not anymore.

CHAPTER THREE

BEN LEANED OVER the bathroom sink, squinting at his reflection in the mirror. He had a sense that the face he saw was his, but he felt mild surprise to see the lines around his eyes, the white hair scattered through the stubble on his chin. There was a dusting of rust-colored blood still in his hairline, and he peeled up the bandage to get a better look at the wound. The doctor had done a good job of taping it up with butterfly bandages, but the surrounding tissue was still puffy and bruised.

Why on earth would he have been driving up this mountain with a blizzard bearing down on him? He didn't know much about himself, but he was relatively certain he wasn't a fool. He'd been heading here—to Mountain Springs Resort. That much was clear to him. And when he'd gotten out of his dented truck, he'd been set on getting to this lodge. At all costs. He remembered pushing through the snow, his boots slipping on the icy ground.

It wasn't just that he'd needed help after the crash. He was convinced that this had been his destination all along, even though it was now clear that he and Angelina weren't connected anymore. They weren't even friends.

"What was I doing?" he murmured aloud.

He turned back to the bedroom and sat on the edge of the bed. He had a few scattered memories, a mishmash of images, and he couldn't make sense of them. A child's lunch box, presumably his. It had a pudding cup inside, and a sandwich, and a juice box, but he'd been particularly fixated on that pudding cup. He must have been pretty young. He remembered a woman's face—his mother's, perhaps? She was bending over him, licking her finger, and wiping something from his cheek. He remembered a tropical beach—busy, full of other people in bathing suits wading out into the surf... He had an image in his mind of a desk—large, imposing, mahogany wood.

Those shards of memory didn't tell him who he was, what he stood for, why he was here. But they did point to his life out there.

He hadn't eaten much at dinner. Now his stomach rumbled.

Maybe there would be something to eat in the kitchen. He could have Angelina put it on whatever tab his father would be paying for. He'd overheard that much—she'd be reimbursed for the expense of taking care of him. And somehow he doubted that even with the hard feelings between them that Angelina would begrudge him something to eat.

He found his key card on the table, then he headed out of his room.

A few rooms down the hall had lights that shone from beneath the doors, but beyond a subdued laugh and some murmuring voices, the sound of a TV—all was calm. The moaning of the wind outside was louder, and he headed down the main staircase toward the foyer and the dining room.

The dining room was empty. The storm raged outside the broad windows, snow whipping past the glass. These windows were obviously meant to give diners a spectacular view of the scenery, but with a storm like this one, it just gave an even better view of the unforgiving onslaught outside, and a shiver ran down his spine.

A light was on in the kitchen, shining through the circular window in the swinging doors, and he paused, looking inside.

The counters and appliances around her were spotlessly clean stainless steel. Angelina had her back to him, leaning against an island. Something about the way she stood, her shoulders raised, made her look vulnerable.

He pushed open the door and stepped inside, and she turned at the sound. He saw that she held a small container of ice cream and a spoon.

"Hi," he said.

"Hi." She licked the spoon off. "Are you okay?" she asked. "Did you need something?"

"I'm not ready to sleep quite yet," he said. "And I was hungry."

"Me, too." She opened a freezer and pulled out another pint of ice cream. She looked at the label. "This one is peaches and cream. It's good."

He accepted the carton and a spoon. She seemed slightly warmer toward him now, and he wondered if that was because of his earlier efforts to talk to her. He didn't think he was a bad man—he should feel that tendency inside himself if it was there, shouldn't he?

Ben leaned against the island next to her as he pried the lid off.

"The kitchen staff are off for the night?" he asked.

She nodded. "I've got four staff members that stayed through the storm—two house-keeping and two in the kitchen. They need their time off, too."

"Are they staying in suites?" he asked.

She nodded. "Yes. We have the space. They'll clean and make up their own rooms, but they'll stay for free."

"You seem like you've weathered storms before," he said.

"I have." He sensed something deeper in those words, but she turned back to her ice cream. "This is a terrible choice of snack." She took another bite. "It's freezing outside, and cold in here…but it's comforting."

"Yeah?"

She nodded. "You used to know that about me."

"Sorry," he said. He wished he still knew these details.

"It's not your fault," she replied.

"Angie…can I ask you something?" he asked.

She shot him a wary look. "Sure."

"Am I… Was I…" He swallowed, uncertain how to even put this. "Was I a bad man?"

She raised her eyebrows. "Bad?"

"You don't trust me—I can feel it. I come

from a powerful family. I asked Warren what he knew about me, and he seemed to tiptoe a bit," he said. "Was I... I don't know...immoral? Or heartless?"

Angelina licked her spoon, then shook her head. "No. You weren't. You were just...born to something different, and no amount of loving you was going to change that."

"And I hurt you," he surmised.

"You broke my heart," she said quietly. "You broke it more deeply than any human being has been able to do to me."

He was silent. He didn't know what to say.

"It was a long time ago," she said. "Thirteen years since our divorce now, so it's not exactly fresh, Ben."

"Okay..."

"And while you were not good for me, I do believe you are decent at heart," she said. "If that's what you're asking."

"That was what I wanted to know."

For a couple of minutes, they both ate their ice cream. It was high quality—creamy, thick, with real peaches rippled through it.

"When I was a kid, I used to get tonsillitis a lot," Angelina said, breaking the silence, "and ice cream was something that I could swallow and that tasted good. It isn't so bad being sick if you get ice cream."

She'd softened somewhat. Was it the reminder that he was basically decent? It mattered to him that she remember it, too.

"What kind do you have?" Ben asked.

"Dark chocolate mint," she replied.

"I imagine your palette has refined over the years," he said, and he took a bite of his own.

"Of course," she said. "When I was a kid it was Neapolitan."

He licked off the spoon, and his gaze flickered up to find her eyes locked on his lips. She looked away when he noticed her. There had been intimacy between them…maybe more recently than thirteen years ago. He could feel it.

"You seem like you're under a lot of pressure," he said. "Do you run this place on your own?"

"I have a general manager and a marketing executive. They're actually married, and at home with their baby boy," she said. "I have good, reliable staff."

"But at the end of the day, the responsibility is yours," he said.

"That's life." She looked up at him again. "It's the same for you."

Maybe it was. It sounded like he'd had a lot of responsibility—people under him, employees, staff.

"I learned a lot from you," she added.

"Yeah?" He smiled at that.

"I watched you managing your business, and I picked up a few of your tricks. All of this—" She gestured with her spoon. "I put this together, but I did learn by watching you."

"Like what?" he asked.

"Hire quality people and pay them well," she said. She spooned up another bite. "Start with quality material, and work up from there."

"Hmm. I sound like I'm good at what I do," he said, and he cast her a smile.

"Like I keep saying, you were born to it," she replied, but she didn't return his smile. She wasn't going to be charmed.

"Is that a bad thing?" he asked. "For you, I mean."

"No, just a fact." She turned back to her ice cream, and he watched as she slowly moved the spoon over the top of it, curling up her next bite. Then her gaze flickered back up to him. "Your family raised you to take over, Ben. You're the eldest son."

"I have siblings, then?"

"A younger sister," she said.

"Huh…"

The information was like hearing a story about a stranger, outlining the family of a man he'd never met. But there was that image in his mind of the woman wiping his face with her thumb…

"Do I have a mother?" he asked.

Angelina's expression softened. "She passed away when you were a teenager."

No one he could call when the phone lines came back, no one to reassure him that he was loved. He'd spoken to his father, and he'd felt an almost formal distance between them. A mother might have been softer. Funny to even be thinking about that right now, but it would be nice to know that someone loved him.

"I think I remember something about her—a lady wiping something off my face," he said.

"Maybe," she replied. "I've only seen a couple of pictures. It might have been the nanny, though. You said that you were really close to the woman your parents hired to take care of you and your sister. Your parents traveled a lot, and left the two of you at home with the nanny."

A nanny. Maybe. Would these memories coalesce into something tangible? Would emotions match faces, and stories become a personal history? Or was he going to be stuck in this whiteout storm in his own head for the rest of his life?

"You know, I now have a small appreciation for the pressure you were under," Angelina said, tugging his attention back.

"Yeah? What kind of pressure?"

"You had a business to run, family to report to, employees to keep happy, stockholders to please… It was a lot," she replied. "And then you had to explain me."

"Did I handle the pressure very well?" he asked with a frown.

"You were a different person under all that pressure," she said.

"Different from what?" he asked.

"From the man I fell in love with." Her face colored and she shrugged. "I'm sorry—that was harsh."

"I don't remember," he replied. "It might also be true."

She shivered. The kitchen was getting cooler, and outside, he heard the far-off whistle of the storm winding through trees. Goose bumps rose up on Angelina's arms, and his first instinct was to put an arm around her—a very stupid first instinct. Instead, he moved closer to her, leaning his arm against hers, sharing some of his warmth. He took another bite of ice cream, and then tipped the tub in her direction.

"Want a bite?" he asked.

She hesitated.

"Come on," he said. "I can't eat all the peach without feeling like a jerk. I feel like I have a lot to make up for, and eating all your ice cream isn't going to help."

She dipped her spoon into his tub and lifted a bite to her lips.

"It's very good," she murmured, then she tipped hers in his direction. "Want to try it?"

He spooned up a bite of hers and when he put it into his mouth she hitched her shoulders up again and settled just a little closer to him, her arm and hip pressed against him.

"It's cold in here," he said.

"Yeah…" She didn't look up, her attention fixed on the ice cream in front of her.

"You can put this on my bill," he said with a low laugh.

"I'm not charging your father for this," she replied, her voice low.

"Why not?" he asked. "I'm definitely an unexpected expense."

"I didn't need a promise of payment to help you."

She was a good person. He could feel that in her—she had a moral compass that guided her.

"Thanks," Ben said. "And honestly, I don't know how grateful I should be for that. Maybe I should be floored by your generosity after our history."

Angelina laughed softly. "You should be."

"Then let me make it up to you." He put down the ice cream and turned toward her. "I'm serious."

"How?" she asked.

"Let me help out. I mean—I can build fires, carry wood, be your muscle around here."

"I should turn you down," she said, but there was something soft in her tone.

"But you won't," he said. "You don't need my messed-up brain. Just use me for my body…and my guilt over whatever I did to make you resent me this much."

Angelina rolled her eyes. "Fine, I will use you for your brawn—not your body. You're no longer my husband, Mr. King."

Ben's head was starting to hurt again—a

dull thud at the front. He put the lid back on his ice cream and handed it over to her. "Let's sneak down tomorrow night and finish this."

"Are you flirting?" she asked.

Was he? He probably needed to take a couple of Tylenol for the pain and sleep it off. But Angelina was beautiful, enticing, interesting... She might be the only woman he could claim to know at this moment in time, but he had a strong feeling that she was special.

"Am I allowed to?" he asked.

"No." She arched an eyebrow at him.

"Then absolutely not." He shot her a grin. "I'm serious about helping you out, though. Tomorrow morning, just tell me what you need, and I'll do it."

"I might take you up on that." Angelina's gaze moved up to the bandage on his head. "I have a feeling that some solid sleep would be good for you, though."

He couldn't argue with that. "Probably. I'll turn in."

Angelina smiled but didn't answer, and Ben headed toward the door. He might not have his memory, but he did have a sense of when to walk away. He liked her. And he liked the way he'd made her smile.

He wanted to do that again.

ANGELINA TOOK ANOTHER bite of ice cream, watching the door swing shut behind Ben. She let out a slow breath.

She couldn't blame him—he didn't remember. But did he have to be so charming? This would be easier if the accident had made him sour or angry. Instead, he was the same smiling, intoxicating man who'd swept her off her feet fifteen years ago, and her heart was reacting the same way it had back then.

"Not helpful," she murmured, and she put the lid on her ice cream and returned both cartons to the large freezer.

Angelina wasn't so easy to impress anymore. She was older, wiser, more cautious. She'd been through a lot, and while she knew that she could survive some incredibly painful things, she was smart enough not to want to repeat them. The point in life was not mere survival. She'd grown too far beyond that to go backward.

Angelina should really get to bed, too. It would be an early morning. The kitchen employees were going to need a hand with the morning prep, and Angelina was starting to worry about the stock of firewood. They'd worked through half of it already, and the next morning, she'd be starting a new fire just to warm the place up. The deep freeze outside was making the old furnace work overtime, and while everything was still technically heated, it wasn't as warm as it could be. The fireplace would help with that.

She made a mental list. They would need to shovel a path to the firewood and restock. There was one section of roof that had always had some trouble shedding snow, too, so they'd need to get up there and shovel the heavy snowfall off. Likely, she'd do it herself, she decided as she flipped off the kitchen light and headed out the swinging door into the dining room.

All was neatly arranged, ready for the next day, and that sight always did something to soothe her. She liked being prepared, knowing what to expect, and knowing that whatever came up, she could handle it. That was what made her a good manager.

Marrying Ben had been her one wild fling, when she'd followed her heart and hoped for the best. It hadn't gone well, and she'd settled back into her well-worn ways, preparing, planning, creating... She was good at this job. She felt safe here at the resort, carefully building up a vacation spot she'd personally love to visit. So far, her strategy had worked.

Maybe even a little too well, considering she had guests who had refused to clear out for this storm.

She headed for the front door and checked it one last time. They were locked up tight. She'd left her office unlocked when her ice cream craving hit, and she went to lock it up now.

Angelina stepped inside to turn off the light, but she spotted Ben's lambskin, fleece-lined coat flung over the back of her visitor's chair.

She picked it up to bring it to him, but as she hung it over her arm, a thick manila envelope fell out of an inside pocket and landed on the floor at her feet.

Ben might need this—once his memory returned, at least. And maybe it would help jog something for him. She picked it up and noticed that the flap wasn't sealed. This was personal—going through Ben's belongings was an invasion of his privacy.

And yet, he was here in her lodge, no memory of his family, of his history, of any pressing responsibilities he might have…

She knew it was wrong, but she peeked inside all the same, and the document she saw not only looked legal, but she spotted Mountain Springs Resort in the lettering. That did it—she pulled out the sheaf of papers and smoothed them out.

Offer to Purchase and Earnest Money Deposit

On this day of ___, King Real Estate Developers offers to purchase Mountain Springs Resort, henceforth referred to as The Property, from Angelina Cunningham, henceforth referred to as The Seller, and delivers to the Buyer's Brokerage, or agrees to deliver no later than four (4) calendar days as Acceptance (as described in Section 23) Earnest Money in the amount of $_____ and in the form of _____...

Her stomach dropped. She recognized these papers—they were an offer to buy her resort, and the amount for the sale was left empty. So that was why Ben King was here—he'd come up to Mountain Springs to buy back the resort.

Her breath caught in her throat, and the first emotion to punch through the fog of shock was blistering anger. He wanted this property back? After she'd grown it, developed it and turned it into the success that it was?

The King family had signed a run-down mountain lodge over to her in the divorce settlement…a settlement that they were only too eager to sign off on because Ben had foolishly, in their minds, married her without a prenuptial agreement, and a run-down lodge was a small price to pay to get rid of her quietly. In return for this lakeside land and the lodge, she'd signed that nondisclosure agreement, agreeing to never divulge any information about Ben or the family that would damage their image. She was allowed to tell people that the relationship hadn't worked—that much was obvious—but beyond that, it was a minefield. She'd agreed—she wasn't petty enough to try to ruin her ex-husband's good name anyway. She'd told her friends why she got divorced—the money got in the way—but anything else she'd kept vaulted.

Besides, it had been kind on Ben's part to give her all this land. She hadn't been able to afford the caliber of lawyer he could in their divorce, and he could have dragged her through court until she was completely broke, but he hadn't. He'd asked what might help her move on, and she'd said she wanted to start her own business. In fact, she'd hoped to run a bed-and-breakfast. All she'd wanted was a house with character in the town of Mountain Springs. The lodge was Ben's suggestion. His family happened to own it.

Was it guilt over how they'd ended? Sentimentality over some residual feelings for her? Whatever it was, with this lakeside property in her name, she'd been able to secure a loan that allowed her to begin renovations, and Mountain Springs Resort was born.

And now the King family wanted it back badly enough that they'd sent in Ben to convince her. That thought chilled her. And if they wanted this land back, how far were they willing to go to get it?

Except Ben had no memory of any of this. If he did, there was no way he'd have left his coat in her office to have those papers discovered. Was that why they were willing to leave Ben here in the middle of a storm?

Angelina's gaze dropped to the papers again, and she flipped through them. That blank space for the dollar amount was brazenly empty, so she had no idea how much they were even willing to offer her to sell them this property back… For just a moment, she did a little bit of mental math.

Did the amount matter? If they threw a filthy amount of money at her, would she take it and leave Colorado? Start over somewhere else?

How much were they talking?

For a moment Angelina stood there immobile, thinking about the number of zeros it would take for her to sell, but she couldn't do it. This resort wasn't a moneymaking scheme. And it wasn't just an investment…it had become so much more than her livelihood. This was her healing, her freedom, her foundation for a whole new life.

This resort had become a place of healing for other people, too. It was as if there was something in the water of Blue Lake, something in the deep mountain springs that fed it, that awakened spirits and reminded women of their worth all over again. The Second Chance Dinner Club, her group of friends who got together on a regular basis to eat amazing food, drink good wine and support each other through the hardest parts of their lives, were a testament to that magic.

Angelina tucked the pages back into the

envelope and slid them back into the pocket of Ben's coat.

When his memory came back and Ben asked her to sell the resort that she'd poured her grief, her sweat, her inspiration and her lifeblood into, she was going to tell him clearly and concisely, no.

Mountain Springs was not for sale.

Angelina Cunningham didn't have a price.

CHAPTER FOUR

ANGELINA STOOD IN the dim light that came in through her open office door, her mind spinning. Ben's memory was gone—she was sure that wasn't a ruse. He didn't know her, and he didn't know about those papers in his coat. She knew Ben and he'd never been that good of an actor.

The coat would be safe enough in her office. Angelina put it back over her chair and locked the door behind her.

Would she tell him that she'd seen those papers? She wasn't sure yet. She'd see how things played out.

Angelina headed down the hallway toward the foyer. This was the quietest this lodge had been since the last snowstorm had whistled through this mountain valley. The empty lodge always unsettled her. As a business owner, every setback, even one caused by uncontrollable outside forces, felt like it could be the last. It was the cautious part of her nature that panicked at times like these, even though she knew that as soon as the blizzard had run its course, they'd fill right back up again.

Angelina headed through the foyer and up the broad staircase. Ben King had come to buy her out… That fact lay heavy inside of her. He knew exactly what the place meant to her. This lodge had been her entire divorce settlement, her fresh start, and he wanted to take it back? How could Ben, of all people, try to do that to her?

At the top of the stairs, she took a deep breath and straightened her shoulders. She was no longer the young ex-wife trying to find her way. Angelina Cunningham had a reputation for excellence now. She'd built something she was proud of. She couldn't forget how far she'd come.

Angelina looked behind her, down the hallway of suites, and she noticed the young woman who was part of the snowboarding group. She was sitting on the floor, her back against the wall. There was something in her posture that spoke of exhaustion, and sadness.

"Is there anything you need?" Angelina asked.

The young woman wiped her cheeks with the palms of her hands and stood up. She'd been crying.

"I'm fine. Just…getting some space," she said.

She was the only woman traveling with a group of rowdy young men, and that in itself was reason to be cautious, in Angelina's experience. She turned away from her own suite and headed in the young woman's direction.

"Are they giving you a hard time?" Angelina asked.

"My boyfriend is being a jerk," she replied with a shrug. "What else is new, right?"

"What's your name?" Angelina asked.

"Elizabeth," she replied.

"Elizabeth…" Angelina nodded. "Do you want your own room? I can arrange that for you right away—"

"No. I'm fine." She looked down at her cell phone. "I was hoping to get some cell service out here."

"No luck," Angelina said softly.

"No…"

This young woman was on her own right now, and there were times when female companionship was a lifesaver. Angelina could wish her a good night and leave her be, but she wouldn't feel right about that.

"How long have you been dating?" Angelina asked.

"Three years."

"Long time," Angelina said.

"Yeah, it is." Elizabeth eyed Angelina hesitantly for a moment, then sighed. "I was expecting a proposal this trip."

There was whooping laughter from one of the rooms and the TV was turned a bit higher.

"With all his buddies around?" Angelina asked.

Elizabeth looked toward that door as there was another eruption of laughter. "It was supposed to be just the two of us. A trip to the most romantic resort in Colorado… His buddies were a last-minute addition."

Angelina nodded. "I see. I'm sorry."

Elizabeth shrugged. "What can you do when his best friends decide to crash the trip and make some 'epic weekend'?"

Dump him was the first thought that came to mind, but Angelina doubted that advice would be welcome. But Elizabeth just might need time away from all that testosterone.

"I'm not quite ready to turn in," Angelina

said. "Do you want to go downstairs with me and chat?"

"Yeah?" Elizabeth frowned slightly. "You've probably got other things to do."

"I'm sure that you'd be calling a friend or texting someone your woes right about now if you could get a cell phone signal," Angelina replied. "Besides, I was your age once upon a time. A very long time ago."

Elizabeth didn't seem to catch the irony in Angelina's tone because she nodded soberly. "Okay, that would be nice."

"So tell me about you," Angelina said as they headed back down the staircase.

"Um… I'm in my last year at University of Denver. I'm taking my bachelor's degree in biology. I graduate in May."

"Nice." Angelina nodded approvingly. "What will you do with it?"

"That's the question, isn't it? It depends on whether or not I'm getting married."

Angelina led the way to the fireside room. There were still a few coals lit in the fireplace, and Angelina added a couple of sticks of wood on top of them, then pulled two chairs up close to the hearth.

Upstairs, the sound of the young men's

laughter and talking was faint, and Angelina sank into the armchair next to Elizabeth.

"You know, I thought the very idea of being a politician's wife was stupid for all of my adolescence," Elizabeth went on. "But then I met Brad, and I fell for him. His family is very political, and he's got several uncles in politics. His grandfather was a senator. He wants to be president one day."

"And you want to be First Lady," Angelina presumed.

"I don't know. Not really. But if that's where Brad's headed, there are worse places to land."

"For Brad it's worth it?" Angelina asked.

"Definitely." But Elizabeth's voice didn't match the enthusiasm of her reply.

"Well… I'm happy for you, then."

Elizabeth leaned forward and put her hands toward the fire.

"What did he say to upset you tonight?" Angelina asked.

"Oh, it was stupid, really," she replied. "He was talking about getting a new apartment once we all graduate, and what *he* was going to do. No mention of me in his plans."

"Didn't use the word *we* once, huh?" Angelina asked.

"Oh, he did, but only in reference to him and his buddies getting together for monthly poker games," she said with a sigh. "He's like that, though. He won't talk about his feelings with his friends around. What guy does, right?"

"Hmm." Angelina watched the blaze. "Politicians' wives can have careers of their own, you know."

"I know."

"So…if you were to have one, what would it be?" Angelina asked.

"That's the problem. I thought I wanted to teach high school biology," she replied. "Or I could go on for a PhD and get into research. My sister became a veterinarian."

"Do you have the grades for that?" Angelina asked curiously.

"Oh, I have the grades," Elizabeth said, shooting her a wry smile. "I just don't know what I would want to pursue, and if I don't know that, I might as well take the next step forward in my personal life, you know?"

"Hmm."

"Brad always said he wanted to get married the year after he graduated his bachelor's degree. It's good timing, politically speaking.

A married man gives the impression of being more stable."

Angelina looked over at her. "So…just being married? The right woman doesn't factor in here?"

"Of course." Elizabeth's gaze moved up to the ceiling. "It takes a real shark to rise in politics, and Brad is definitely a shark."

Angelina knew a thing or two about well-positioned families, and looking at this young woman—a little younger than she'd been when she met Ben—she felt a wave of maternal protectiveness. Elizabeth thought she was ever so grown-up, and legally speaking, she was certainly an adult. After three years of dating this young "shark," she should know what she was getting into…but then, did anyone?

"Are you a shark, too?" Angelina asked.

Elizabeth laughed. "No. Not at all. I leave all the carnage to him."

"Do you get along with his family?"

"His parents love me." Elizabeth moved her hair away from her face. "I think his dad thinks I'm more wonderful than Brad does! He tells Brad not to lose me, because I'm utterly irreplaceable."

"That's sweet," Angelina said with a smile.

"And his mom is great. She sometimes comes to Denver and takes me out for lunch and a pedicure or something," Elizabeth went on. "You know, she's the one who told me that I really bring out the best in Brad. I make him kinder and more considerate."

So this was the best version there was of the young man… But Angelina could see what would draw a young woman in. He was good-looking, from a wealthy family and confident. Many a mediocre man had gone for miles on those characteristics alone.

"What did Brad take in school?" Angelina asked.

"Political science."

"That makes sense."

"With a minor in criminology. He's really passionate about the prison system. He wants to see it reformed."

"Oh, that's a positive thing," Angelina said.

"He's brilliant, you know," Elizabeth said, looking toward Angelina. "He's smart. I know he hides it well on vacation—trust me, I know how he comes across. But under that party boy exterior beats a really patriotic heart. He wants to make our country better for our children."

"I was married to a man who was from a

very wealthy family," Angelina said softly. "And it was hard. Really hard. I think you might have it easier because Brad's parents like you, but I didn't have my in-laws' good opinion to start with, and the pressure was too much."

"What happened?" Elizabeth asked.

"Oh…it's a long story," Angelina said. It was also a story protected by a nondisclosure agreement. "But suffice to say, we didn't last. The thing is, it's easy to lose yourself in all the expectations and the demands on you. Be careful not to make that mistake."

"Oh, I won't," Elizabeth said, but her expression grew more sober. "So are you single?"

"Yes, I am," Angelina replied.

"It must be lonely. Do you miss being married?" Elizabeth asked.

Angelina was silent for a moment. "Marriage was far more complicated than I realized going into it. I have this group of friends who all went through a divorce, and the one thing we all missed the most was that younger, optimistic version of ourselves. I really loved my ex-husband, but I'm happy single, too. Once I was on my own, I could get back to things I'm passionate about…like this resort."

"This is a really beautiful location," Elizabeth said. "You're the general manager, right? How long have you worked here?"

"Sweetie, I own it."

Elizabeth blinked. "Oh!"

Angelina smiled. "The general manager is at home with his family right now. No, I'm the one who looked at an old hunting lodge and thought that with some wood refinishing and some beveled glass, something beautiful was possible."

"I'm sorry, I didn't mean to underestimate you," Elizabeth said. "This is a really amazing resort."

"Thank you," Angelina replied. "I appreciate it. If you have any ideas of how to improve things for a guest, just let me know."

"It's perfect the way it is," Elizabeth replied.

Upstairs, footfalls creaked down the hallway. A faint voice called, "Betsy?"

Angelina looked over at Elizabeth. The young woman sighed.

"Betsy?" Angelina asked.

"It's what Brad calls me. It's a private joke—" She shrugged. "He thinks it sounds more like a senator's wife."

"Betsy?" The voice came from the direction of the main staircase now, and he sounded worried. "Where are you?"

Brad came around the counter into the fireside room. He wore a pair of jeans and a football jersey. His wavy blond hair was tousled, and his glittering gaze raked over the room and landed on Elizabeth.

"What are you doing down here?" he demanded.

"I'm surprised you noticed," Elizabeth said.

"Yeah, well, I did. So what's the matter?"

"Nothing." Elizabeth rose to her feet. "I'm glad to be missed." She turned to Angelina. "Nice to meet you. I didn't catch your name…"

"Angelina," she replied.

Brad reached for her hand and tugged Elizabeth against him. He looked down at her with a possessive gaze, and then glanced up at Angelina.

"Oh, and we need new towels up there," Brad said. "If you could bring some, that would be great."

Elizabeth nudged him. "Brad…"

"And I know you said the kitchen is closed, but we'll pay for it. We need pizza," Brad added. "And wings, too."

"The kitchen *is* closed until breakfast," Angelina replied. "You can use the bar fridge for snacks."

"You can't just...whip something up?" Brad asked, and he shot her a hopeful smile. "We're pretty hungry, and some macadamia nuts aren't going to cut it."

This was a young man used to being obeyed, and as Angelina eyed him, she was reminded of the young man who'd swept her off her feet when she was only a few years older than Elizabeth was now. Brad and Ben had the same confidence that all would go the way they dictated.

"Brad, she's the owner," Elizabeth said, raising her voice.

"I know who she is." He paused a moment. "So where are we on the pizza and wings?"

Elizabeth blanched, and Angelina chuckled. This was a power play. Brad had decided that she was below him.

"I strongly suggested that you all relocate to Denver for this storm. You chose to stay. The pizza and wings are in Denver. I suggest you make do with the macadamia nuts and get up nice and early for a hearty breakfast."

She watched conflicted feelings flicker across his handsome features. He wasn't used to being told where to get off, she could tell, and his expression went from irritation to mildly impressed. He landed on the latter and shot her a rueful smile.

"Okay, okay," Brad said. "We'll behave. Thanks for entertaining Betsy here." He gave Elizabeth a squeeze. "Come on. Let's watch that movie you wanted to see. I'll kick the guys out."

The couple headed out of the fireside room arm in arm. Angelina could hear their soft voices heading back up the main staircase. Once upon a time, she'd been just as naive and hopeful as Elizabeth was, and her heart had been at the mercy of a wealthy, handsome man, too.

Ben had been right to hide his wealthy family from her until after the elopement, because if she'd known exactly how powerful his family had been, if she'd had a brain cell left in her head that wasn't soggy with dopamine, she would have insisted on a much longer engagement at the very least.

Angelina couldn't judge young love. She'd been there before. All she could hope was that it went better for Elizabeth than it had for her.

BEN WOKE UP the next morning to the low moaning of the wind outside. The room was warm, though, and when he tossed his covers and went over to the window, he could see the faint outline of mountain peaks through the blowing snow.

The blizzard hadn't let up, and the lacy fingers of frost spread from the edges of the window. He stood there for a moment, searching his memory for more information than he'd fallen asleep with. He'd finally drifted off last night with the vague hope that a solid rest would improve matters inside his own skull.

"Who am I?" he murmured aloud, hoping for an answer to spring to mind that was more than the words of other people. There was nothing.

When was his life going to come back to him? Facing hour after hour without his memory was exhausting. The constant effort to remember, even if he didn't realize he was trying to do so, was draining. And yet, here he was in a mountain resort with a storm howling outside his window, and nothing better to do with himself than to try.

He picked up his phone and looked down at it. No bars. No connection… He could see the phone calls he'd received over the last couple of weeks—some just numbers, some with names attached. One that came regularly, every couple of days, was listed as Dad.

His texts weren't terribly enlightening, either. The texts from his father tended to be things like "Call me" or "What's your ETA?" Apparently, there wasn't a lot discussed via text with his father. The other messages seemed to be work related—questions about reports or meetings. One woman, though—Hilaria—texted more personal things...

I still love you. Are we doing the right thing here in calling off the wedding?

Why are you so cruel to me? We want the same things! Can't that be enough for you?

I'm not talking to you right now, Ben. You're being impossible. Your mother is right—I'm the best thing that ever happened to you.

Is this about your ex-wife? Honestly, Ben, get Angelina out of your system already. You know exactly why it didn't work, and you're ruining a good thing here.

It was more of the same. He didn't see any responses from himself. Maybe he called her and spoke on the phone, instead? This was like scrolling through a stranger's phone. Hilaria was just a name, someone he didn't have a mental image of. But apparently his ex-fiancée thought he had some unresolved feelings about Angelina.

Ben looked through his phone and found a number under the name Angie. He checked for texts—there were none.

Angie... Did he remember something about her? It was just the shine of golden hair. Was that an actual memory, or just his thoughts surrounding the woman he'd met when he stumbled into this lodge? He couldn't tell. She'd told him they got divorced over a decade ago. Angelina didn't seem to be holding any torch for him. Maybe his feelings had been one-sided.

His stomach rumbled and he looked down at his watch. It was almost eight. He'd head downstairs and see if he could order breakfast. And maybe he'd see Angelina, as well. He had to admit that he was hoping to. She was his one connection to the life he couldn't remember, and she was both beautiful and likable.

Yeah, maybe Hilaria had had a point. Even

with his memory addled, he seemed to be drawn to Angelina.

Ben pulled on a pair of jeans and a long-sleeved grey Henley shirt that had seen better days. In the mirror he looked downright rustic. His boots were dry now, and he found a pair of socks in the pile of clothes Angelina had given him, and it felt good to pull his cowboy boots back on. His black hat lay on the little writing desk, and he picked it up, rolling it around between his palms.

Did he remember this hat? He felt like he did. He remembered the feel of it, the slight weight of it. He put it on his head and it felt like it completed his face, somehow.

"That's a memory..." he murmured. Sort of. It was the best he had so far.

He took the hat off and tossed it onto the desk again. He knew exactly how hard to throw it to have it land in the center. A man's hat felt like a personal thing.

He headed out of his room and pocketed the key. There was a do-not-disturb sign put on one of doors that Ben passed, and as he headed down that main staircase, he felt a surge of anticipation for some breakfast. He wanted eggs Benedict and a cup of hot coffee with cream and sugar. The mental image was so sharp that it startled him. Strange, the detailed memories that had somehow dug in. If only he could reach the rest in his head.

The dining room was nearly empty, except for a table at the far side of the room next to a window. Angelina sat with a teacup in front of her, dressed more casually in a pair of jeans and a pale pink cowl-necked sweater. She looked softer, somehow, more approachable than she had before. He looked down at his own clothing—maybe he was more approachable than usual, too.

He wound his way around the tables, and when he got to hers, Angelina looked up.

"Good morning," she said.

"Good morning." He pulled out a chair, not waiting for the invitation.

"How are you feeling?" she asked.

"You mean, how much do I remember?" he asked, raising an eyebrow.

"Exactly." She met his gaze frankly.

"Nothing more," he said. "Unless you count a fondness for my hat. I seem to remember that hat."

She smiled faintly. "I don't think that counts."

"Well, then…" He shrugged. "I'm still at your mercy."

"Do you want breakfast?" she asked, and she beckoned to a server.

"Joel, I'll have oatmeal, wheat toast and a bowl of yoghurt," Angelina said, then turned to Ben. "What will you have?"

"Can I get eggs Benedict?" he asked.

"Yes, not a problem," Joel replied.

"And coffee—cream and sugar," Ben added.

"Right away, sir."

Joel disappeared and Ben noticed Angelina's attention was fixed on him in a rather pointed way. He shot her a curious look.

"What?" he asked.

"You always ordered the same thing for breakfast. I guess that hasn't changed."

"I seem to remember really liking it." He paused for a moment. He had other questions that were more pressing than his breakfast preferences. "Is Hilaria my ex-fiancée?"

Angelina's composure faltered a little. He'd surprised her.

"Uh—" She nodded. "Yes. Hilaria Bell. You were engaged for about six months. Are you remembering her?"

"No, I was reading my texts," he confessed. "And she had some real thoughts about you."

"Me?" Angelina's eyebrows went up. "Why?"

"We were married," he said.

"Thirteen years ago," she replied. "That's a lot of water under the bridge."

He nodded. "I know. And again, I have no memory of this stuff. I'm just going by her texts. She seemed to think..." He watched Angelina's face for some confirmation. "She seemed to think there was something between us still."

"Why?" she asked bluntly.

"Was there?" he asked. "She seemed to think that me breaking off the engagement was about you."

Angelina let out a slow breath, then shook her head. "She's wrong."

"Okay, I'm willing to believe that," he said. "But what would give her that impression? You said I came to tell you about the engagement...obviously you and I had some connection still."

"I was your first wife," Angelina said. "I think there will always be a connection between us. But it doesn't mean I had any interest in breaking up your relationship."

Maybe she wasn't the one who was crossing lines...maybe it was him. Ben wasn't sure how he felt about that possibility.

"Did I seem like I was hung up on you?" he asked.

Angelina met his gaze, and then her cheeks pinked slightly. "No."

"Would you tell me if I had been?" he pressed.

"Ben, you were marrying a much more appropriate woman. Your family loved her."

But had Ben felt the same way?

"That doesn't answer my question, though," he said. "Would you tell me? I mean, if I had my memory, I can understand trying to spare my feelings, or save me embarrassment. But I have nothing here. So you're not going to embarrass me."

In fact, looking into her clear, thoughtful gaze, he could understand still holding a torch for this woman. It wouldn't surprise him in the least.

"We've always had some…chemistry," she said quietly. "We both knew it didn't matter, though."

"But we stayed in touch?" he pressed.

"We talked maybe twice a year, and when we did, we…" She sighed. "We had a way of getting right to the heart of a matter. You appreciated that."

"I think I would."

"Your life was always much bigger than me," she added.

Ben fished his phone out of his pocket and opened up the photo album. "Would you do me a favor and tell me who people are?"

Angelina flicked through the photos and held up one of him standing arm in arm with a dark-haired woman. He was in a suit, and she was in a blousy, nude-colored dress.

"That's Hilaria," she said.

"Okay..." He took the phone back and looked closer. He couldn't connect any emotions or memories to the photo. Hilaria was just a woman. She was slim, well-dressed, pretty.

Angelina took the phone back and flicked through another few photos, and then held up another shot of the man who'd said he was his father standing next to a different woman— late thirties. She wore a pantsuit, and her makeup was understated.

"That's your dad."

"Yeah, I recognize him from the video call."

"That's your younger sister standing next to him," she added.

"What's her name?"

"Cleo," she replied.

"Are we close?"

"Not particularly," Angelina replied. "You see her on holidays, and once in a long while you chat. Unless that's changed over the years."

He hadn't seen her name in the list of recent phone calls or texts.

Angelina flicked through a few more pictures, and then she froze.

"What?" he asked.

She turned the phone so he could see the picture. It was one of him and Angelina together. It was a selfie—him shirtless and bronzed by the sun, and her in what looked like a bathing suit top. They both looked younger…happier.

"That's us," he said.

"Yeah…" She handed the phone back. "I didn't know you kept that one on your phone."

Ben looked at the photo, and it was almost like he could smell the surf and feel the warmth of the breeze against his skin.

"When was this?" he asked.

"It was on the cruise when we met," she said. "We got married two weeks later."

"We look really happy," he said.

"We were naive," she replied with a low laugh. "And you'd hidden that you came from a wealthy family from me. Maybe the fact that you could just take an extra couple of weeks off work should have been a tip-off for me. I thought you were as ordinary as I was."

"I'd hardly call you ordinary."

Angelina looked at him for a beat, then a smile tickled her lips. "You shouldn't do that."

"Do what?"

"Flirt."

"I said I wouldn't do that, didn't I?" he said.

"Mmm-hmm."

"And there are probably really good reasons that we're no longer together…"

"There are excellent reasons," Angelina replied, but a smile curved up her plump lips. "Just trust me about that."

The meal came then, his coffee cup was filled, and they both fell silent as the server gave them their plates. His eggs Benedict looked perfect, and he poured a dribble of cream from a small ceramic jug into his cup of coffee.

He picked up his fork and looked at her thoughtfully. "You know what? I think Hilaria had a point. It appears that I was very much hung up on you still."

"The picture?" she asked.

"And the texts where Hilaria talked about

you," he said. "Then there's the fact that I was hell-bent on getting here, specifically. I don't know why I was coming, but…you have to admit, it's mighty coincidental."

"You forgot your coat in my office," Angelina said suddenly.

"Oh…" That was a weird change of topic.

"Do you want to get it now?" she asked.

"Uh—" He nodded toward his plate of food. "Can it wait until after breakfast?"

"Can it?" she asked.

He shot her a quizzical look. "Are you trying to get me alone? Or am I particular about my coats, too?"

"Just wondering if you had missed it," she said. "It's a very expensive lambskin coat. That's all."

"No, I hadn't even thought of it," he replied. "How nitpicky am I?"

Angelina relaxed slightly, then laughed softly. "Not that bad."

"Good."

Angelina looked like she was about to say something more, then she shrugged.

"Anyway, maybe you'll sort things out with Hilaria yet," she said.

Would he? Right now, he couldn't remember meeting either woman. He couldn't remember his own mother...

"I'm in no state to offer myself to anyone," he replied, and he took a bite, chewing slowly. "But by the looks of things, I have some very inconvenient, unresolved feelings for you."

He shot her a grin, and she blushed again.

"I just can't remember them," he added.

Ben liked making her blush. Was it thoroughly inappropriate for him to be hoping she returned a few of those unresolved feelings? Maybe there was no future, and no hope for it, but it would be soothing to his ego if he weren't the only one. Otherwise, he'd just be a guy who broke off an engagement to a perfectly nice and appropriate woman for a memory.

"It would be in your best interest to resolve them," Angelina said.

"I have no hope of winning you back?" he asked.

And for just a moment, he felt a strange surge of longing so strong that it nearly rocked him. He had more than unresolved feelings for this woman...

"No hope," Angelina said, and she laughed softly. "Trust me, Ben. You have a whole life out there. I'm not going to lie to you about that, even if—"

She didn't finish the thought.

"Even if?" he prodded.

Just then, the overhead lights flickered twice and went out.

CHAPTER FIVE

ANGELINA WASN'T GOING to lie to him, even if it might be tempting to pretend that she was more central to his existence. She'd been about to say that before the lights went out.

But her mind was caught on the words that hung in the air between them. Ben had feelings for her? Enough that he'd been able to sleuth it out on his cell phone thirteen years after their divorce? But he'd never let on to her!

Angelina pushed back her chair and rose to her feet. She heard some muffled voices of frustration from the kitchen just as the doors opened and Dr. Thomas came into the dining room. The rest of the snowboarders wouldn't be far behind, and they'd need at least some electricity back.

"I've got a generator in the basement," Angelina said.

"Do you want a hand?" Ben asked.

Being alone with Ben wasn't going to get

her emotional balance back, but Angelina was running this resort on a skeleton crew.

"I'd appreciate the help," she said.

Ben shoved a bite of food into his mouth and took a swig of his coffee.

"You might as well finish up first," she added. "We can take a couple of minutes to eat."

Warren came through the dining room, looking around in mild confusion.

"The electricity just went," Angelina called to him.

"Ah." Warren looked behind him toward the door. "So that was what I heard up there—shouts of anguish."

Angelina laughed softly and took a quick bite of toast. She shot Ben a rueful smile. "And the generator will only supply the kitchen, offices and basement. The rest of the resort will be dark until the electricity is back."

Ben raised his eyebrows. "That's...not good."

"I did strongly encourage everyone to head out of the mountains," she said.

"But you will have to deal with complaints, regardless," he replied.

"True."

And she wasn't looking forward to trying to curb the natural instincts of a group of snowboarding college students. She finished the last of her toast, then turned her attention momentarily toward the doctor. "Warren, there is a large pot of oatmeal already cooked, and there is dry cereal, bagels and cream cheese, fruit… You'll get a decent breakfast if you're okay with those things."

"I'll eat just fine," Warren said with a nod. "Don't worry about me. Is there anything I can do to help?"

"Would you mind starting a fire in the fireside room later on?" she asked.

"I could probably figure that out," Warren replied. "Consider it done."

Angelina glanced over to Ben, who was regarding her with a thoughtful expression. One of these days he was going to remember everything, and she had a feeling that his warm interest in her would fade away. She was a curiosity right now. Once he remembered their marriage, she'd just be the ex-wife again.

"Let's head down there," she said.

Angelina led the way out of the dining room, stopping at the front desk to pick up a couple of flashlights. She handed one to Ben, and glanced over his shoulder toward the windows where the snow was still whipping past the glass.

"Ben, I don't think you had as many unresolved feelings toward me as you suspect," she said, meeting his gaze.

"Why's that?" he asked.

"I would have known." And he wouldn't be here to buy her out of the business that meant so much to her if he did.

"I don't think it really matters right now," he said. "Unless you had a few unresolved feelings of your own."

He shot her a teasing smile and she met it with a chilly look.

"No," she said curtly. "I don't."

At least, she was trying very hard to subdue them. At this point in her life, she wasn't interested in emotional games. She knew where this led.

"Then we're fine." He shrugged.

Were they? She sighed. She didn't have time for this… Ben with his memory intact might have been a worthy adversary to argue with. Ben without his memory? Actually he was just as charming, just as handsome, and interestingly, just as confident.

"Let's go," she said, and she led the way to the basement staircase.

Angelina pulled open the door and shone her flashlight into the darkness. All was silent, and she started down the stairs, Ben's footfalls creaking behind her. She knew this lodge inside out—the nooks and crannies, the back rooms and the basement labyrinth. But she'd never navigated the basement in the dark before.

When she got the bottom of the staircase, she felt Ben's hand on her shoulder, warm and strong. It transported her back to those early days of marriage when they'd arrive at a function, and Ben's hand on her shoulder or just on the back of her neck had been reassuring, knowing he had her back.

In the end, it hadn't been enough, but his touch brought with it the memory of sweeter days.

Angelina shivered, and they moved together into the dark depths of the basement, leaving the light from the open door behind them. His hand dropped from her shoulder, and she paused, shining the paltry flashlight beam down a hallway. The skitter of a mouse's feet scratched to her left.

"I hate mice," Ben muttered behind her.

"No, you don't," she said.

"If I actually remember it, I think there's a

pretty high probability that I do," he retorted, and he flashed his beam around the hallway.

"You told me they didn't bother you," she said. "When I first got this place, you emptied the traps for me."

Angelina could hardly see him in the dim light, but his deep laugh rumbled close to her ear. He'd been a kind ex-husband—she had to give him credit for that.

"I must be quite the hero, then," he said. "Because they give me the heebie-jeebies." The warmth of his chest emanated against her. "I did that for you?"

"You did," she said.

"Was I...around a lot after the divorce?"

"No, you'd come with some papers for me," she replied. "You were a decent ex, Ben. I'll give you that."

"I guess that's...a good thing."

"My grandmother once told me that a woman should marry a man who'd make a good ex-husband."

He grunted. "I'm not sure I agree."

Angelina smiled. "It sounds pessimistic, but I think the idea was, if a man will still be kind to you and reliable after a divorce, he's a truly decent guy."

He was silent for a moment, then she felt

his fingertips touch her temple and move through her hair. She closed her eyes.

"Maybe the husband would be worth keeping around then," he said.

"It's not always that simple," she whispered.

He ran her hair through his fingers, and then his touch was gone. But she could feel him close to her.

"I don't remember any of that," he murmured. "But I do remember your hair."

Her breath caught. "What?"

"I remember it," he breathed. "How it felt on my fingers. How it looked in the sunlight… The way it smelled on a pillow…"

"Ben…"

His hand closed around hers—strong, warm.

"I don't think the measure of a man ought to be what kind of ex he makes, either," he murmured. "It's a little underachieving if you ask me."

She should tell him to stop, but somehow the words didn't come out, and for a couple of beats, they stood there in silence, the air between them tingling. His fingers tightened around hers, and the warmth of his breath tickled her cheek. If she let this continue…

She swallowed, tugged her hand free and took a step back.

"We can't do this," she whispered.

"Do what?"

She smiled ruefully. She wasn't going to play this game. She knew exactly where this would go...their chemistry was nothing but predictable, and the memory of his searing kisses was enough for her.

"We've had a couple of lapses in the past," she said.

"Oh?"

"Just two." She paused, remembering her moments of weakness when the yearning between them had just been too much.

He stepped closer so that the front of his shirt brushed against hers, and his hand moved up her arm. "How much lapsing did we do?"

"Some kisses," she said. "Some cuddling. Some wondering if we could patch things up... Spoiler alert, we couldn't. It just took a few tries for us to make our peace with that."

"So this attraction between us is just what we do?" he asked.

"We used to. Not anymore." Angelina shone her flashlight toward a far door. "That's where the generator is."

She longed to reach back and touch him—take his hand, or grab his shirt, anything. But she wouldn't.

"The snowboarders are waiting..." she added.

"Right." A smile tickled the corners of his lips.

Angelina would have to be the one who rescued him—both from the mice, and from himself, it would seem. They'd followed their feelings before, and it didn't end well.

"Come on," she said.

Angelina led the way toward the door and pushed open the door with a creak. The generator looked like a large metal box with a few doors on the sides. She hadn't been able to afford the biggest or the fanciest, and she didn't have the space in the electrical room for anything too large. That left them with a moderate generator that would keep the kitchen and offices in power.

"The instructions are here somewhere," she said, opening the side door and moving the beam of her flashlight over the small lettering on the inside panel. There was a key already inserted in the ignition. Ben's beam came over her shoulder giving her a better view as she scanned the directions.

"Have you used this before?" he asked.

"No, this is the first time… So, I flick the fuel valve on, the choke switch…" The installer had walked her through this a few times, but it felt different in the dark. "Turn the key in the ignition and—"

His hand came beside her and he pushed the red button, the generator chugging to life.

The machine was loud, but a moment after it started, the lights flickered and then popped back on, illuminating the room. Angelina blinked in the sudden light, and she found Ben so close that she was remembering those kisses again…

She pulled her mind back from the precipice.

"Thanks," she said.

His gaze moved down her hair, and he reached out and fingered a tendril, a smile touching his lips.

"Yeah, I remember your hair," he said quietly, then he stepped back.

Would he ever remember more than her hair? But then, he'd always underestimated her. He'd always thought she was beautiful— he'd told her often enough—but she'd also been capable of so much more than he'd even considered. She'd been a woman with ideas and dreams, and never quite enough capital behind her to make them into a reality. Well, this resort showed exactly what she was capable of, and her looks had very little to do with it.

"You remember my hair," she said quietly. "But do you remember my heart? Or my loyalty? Or my talent? Or my temper?"

Ben met her gaze, his expression clouded. No, he didn't, apparently.

"It'll come back," she said. "I drove you crazy. I've always been more than a pretty face and great hair. Thirteen years hasn't changed the reasons why we'll never work."

Ben blinked, then nodded.

"I'm sorry. I'm not asking for anything," he said. "I'm just trying to remember...and when something comes back, it's like a piece of me returning."

A piece of him...did Angelina still count as a piece of this man's heart? After all this time, after the choices they'd both made, after asking another woman to marry him...

No, she wouldn't let Ben pull her back into this. He was just grasping at some memories. She remembered all of their history together, and there were papers upstairs in the inside pocket of his lambskin coat that suggested he *would* be asking for something—her entire resort.

Angelina took a step away from him, away from temptation.

"Let's get back upstairs," she said.

Their chemistry had never been enough.

BEN WATCHED AS Angelina headed for the door. Had he offended her? At least he had one concrete memory now. He did remember her golden waves, the way they'd slip through his fingers, the silkiness against his hands... and that was associated with warm, soft, safe feelings. That was a good memory.

For him, at least. But he'd overstepped.

They were broken up, so maybe it was stupid of him to assume that her memories of him would be pleasant ones. Apparently, he hadn't been a great husband and made a significantly better ex. He'd obviously messed up in a big way.

Angelina looked over her shoulder, meeting his gaze. "You coming?"

"Yeah."

He followed her out the door, and she flicked the light off, then pulled it shut after her.

"Angie—" he started, and she turned to face him.

"Don't call me that, Ben."

"What?" He eyed her uncomfortably. "What do I call you?"

"You call me Angelina like everyone else does, and you're damn grateful that I'm civilized to you," she said. "That's our dynamic. Between us, we don't play games. You know what you did to me, and you're deeply thankful that I'm not the vengeful sort. You respect me and you don't sweet-talk me, because you know I'm smarter than that!"

Her gaze flashed fire, and then she sucked in a breath, and everything about her stilled. She was back in control, but that was the most honest reaction he'd seen out of her yet.

"Okay…" he said quietly. "What did I do to you?"

"It'll come back, I'm sure," she said.

"Why don't you just tell me?" he asked. "I want to know. Maybe I'm not quite so self-aware as you think."

"You swept me off my feet," she said, "and then you married me. But when it came right down to brass tacks, you chose your family over me."

"I did?"

"And you broke my heart."

Ben swallowed. "What happened…specifically?"

"It doesn't matter!" she said. "It's done!"

"Maybe it matters to me," he shot back. "Because my head is empty except for a few fleeting memories I can't pin down. And the one memory I can identify has to do with you, but you're telling me I did you wrong in some pretty big ways! So maybe I want to know what I did!"

"It was a hundred little things," she said. "It was brushing off their snobbish attitudes and explaining away your crotchety grandfather. You spent more time trying to teach me how to fit in with them than you did trying to teach them how to understand me! I was the problem to be solved, the one who would never quite be good enough, and you let that go. And then one day, your grandfather called a family meeting that included all the other spouses and told you that I wasn't invited to it."

She met his gaze meaningfully, and his heart sank.

"Don't tell me I went without you?"

"You did." She sucked in a slow breath. "And that was the end. When you got home, we had it out, we both said what we really felt and we decided to break up."

It was like hearing a story of two heartbroken strangers, but it still tugged at him.

"What did we...really feel?" he asked at last.

"I felt ignored and unappreciated," she said. "You felt like I wasn't doing enough to fit in with your family. We both realized that I wasn't going to be what you needed. Love wasn't enough."

"I feel like love *should* be enough," he countered.

"We both did when we eloped after the cruise," she replied. "But it wasn't. I was a bookkeeper with dreams of opening her own bed-and-breakfast with a view of the ocean in California. You were Colorado royalty. We were...opposites."

And he'd chosen that Colorado royalty family over her. He let out a slow breath. Granted, he didn't remember his family, but standing with her in the basement of her resort, he couldn't imagine why he'd make such a choice.

"You seem pretty incredible to me," he murmured.

"Oh, Ben..." She smiled faintly. "Your

family disagreed, and you needed their approval."

"Why?" he asked.

"Because in your family there was the good sibling and the bad one. Your sister was the black sheep of the family. She traveled a lot, she partied hard and she caused your father no end of grief. She spent money, she didn't make it. You were the one everyone pinned their hopes to, to keep the family wealth growing, and you took that role incredibly seriously."

"So seriously that I'd choose them over you?"

She didn't answer, but she did meet his gaze. So that was what it came down to, apparently. He tried to remember faces and connections, but he wasn't coming up with much. All he had were some cryptic warnings from his father about people who might want to take advantage of his amnesia—warnings not to sign anything until his memory was intact. Was his father protecting him or manipulating him?

What kind of family did he come from?

"It was thirteen years ago, Ben," Angelina added after a moment of silence. "I know this all feels really new for you, but it's not for me. I've gotten over it. I've hashed through everything with my therapist, and I've put it all to rest. In fact, I have you to thank for the woman I've become. It was the deepest pain of my life when our marriage ended, but it was also the pain that pushed me to achieve my dreams, to be the woman I always knew I could be."

"And me?" he asked. "What did I do with that time?"

She was thoughtful for a moment. "You did the same. You focused on learning the business and you've gained a really solid reputation in the business community. We both grew up."

"Do I have you to thank for any of it?" he asked.

"Of course." She smiled then. "I made you face a few uncomfortable truths about the silver spoon you were born with. And I think you've got a better understanding of ordinary people. And you know that—or at least you will again when your memory comes back. I might not have been your partner for the rest of your life, but I was good for you."

He believed it. She seemed like she'd be good for anyone who came into contact with her.

"I'm sorry I wasn't the husband I should have been," he said.

"It's been a long time—"

"Still," he said. "I mean it. I don't remember any of this, but I can see that I was…less than I should have been for you. And I'm sorry."

For what it was worth. Did an apology even count coming from a man who couldn't remember who he was?

Angelina smiled, and for a moment, he could see emotions flicker behind that clear gaze.

"You haven't lost your charm, Ben King," she said at last. "Come on. Let's head up."

Angelina went first, and Ben followed her. An employee came down the stairs just as they were heading up.

"The kitchen is working again, Ms. Cunningham," the young man said. "So we're starting lunch now, just to make sure we've got food available."

"That's a good idea," Angelina replied. "Make a couple of platters of sandwiches to keep in the fridge, too, just in case we need something quick."

"Okay, will do."

They all emerged onto the main floor together, and the young man headed in the direction of the kitchen. From the fireside room, Ben could hear the murmur of voices and the crackling of flames. They walked over to the room.

Ben moved up behind her, looking over her shoulder at the young people inside. A couple of young men were stoking the fire, and another two stood by the tall window, looking out at the falling snow, arms crossed as if they could dare the weather to stop.

There was one young man who stood apart from the rest. He leaned against the hearth, watching the fire with a closed-off expression. The one young woman in their group sat cross-legged on an armchair, looking moodily into the fire. She said something, and the man turned to look at her. His gaze didn't soften, but he answered her and turned away again.

There was something about him that rubbed Ben the wrong way.

"I don't like that guy," Ben said softly. "The one in the gray shirt."

"Oh, him…" Angelina's voice was so low, that only he could catch her words. "His name is Brad Smythe. He's a fourth-year political science major at U of Denver. According to his girlfriend, he's from a rather affluent political family."

"Oh…"

"He'd asked his girlfriend to come on this romantic trip to my resort," Angelina went on. "She was expecting him to propose, but instead he brought his snowboarding buddies along."

"Did he change his mind about marrying her, maybe?" Ben asked.

Angelina turned around and gave him a surprised look. "I didn't think of that. Do you think?"

Ben shrugged. "I don't know. That would be my assumption. He planned a proposal, but changed his mind so brought his buddies to change the tone of the trip."

"Is that the sort of thing you'd do?" Her eyes narrowed slightly.

"Angie—" He stopped. "Angelina, I mean. Apparently, I married you after two weeks. I think we've established that I'm not the kind of guy to back away from commitment."

She smiled at that, and then turned back to survey the room. "You're right about that. Except for your last engagement."

"Who called that one off?" he asked.

"You did."

So maybe he had it in him, after all. And Angelina knew him better in the present than she'd been letting on. All this talk about thirteen years ago...

"How do you know?" he asked.

"You called me." She looked at him over her shoulder again.

"And why did I do it?" he pressed. "Why did I break it off?"

"You said that she was perfect for your family, but she didn't really understand you," Angelina replied. "You wanted a woman who really got you, and she wasn't it."

Who was the woman who really understood him? Angelina seemed to know him well, and Hilaria seemed incredibly intimidated by her. He thought he could understand it now. Angelina might have no desire to connect with him romantically, but she seemed to be the one who knew him best.

"In my text messages, Hilaria is still trying to talk me back into that wedding," Ben said.

"And she might yet," Angelina replied.

"What makes you say that?"

"You're underestimating your family's influence. They like her. They want her to be part of the family, and she can be counted on to work well with them," Angelina replied.

"The deepest longings of your heart aren't really part of this."

Ben started to laugh, but then he sobered. She wasn't joking. "You hate my family."

"No, I don't hate them."

"You sure sound like you do," he replied. "Are they such terrible people?"

"They're predictable," she replied. "They have something more important than hearts to protect."

"Which is?" he prodded.

"Money."

Ben swallowed. "My father warned me in that video call to be careful. Was he worried about you?"

Angelina blinked, and it felt good to finally have the upper hand. She shook her head.

"I'd be flattered if I thought I intimidated the great King family, but I don't. I'm not someone they need to be worried over."

"We had a few lapses, you said before. Did you break up my engagement?" he asked softly. Was he going to remember having an affair with his ex-wife when it all came back again?

Angelina shot him an annoyed look. "I'll forgive that because you don't remember any-thing. But I'm not the kind of woman who meddles in *any* man's love life. I have personal standards for my behavior."

"And Hilaria's concern over you?" he asked.

"Another woman's insecurity isn't my fault," Angelina said quietly, but there was ice in her tone. "That was on you. If she didn't feel secure in your relationship, you should have fixed it."

Angelina brushed past him and headed across the foyer without another word. He'd ticked her off, it would seem. She disappeared down the hallway that led toward her office, and he stared after her for a moment, his own frustration simmering.

His lost memory wasn't her fault, but Angelina was holding back on him, too. He needed to piece his life back together, and Angelina had been a bigger part of it than she was letting on.

Ben turned back to the fireside room and that unlikable young man. Brad's gaze was brooding, and Ben noticed how the young woman looked at him. Her hair was pulled away from her face, making her look younger than she probably was. She wanted something from that brooding college student—something he was refusing to give. Had Brad been hinting at an engagement, and then decided against it? Had he come to the realization that the rest of his life was a very, very long time to promise to another person?

Did he even noticed that he held that woman's heart in his fist?

CHAPTER SIX

ANGELINA HAD ENOUGH to keep herself busy that day, and Warren and Ben spent the rest of the afternoon together.

Later that evening after dinner, Brad sat down with Ben and chatted for a while. It turned out their families knew each other. So much for keeping Ben's presence here under wraps, but she'd warned Karl that it might not be possible. The Kings were recognizable.

Brad, the snowboarding college student with political aspirations, was actually closer to Ben's social circle than Angelina had ever been. Angelina's parents were both hard workers. Her mother had been a high school teacher, and her father was a mechanic. All her grandparents had been ranchers—not the wealthy kind like Ben King, either. The family land was long gone.

After checking on the rooms to make sure they had all been cleaned, Angelina paused in the dining room doorway to see Brad showing Ben some pictures on his phone and chatting away as easily as if they'd known each other for years.

"That's Ben King."

Angelina turned to see Elizabeth at her elbow.

"Yes, it is," she confirmed. "Do you know him?"

"Brad said he sort of does. He didn't recognize him until tonight. People are different when they're on vacation instead of when they're officially representing a company or a family."

"Hmm." Angelina watched the men chatting amicably together. Was she supposed to be running interference here until his memory was back? Karl might think so, but maybe this would help jog some memories loose.

"Brad thinks that Ben King might be able to help his father get a business deal with the Kings," Elizabeth said. "I hate that."

"The constant schmoozing?" Angelina asked.

"The constant using," Elizabeth replied. "Brad can be incredibly charming to people he needs."

"And you feel like he doesn't need you anymore?" Angelina guessed.

"Well, he's more fun with Ben King than he is with me these days," Elizabeth replied. "Is that what it would be like to be married into a wealthy family?"

Not at first, Angelina realized. And she'd also seen strong, healthy marriages among the friends of the King family. But over time, her own importance had started to slip. She couldn't blame the failure of her own marriage on money, and there was no added virtue in having less money, either.

"It depends on the marriage," Angelina replied. "It depends on the people involved."

"I even got my nails done," Elizabeth said softly. "For the pictures of the ring on my hand..." Tears welled in her eyes, then she blinked them back. "I'm an idiot."

"No, you aren't," Angelina said. "Let me see—"

She took Elizabeth's hand in hers and looked at the immaculate French manicure.

"Beautiful," Angelina said and held out her hand. "See mine?" She'd done her own nails in ballet slipper pink.

"Very nice," Elizabeth said.

"Sweetie," Angelina said quietly, "don't ever think your manicure isn't worth the time or money because a man isn't there to appreciate it, or a ring isn't there to draw eyes. You are worth a nice manicure. That's a lesson from this side of forty."

Elizabeth looked over at her, a glimmer of understanding in her gaze.

"And when I go home in a few days, minus an engagement ring?" Elizabeth asked.

Angelina sighed, her gaze swinging back over to Ben and Brad. She had her own disappointments with a handsome heir to a fortune.

"It will sting," Angelina said at last. "But you won't die of it, and it will become part of your story—the tale you tell when you get together with good friends over a fine dinner and an expensive bottle of wine. You aren't alone, Elizabeth. Women everywhere are getting their hearts mangled, facing tough choices, and putting one foot ahead of the other again."

"I have a friend getting married this upcoming summer," Elizabeth said. "I'm green with jealousy."

"And you probably have fifteen friends who aren't getting married this summer," Angelina replied.

"You sound like my mother."

"Wise woman." Angelina shot her a smile. "Trust me, we get older and you probably just see us as dinosaurs, but we've been through a lot. We know what we're talking about."

"You're no dinosaur," Elizabeth said.

"Thank you for saying so," Angelina replied, nudging her with her elbow. "Anyway, I'd better get back to work."

The day slipped away, and Angelina was tired by the time it was eight o'clock. Without electricity and cell phone service, she'd expected the younger crowd to be a little squirrelly, but Warren had settled into the fireside room with them and they'd started a few board games, and in one corner, Brad and a couple of friends were playing cards, betting with pocket change.

Ben had already gone to his room, and Angelina headed up the stairs toward her own suite with a small lantern to light her way. She'd have to go back later on to make sure people got into their rooms without leaving lit candles anywhere. She paused as she got to the second floor, considering, and then turned down the wing toward Ben's room. She owed him this much…

Ben opened the door a moment after Angelina knocked. He held a book in one hand, and couple of candles flickered behind him.

"Angie?"

He was still calling her that, but she didn't have the energy to tell him not to tonight.

"Is everything okay?" she asked.

"Yeah, I'm—" he looked down at the paperback in his hand "—I'm seeing who killed the soulless millionaire here."

She smiled ruefully. "Well, enjoy that. I just wanted to let you know that Brad might have a few ulterior motives to his friendliness."

"Speaking of soulless millionaires?" he asked with a small upturn of his lips.

"Or the sons of millionaires," she replied.

"He was just showing me pictures of people I might know," Ben said.

"Did you recognize anyone?" she asked.

"Not directly. I kind of got a familiar feeling a few times, though, with the locations. Like one restaurant felt familiar."

"It's a start," she said. "Did you tell him you have no memory?"

"I just said I didn't remember *him*," he replied.

That was the shark coming out in Ben. He knew how to smooth people over, but he also knew how to make them feel about two inches tall when he needed to.

"That might be for the best," Angelina said

with a rueful smile. "Apparently, Brad's father owns a business that wants a deal with one of your businesses. I have no idea if that's a good thing or not."

"Neither do I," he replied.

"Just…" She cast about, looking for the advice she wanted to give. "Don't sign anything. Or promise anything… Not until your memory is back and you know what you're doing. I'd hate for you to get taken advantage of on my watch."

Ben gave her a funny look. "That's the exact thing my father said."

Angelina smiled wanly. "It's solid advice."

"Look, I'm sorry about earlier," he said. "I'm sorry for suggesting you broke up my engagement. I don't remember anything, and you're right—if I had an insecure fiancée, that was my responsibility."

"Thank you," she replied. "One thing you should know is that I have integrity."

"I appreciate that," he said, his voice low.

Ben met her gaze, and he smiled faintly. It was that old, uncertain look of his that used to melt her heart. When he was confident and charming, Ben was hard to resist. But there was something even more devastating about him when he wasn't so sure of himself…when he was looking to her for some reassurance.

"That's all I wanted," she said. "I'm going to relax for a while. I'll need to check the fireside room in a couple of hours, but I'm wiped."

"Sure."

He'd be fine. And maybe he'd been right about her being in a little too close. She'd hate to give Hilaria evidence of overstepping if Ben and his ex got back together.

Angelina let herself into her suite. It had been a long day. Ironically, it was less work dealing with a full lodge and full staff than it was with this current situation. Inside, it was dark, and the lantern threw long shadows. She spent a few minutes starting a fire in her little fireplace, watching as the first flames flickered upward in a cozy orange glow. Then she turned off the kerosene lantern to save the fuel for later on.

All she wanted was a little time to herself. She hadn't had much of a chance to sort through her feelings since Ben's arrival, and whenever she wasn't busy, her thoughts kept slipping back toward him.

Ben needed her right now—that was her official excuse for her preoccupation with her ex-husband. She was remembering the good times they'd had and how easy it had been to fall in love with him. Ben King had been the love of her life, whether or not he deserved the designation. In the years before him and all the years since, she'd never loved a man like she'd loved Ben. She'd tried to replace him—it was the smart thing to do—but he'd touched a part of her heart that no man had been able to get at.

There was a knock at her door, and Angelina sighed. Did the staff need her already? When she pulled the door open, she saw Ben standing there in the darkness.

"Hi," he said quietly.

"Ben…" She stepped back to let him inside, and he shot her a smile.

"The candles are blown out in my suite so no worries about that," he said. "I came by because something occurred to me."

"What's that?" she asked.

"You probably have pictures," he said, and he caught her gaze. "Of me. Of us. Of…our time together."

"I do," she replied. "I don't tend to look at them, though."

It was harsh, but true. Ben was supposed to be in the past.

"That's understandable," he said. "It's just that I'm remembering a little bit of you, and I thought it might be a good place to start to try and jog my memory…if you don't mind."

It was so rational that she couldn't think of a reason to turn him down. Besides, she realized in a devastating rush, she wanted a little more time with him tonight.

She gestured him toward the fireplace. "I'll see if I can root out our wedding album."

If this was where he wanted to start, who was she to argue? Besides, maybe it would do her some good, too…get him out of her system.

Angelina went to a closet and found the album near the top. She'd been tempted to destroy the album in some symbolic way several times over the years, but something had always stopped her. Ben was a part of her history—no album burning by the lake was going to change that. She carried it to the couch and the soft glow of the fireplace.

"Here we are," she said.

The room was chilly. The generator was keeping the furnace running, but the cold from outside still seeped in through the tall windows. She grabbed a throw blanket from the back of the couch and sank down next to Ben.

"Do you want some blanket?" she asked as she pulled it over her legs.

"Sure." He slid an arm along the couch behind her and she tossed the blanket over his knees, then opened the album across their laps. The light from the fireplace flickered over the first photo—a shot of Angelina in her simple wedding dress. It was a lacy cocktail dress, just past knee length, and it had suited her figure perfectly.

"Wow…" he murmured.

Their wedding had been a tiny one at a small-town California courthouse. She allowed herself a peek at his profile as he scanned the photos, unable to tell what he was thinking.

Ben turned the page.

"We met on a cruise, and you asked me to marry you out on the deck near the end of our two weeks at sea," she said. "When we landed, we stayed in California together until we got our wedding license, and then we went to a courthouse and made it official. We didn't tell anyone—we said we'd wait till after it was done."

Her parents would have tried to get her to

think it through. She'd known even then that she was taking a massive risk.

Ben tapped a picture of the two them holding hands, their heads together as they shared a quiet moment before the ceremony began.

"How did we get these pictures?"

"We hired a photographer," she replied. "He was local, and very good. We were just lucky he was available for the day."

"What were we saying?" he asked.

Angelina looked down at the picture of them whispering together, and she smiled. Their wedding had been thrown together. She'd found the dress in a little seaside shop but she hadn't been able to find something blue to go with it. She hadn't even cared. Ben had chosen gray pinstripe dress pants and a crisp shirt, the kind she'd learn to associate with him. They'd been so excited, feeling like they were creating the biggest surprise ever.

"I don't remember what we were saying anymore," she said. "I just remember how I felt."

"And how did you feel?" His voice was deep, soft…that same tempting tone that had always pulled her in.

Angelina looked found his dark gaze locked on her. This wasn't supposed to matter anymore. She'd felt all sorts of heady emotions that day, and she'd been certain that she'd never forget a single detail, from their impatient wait for the judge to their simple vows and the exchange of those plain gold bands.

"I was headlong in love with you," she said. "But this isn't supposed to be about me. It's about you. Does it spark any memories?"

BEN LET OUT a slow breath. She'd been in love with him. He could see in the picture that they'd both been in love. They were leaning together as if something invisible was tugging them together.

He sifted through the fragments in his mind, looking for a puzzle piece, or some sort of connection. There was sunshine in his memory, and her glistening honey-blond hair. He remembered pushing it behind her ear, and her blushing, looking down...

Was that the wedding? It was hard to tell, but it was like scrolling through pictures on a cell phone and coming across a video— just the tiniest glimpse behind the pose. He couldn't remember what she'd been wearing, just her hair, the warmth of sunlight, her downcast gaze.

"I'm not sure..." Ben murmured. "Almost..."

It was hard for Ben to describe the feeling, both familiar and utterly foreign at the same time. But those pictures did spark something deep inside of him…like she said, more of a feeling than a memory. Because attached to that image in his mind of Angelina looking down, him pushing her thick hair behind her ear, was a feeling of overwhelming tenderness. He studied the picture of Angelina—young, refined, stunning. Time had deepened her beauty, and Ben glanced between the picture and the woman next to him.

"It's been a few years," she said, as if reading his mind.

"You've gained something," he said.

"Gained what?" she asked, and he could see a challenge in her gaze. He'd almost insulted her.

"You're more beautiful now," he said. "You seem deeper."

"Fifteen years will do that," she said. "As for being more beautiful—"

"Hey, I call it like I see it. For me, this is like seeing pictures of someone who's almost a stranger…"

"Almost?" she asked.

"Like I said, I remember your hair…" And

the tumbling cascade of love associated with it. "So we're not quite strangers, are we?"

"You always were smooth," she said with a low laugh.

"Maybe I'm honest," he replied. "Because I'm just saying what I see."

She smiled ruefully at that. "I know you better than you know yourself right now—well enough to be careful of you."

Ben chuckled. "I'm a fox, am I?"

"A bit." She rolled her eyes. "Who says fox anymore?"

"Me, apparently." He shot her a grin.

He flipped the page and saw a photo of himself standing by a window looking serious. He looked younger than he appeared in the mirror now, but whether or not he'd improved over the years, he couldn't tell.

He noticed his cuff links in the photo and he looked closer. The one he could see was the shape of a sailing ship, and he had an image in his mind of slim, manicured fingers helping him to put them on.

"Those cuff links," he said. "They seem familiar."

"They're a family heirloom," Angelina replied. "They were your grandfather's and he gave them to you when you graduated from college."

It wasn't the cuff links, exactly, that were familiar. Again, it was a connection to someone else—those hands.

"Those cuff links are antique," Angelina went on. "They were made in the early 1800s, I think, by some British menswear company—I don't recall the name."

At mention of his grandfather, he saw a face, watery blue eyes, white hair neatly trimmed and a brush of a mustache.

"Did I call him Granddad?" Ben asked.

"Yeah…" Angelina nodded, a smile on her lips. "You also called him a lot of things a lot less complimentary."

Ben cast her a surprised look. "What? We didn't get along?"

"It was complicated between you," she replied.

But still, the thought of calling an old man names felt…wrong. Crass. Inappropriate. He felt some stirrings of guilt.

"Am I…kind of a jerk?" he asked, feeling oddly nervous.

"Your grandfather isn't quite the frail old man," Angelina said. "I mean, he is. He's in his midnineties. But he's got a tongue like a viper. He's blunt. He thinks you're too young to be useful yet. You think he's…oh, a whole slew of things."

He let out a slow breath. "I wish you could say I was better behaved than that."

"Well…he pushes your buttons," she replied.

"You're being kind," he said. "I *am* a jerk, aren't I?"

"No…" She sighed. "You're actually a really decent man. Your family is rife with these complicated relationships. You all love each other, and you're loyal to a fault, but you have a hard time liking each other sometimes."

Ben ran that thought through his mind, and he tried to pull up the memory of the old man again, but he couldn't bring it back.

"That doesn't sound like a fun family relationship," he admitted.

"You always understood that dynamic better than I did," she replied.

Ben looked closer at the cuff links in the picture, and they looked like they were made of sterling silver, rubbed and softened over the years. And in his mind's eye, he could see those cuff links, but they weren't connected to the old man, but those slim, feminine fingers affixing them to his cuffs.

"Did you help me put those cuff links on?" Ben asked. "On our wedding day, I mean?"

"I always helped you with your cuff links," she replied. "Even after our wedding day."

There was something tender in her voice.

"Like tying a tie for your man?" he asked.

"Very much like," she said quietly. "Except you always did prefer a bolo tie. You didn't need my help with that."

Ben's fingers moved to his wrists—but there were no cuff links to touch, of course. His breath lodged in his windpipe, and he looked at her, her blue eyes glistening almost navy in the flickering firelight.

"I remember a hand," he said. "May I?"

He held his hand out for hers, and she hesitated a moment, then put her hand in his palm. Her fingers were cool and slim. She wore a diamond ring—not a solitaire, but something that gave the impression of vines and leaves. Those were the fingers he remembered, right down to the immaculate manicure.

He instinctively turned her hand over, and an image materialized in his mind of the inside of her wrist, and him pressing his lips against it softly.

Angelina's hand trembled in his, and he looked up at her, searching her eyes for more… Why couldn't he remember more than a glimpse?

"I used to…" He swallowed. "I used to kiss your wrist…here—" He ran his thumb over a tender spot, and her pulse beat hard beneath his touch.

"You remember that?" she whispered.

"I remember how your fingers felt twined with mine, and how I'd lean over your wrist and I'd smell…"

That perfume. He'd suspected it before, but now he knew beyond the shadow of a doubt. It was a scent locked in his mind with her.

"That scent that I remembered before was you, wasn't it?" Ben asked. "I don't know what it is about that perfume, but I remember it. It's like it lingers around any memory I have of your hair, or your fingers, or…" He brushed his thumb over her skin once more. "Your wrist."

Angelina blushed and pulled her hand back. He let her fingers slip out of his grasp, but she was still only a couple of inches away from him. He felt her shift beneath the lap blanket over their knees.

"Yes," she said.

"Why didn't you tell me that before, when I asked about it?" he asked.

"I didn't want to," Angelina said simply. "I'm more than a signature scent."

"It's pretty," he said. "You shouldn't have stopped wearing it because of me."

"My grandmother wore it, too," she said. "It's Chanel No. 5. In fact, she gave me this old perfume atomizer from when she was a young wife. She got married in 1950, and my grandfather was an alcoholic. She had seven children with him, and one night after he'd gotten into a violent rage, she kicked him out. She never took him back, either."

"How did she survive?" Ben asked. "Back then it wouldn't have been easy."

"She remarried," Angelina replied. "And her second husband was much nicer, but my grandfather caused trouble for her up until his death. Hence, her advice to marry a man who would make a good ex-husband. Her second husband, the only grandfather that I knew, was kind and sensitive. He was a real teddy bear."

As a man, Ben wasn't sure that was a great way to be remembered, but the second husband had been the one to stick.

"There's something inside of every man

that wants to be known for his strength, his ability to protect the ones he loves," Ben said. "I want to have a little more steel inside of me. I'm not sure I want to be remembered as a teddy bear."

"Don't worry," she said with a rueful smile. "You aren't."

A piece of wood on the fire popped and an explosion of sparks sailed upward into the chimney. A swirl of cold air swept down to meet them, and there was a tangle of swirling red dots above the flames.

"But you are a decent ex-husband." Angelina eyed his bandage for a moment, winced slightly, then lifted her hand to his forehead. "How is your head?" she asked.

"It's okay," he replied. "Why?"

"There's some blood showing through."

He didn't know why he did it, but he ran his fingers down her bare arm, leaving goose bumps trailing behind his touch, and then tugged her arm closer. His lips found her pulse, and for a moment, he stayed immobile, his kiss pressing against the soft patter.

She moved into his touch instead of drawing away. Her eyes shone with suspended tears.

"I just—" He hadn't been able to help himself.

"You're the only one who did that," she whispered.

"Good…" he said. "I should have something in your memories that's only mine."

"You always were a little too confident," she said, a smile teasing at her lips.

He reached for her wrist again and pressed another kiss against her pulse.

"If I'm not a teddy bear, then what am I?" he asked.

She considered him. "You're the one that got away."

His gaze dropped down to her lips, and for an agonizing moment, all he could think about was pulling her close against him. He rubbed his thumb over the delicate inside of her wrist, and he felt her pulse speed up under his touch. He started to lean toward her, but she pulled her hand away again and cleared her throat, breaking the moment.

"I should probably go, shouldn't I?" he murmured.

"Yes," she said, and she pressed her lips together. He put the album down with some reverence.

Angelina rose, too, and walked him to the

door. Ben turned. They were in shadow, the light from the fire flickering a few paces away, and he looked down into those eyes that looked midnight blue in this lighting, and he felt a longing to kiss her so strong that it nearly rocked him.

"It's coming back, Angie," he murmured.

"I can tell," she said.

"I'm not remembering anything bad yet, though," he said with a small smile. "And that's the problem."

"You will," she said.

"Well, right now, I'm just a man…and I've got shreds of memories swimming in my head, but for the most part, you're new to me."

She smiled. "That's…ironic."

"I don't know how I messed everything up," he said. "But I must have been some fool."

"We can agree on that." She met his gaze and then she laughed. It was a relief to see the humor in her eyes. He probably deserved worse than that.

"You should go," she said.

"Good night, Angie."

He opened the door into the dark hallway. "Ben?"

He turned back.

"Don't call me Angie."

Ben shot her a grin. "It was a pleasure, Ms. Cunningham. I'll see you…"

But she wasn't Ms. Cunningham in his resurfacing memories. She was delicate, soft, tender, beautiful—she was *Angie*…

Ben headed down the hall, and it took a couple of beats before he heard her door shut behind him.

ANGELINA CLOSED THE door and leaned against it. Her wrist still tingled where his lips had touched her, and she let out a slow breath. It was just like meeting him on that cruise ship—the immediate chemistry between them, the depth of his longing for something real…

If only she'd known then just how complicated his real life had been. He'd been on that cruise as a way to clear his head. His father wanted him to start taking over part of the business, and they'd also been strongly suggesting it was high time he got married and started on a family. Cleo was up to her usual antics, and they weren't looking to her to get serious with the business. It was all on Ben. He'd been frustrated and felt locked in, and he told her that he realized that the freedom he was longing for was right there in front him…*her*.

But Angelina had been more of an annoyance to his family than the breath of fresh air she was supposed to be for Ben. And the novelty of a "commoner" wife had worn off. Truthfully, it had worn thin for her, too. She got tired of being the constant representative of "regular people," and tired of messing things up—not knowing the right fork, or the right honorific for whatever guest was at dinner. She was tired of the backhanded compliments and quips—the general reminders that she wasn't good enough for the Kings' oldest son.

And yet here Angelina was, stuck in a snowstorm with Ben, and the chemistry was still there… There was something incredibly intoxicating about a man who was drawn to her that powerfully. And he was still just as good looking, just as charming, just as sweet…

If only their divorce could have been because he was surly and mean, and not because he needed more than she could give. Being the woman who came up short all the time—that was a feeling she didn't want to revisit. At least here in her resort, she was enough—she was the heart of this place in a way she'd never been able to achieve in her home with Ben.

Angelina went back to the couch and looked at the closed photo album. It was a lifetime ago, but she'd never fully turned off her feelings for Ben, either. It didn't seem possible, but at least they'd both carried an understanding of exactly why their chemistry wasn't enough. And now, she was the only one who knew that in the face of an attraction that never had tamped out.

She glanced at her watch—it was almost nine. She had a few duties to see to yet this evening. And hopefully by morning, she'd have a better handle on the feelings that Ben simmered up inside of her. Cold nights and firelight were never good for emotional balance.

CHAPTER SEVEN

THE NEXT MORNING, Angelina ran into Warren on his way to breakfast.

"Have you seen Ben?" Angelina asked.

"I'm just coming from his room," Warren replied as he came to the bottom of the staircase. "He's doing well. His head is healing—although, it really could use some proper stitches. He says a few memories are coming back."

Yes…she'd seen that last night. Angelina nodded. "Good. I'm glad to hear it. Thanks for stepping up like this."

"Oh, it's no problem. Once a doctor, always a doctor. Even if I weren't asked, I'd still be poking my nose in," Warren said with a smile. "But I was going to ask you about something."

Angelina paused to give him her attention. "Sure."

"Do you know of any links between Blue Lake and Camp Hale?" Warren asked.

"Not directly," she replied. "We're about forty miles away from Camp Hale."

"I had heard that they did a march out to Blue Lake a couple of times," Warren said. "Have there been any WWII-era artifacts discovered in the woods? People used to be able to find bullet casings from soldiers' target practice."

Angelina shook her head. "Not that I know of, but I do have a marketing manager who would be just ecstatic if we had any proof of connection to Camp Hale. I'm sure she could use that in our next ad campaign."

"I was hoping you'd have some little nugget of information," Warren said.

"I'm afraid not." She shrugged. "Sorry."

"I'll go see about some breakfast," Warren said. "The food is smelling great."

"Yes, please do. Enjoy." Angelina returned his smile, and she turned toward the fireside room.

The wood box was nearly empty—a few sticks of firewood left, and some chunks of dry bark. The smaller box of kindling was completely empty. The furnace was still running, but a big roaring fire was going to come in handy later on.

Warren's questions about WWII history

were running through her mind as she went over to the bank of windows and looked out into the snow. She'd never seen any antique bullet casings out there, and it was possible that all that time and the weather had simply rusted them back into the soil. But if there were a connection to Camp Hale, that would be interesting. It would be nice to have this place connected to more history than just the King family. It would be a relief, actually, especially after the way Ben had kissed her wrist in her suite last night…

Her stomach gave a tumble at the memory. What was it about that man that could still turn her heart upside down?

The snow had gotten significantly deeper out there—a soft, marshmallow mantle covering everything. If she didn't have to worry about this old building, she might enjoy the sensation of being snowed in for a while, but she had more things to worry about.

"Angie?"

She turned to see Ben in the doorway. He was dressed in a pair of jeans and a slightly too-small long-sleeved undershirt that only accentuated his muscular physique. And his black hat—the one she'd grown to associate with him. He replaced it from time to time, but Ben King was always in a black cowboy hat.

A smile quirked up one side of Ben's mouth. "Are you okay?"

"I'm fine. Why?"

"You look…pensive," he said.

"I'm thinking about firewood," she replied. "We're low, and I need to get more inside."

Among other things, but she didn't want to talk about those.

"You want help?" he asked.

"Actually, I do," she replied. "Thank you. The thing is, we're going to have to shovel a path to the woodshed and then bring a few loads back inside. I normally have a fair amount of wood stacked against the side of the building here, but I didn't get to replenish it before the storm hit."

"You had other things to think about," he said.

"Mostly trying to get guests checked out," she said, then shrugged. "Okay, well… There are a couple of coats that the employees use for outdoor work, and we can use those. This will probably ruin any good jacket."

"Sounds good."

He didn't even blink at the mention of coats, and she eyed him for a moment, waiting for a reaction to that lambskin coat in her office. How long would it take for him to remember why he was here?

"What?" he asked.

"Nothing," she said. "Let's go. Unless you wanted something to eat—"

"No, I'm fine," he said. "I mean, I have an in with the boss, so maybe she'll let me forage in the kitchen after we're done with the wood."

Angelina chuckled as she led the way to the employee lounge. Four winter coats with the Mountain Springs Resort icon emblazoned on the breast pocket hung on pegs on the wall, and Angelina passed him one of the bigger ones.

"That should fit," she said.

She found them thick work gloves and waterproofed winter boots, too. Her employees were always well-defended from the weather. Maybe it would do her good to get outside and breathe in some fresh air. They'd all been cooped up for too long.

Armed with snow shovels, she and Ben stepped through the side door. Brisk wind whipped in with a cloud of snowflakes, and Angelina put her head down and pushed outside into the onslaught, Ben close behind. Together they started to work.

"The path leads up toward that brown shed—you can just see it," Angelina said, pointing in that direction.

"Yeah, I see it," Ben said, and he bent to the task at hand.

Ben was stronger than her and he was able to clear more snow than she could with every shovelful; the job was getting done much faster than if she was working at it alone. The steadily falling snow left a velvet cover behind them over the pathway that they cleared, absorbing sound around them and muffling the scrape of their shovels.

"Angie, I—" Ben started. Angelina shot him a wary look, and he caught himself. "Angelina. Look, I know overstepped last night."

Angelina straightened. "We were always like that, Ben."

"You mean...drawn to each other?" he asked.

She shrugged. "Yeah, I'm afraid so. But... it doesn't work. We learned that the hard way. No relationship is about two people alone. They have to fit in somewhere, and you and I didn't work when we were a part of your family or your world."

"I'm remembering more," he said.

"Like what?" she asked.

"Just fragments. I don't know where they fit in. I remember making you dinner one night. It was steak."

"Are you sure it was for me?" she asked, attempting to sound lighthearted. Surely he'd made his famous steak dinners for more women than her… She was the only woman in his world right now, and it was too easy to get tugged into this.

"You were wearing a floral summer dress," he said. "And your hair was down. You were leaning over the counter with a glass of champagne, and your eyes…"

Angelina held her breath. Ben cleared his throat, then smiled awkwardly. Yes, he was remembering. She turned back to the shoveling. It was safer than meeting his gaze.

"There was some kind of baseball game, and I was playing outfield," he went on. "That's a memory from childhood. Nothing more to it—just me in the outfield, chewing gum and waiting for a hit."

"That's a nice memory," she said, and she heaved another shovelful of snow to the side. "You also did rock climbing."

"Yeah?" He sounded mildly surprised.

"No memories of that?"

Ben shook his head. "Nothing."

"Well…something for you to look forward to, then," she said, and she shot him a teasing smile.

They were getting close to the woodshed now, and for a couple of minutes Ben put his energy into clearing the snow. When they got to the overhang, they were both breathing a little quicker, and Ben's cheeks were reddened from the cold.

"There's…um…one more thing I remembered last night," Ben said. He straightened, but he didn't quite meet her gaze.

"What's that?" she asked.

"You said I'd eventually remember the tough parts of our relationship," he said.

Angelina's heart sank. So it had finally come…

"I don't know what it was about," he said, his voice gruff, "but I remember shouting, and you yelling something back, and—" he paused, winced "—and then you cried. Tears just welled up, and you looked like you were holding it back for a second, and you just sank into a chair and…cried."

A finger of wind lifted a tendril of hair away from her face.

"Yeah…" Angelina said softly. "We did that a lot toward the end."

"What were we fighting about?" he asked.

"I don't know. It would start with some silly thing or other and snowball into something bigger," she said. "One of us would make a cutting, hurtful remark and the other would walk away."

"But we loved each other," he said quietly. "I know that."

"We did," she said with a nod. "But the pressure was too high. It was hopeless. We both knew it."

"Look." Ben's voice was low, rough, and he stepped closer, blocking the last of the wind from touching her. "I'm sorry. I really feel like I owe you an apology for ever raising my voice to you, or saying anything that could make you…" His voice caught. "I'm really sorry."

"Oh, Ben…" She felt her own restraint begin to tremble.

"I didn't want to remember something like that," he murmured. "But I knew it was coming… You told me, didn't you? I just…"

"It's okay," she whispered.

She was going to say something more, explain that that was why they hadn't worked out, or tell him that she'd forgiven him a long time ago, but the words just wouldn't form. His eyes were filled with misery, and their breath hung in the air between them. Fighting had always been as painful as tearing flesh. She hated those memories, too.

"I don't remember kissing you, though," he said. "I remember breaking your heart, but never kissing you—"

Before she could think of anything to say, Ben leaned in, his mouth just a whisper from hers, and when she didn't move away, he closed the distance.

BEN WRAPPED HIS arms around her, tugging her against him as a flood of relief swept over him. He didn't know why, but he needed this—to kiss Angelina, to hold her, to make up for some fight they'd had over a decade ago that he couldn't remember ever making right. And if he couldn't remember kissing her even once, then maybe it was time to kiss her properly.

It was the link he needed between too many of those fragments of memory—her hands, her hair, her smile, her perfume... His shattered memories all seemed focused on the woman in his arms, and as he pulled her against him, every beat of his heart was telling him that this was the connection.

He could just feel her curves under the bulk of her coat, and she leaned into his embrace. When he pulled back, Angelina blinked up at him. Her cheeks were pink, and her hair ruffled in the cold wind.

"I needed to do that," he breathed.

"Me, too—" She sucked in a breath, and he was about to kiss her again when she pulled away.

"Should I apologize now?" he asked uncertainly.

"No apologies." She blinked back the mist in her eyes. "We can't be doing that, Ben."

"I don't know… We're both adults, and single," he said. "We very well can."

"I've gotten over you. I've gotten to the point where you can walk into my resort and tell me you're marrying someone else, and I can summon up some happiness for you. But that didn't come easily."

What kind of a callous idiot was he to do that to begin with?

"Good," he said. "It shouldn't come easily."

She was embedded in his psyche, too. None of this *should* be easy.

"So kissing me like this—it's not fair," she

said. "We always did have a connection, Ben. We always will! But I have to keep you—" She took a step back. "I need to keep you over there."

It felt like a gulf between them, and it tugged at something inside of him. He couldn't even put into words why that kiss had been so necessary. Kissing her shuffled something inside of him that brought those old memories together like the cement between bricks. It made the things he was feeling inside of him make sense. And maybe it was an apology, too, for all the times that he couldn't even remember where he'd fallen short.

"You make the rest of my memories make sense," he said.

A smile touched her lips. "I keep telling you your life was much bigger than me."

Well, tell his shards of memory that, because most of what he'd gotten back centered around this woman. But that memory of her tears was still tugging at him uncomfortably.

"Why don't I finish up?" he said. "I'll bring the wood inside and stack a bunch up next to the door."

"I couldn't ask you—"

"Yes, you could," he replied firmly. "You

could ask a whole lot of me. You always could. And I don't know why I wasn't telling you this a long time ago, because it's clear enough to me right now. You can ask me to make things easier for you. Okay?"

Angelina stilled, her gaze meeting his for a moment uncertainly. She was beautiful, but that arm's length she'd put between them had reached her eyes, too. She didn't trust him—that much was clear.

"I'll finish up," Ben repeated. "I'm sure you have more important things to be doing right now than carrying wood."

"I have some things waiting for me," she said.

"Go on, then."

Angelina smiled, and as she walked past him, she put her hand briefly on his arm. She headed on back through the blowing snow, her head bent, and he wondered if he would come to her conclusion when all his memories came back, that there was no way for their relationship to have worked. Because while he could accept too much time may have passed for anything to reignite between them, he wasn't sure that their relationship had been doomed from the start. He couldn't believe that a love that passionate had been hopeless.

For the next few minutes, Ben piled wood into a wheelbarrow and brought it back into the building, stacking it inside the wood box. He repeated the loop until the wood box was overflowing. It was when he was wheeling wood over to the side of the building to stack it for easier access that the side door opened and Brad Smythe appeared wearing a ski jacket, boots and a pair of work gloves.

"Hey, do you need a hand?" Brad asked.

"Sure," Ben replied. "Just stacking wood."

"You get bored enough that manual labor gets appealing," Brad said with a laugh. "You know what I mean?"

"I guess," Ben replied, unsure of how to answer that. He wasn't out here out of boredom.

"You and I should do some golfing this spring," Brad said. "You golf, don't you?"

Did he? Ben shrugged. "Why, are you wanting to talk business, or am I really just such fantastic company?"

Brad grinned. "Hey, we can genuinely like those we do business with, can't we?"

"I'm not talking business today," Ben said. "Just to be clear. Not here."

"That's fine," Brad said. "We'll haul wood. It's a manly occupation." Brad looked up at the second-floor windows. "Maybe Betsy will find me rugged and irresistible."

It would seem that Brad's friendliness did have more selfish motivations after all, and he was grateful for Angelina's earlier warning. As it had before, something about this young man rubbed Ben the wrong way.

"So how did you end up on a trip with your girlfriend and all your buddies?" Ben asked, and he picked up a cord of wood and dropped it with a hollow clang into the bottom of the barrow.

"Oh…" Brad grabbed some wood, too. "It's a long story."

"I've got time," Ben said.

Brad eyed him for a moment, then shrugged. "Okay, well, Betsy wanted a romantic getaway, and when I agreed to it, I'd forgotten about my buddy's birthday, and we'd all agreed months ago that we'd do something to cut loose a bit on his birthday weekend. So, I just kind of brought the two together."

"Huh." Ben added a few more pieces of wood, balancing them on the top.

"Why?" Brad asked.

"It's just, I've been watching you all—" Ben shot him a wry look. "And don't take that the wrong way. I've got nothing else to do, right? But she seems… I don't know… unhappy."

"What?" Brad shook his head and picked up the handles of the wheelbarrow. "She's fine."

Ben might have lost his memory, but he hadn't lost his powers of observation. He grabbed a few extra pieces of wood and headed after Brad in the direction of the lodge. A gust of frigid wind whited out his view and he stopped in his tracks until it cleared.

He had a vague memory of having done this before—but in his memory, he saw cattle, a horse and his stern grandfather with a bristling white mustache. That was all.

A memory from his ranch? He hated this feeling—fragments floating around with absolutely no context.

"So, why do you think she's not happy?" Brad asked with a frown as Ben stacked the wood in his arms against the wall.

Ben looked over at the younger man. "Her face. Her body language. You can't tell she's miserable?"

"I mean, I guess I could take some more time with her alone than I've been doing, but these are her friends, too. They all really like Betsy. She's got a wicked sense of humor."

Ben sighed. It really shouldn't matter to him whether Brad made that young woman happy or not, but there was something about the dynamic that felt uncomfortably familiar. Had he been like that with Angelina?

"She seems great," Ben agreed.

"It's just the stage of things," Brad said. "She wants to start planning a wedding and stuff. Her older sister just got married, so she's got weddings on the brain."

"How long have you been together?" Ben asked.

"Three years."

"So, long enough," Ben said.

"What? No, I mean, three years is nothing. My cousin dated the woman he married for eight years. Time is important. I want to be a senator someday, and I need the right woman at my side to make that happen."

"What kind of woman?" Ben asked.

"Sweet, cooperative, undemanding," Brad said. "And discreet. You know? I need a woman who can keep our disagreements private. We need to have a perfect, presentable image."

His wish list sounded more like a paper

doll than a real woman, capable of being folded up and put in a drawer.

"The thing is," Brad went on, "I'm not sure Betsy is the kind of girl who can do that. I mean, she loves me, sure. And she's beautiful, smart, quick-witted… But she isn't exactly undemanding."

"So, she's got some expectations, too," Ben replied.

"Yeah, well…if she marries me, she'll get comfort and position. But I can't be there to hold her hand the whole time, you know? She'll have to be tough enough to navigate on her own and not embarrass me in the process."

Something about that tickled the back of Ben's mind, but he couldn't quite grab onto it.

"Are you going to marry her?" Ben asked.

"Maybe." Brad was silent a moment. "Probably. I mean, she's great, right? She's great!"

They headed back toward the woodshed, and Ben squinted through the falling snow. Their footsteps had almost disappeared already, and the shoveled walk had an inch of snow on it.

"You're getting married next summer, aren't you? To Hilaria Bell?" Brad asked.

They started reloading the wheelbarrow,

the wood landing with the reverberation against the metal.

"No, we broke up," Ben said.

"What? You two—" Brad's eyes were wide. He shook his head in disbelief.

"Yeah, well, it doesn't always work out," Ben replied. He didn't even know all the details, but Hilaria's texts had enlightened him to the broader strokes.

"So you get it," Brad replied. "I mean, we have to be careful, right? We have to make sure that we get a woman who can keep up, and make things easier for us. It's teamwork, but you've got to be careful who you pick for your team."

"That sounds more like backyard football than romance," Ben said with a laugh.

"Yeah, yeah. Add in some new jewelry and a weekend away here and there, but you've got the gist," Brad said.

Had that been what Ben had been looking for? Was that what he'd been expecting of Angelina—that she'd anticipate his needs and settle into a life of being his understudy? That idea was almost laughable when he saw what she'd done for herself without the benefit of his input. She'd built a world-class resort, and she seemed to command a fair amount of respect.

"What happened with Angelina Cunningham?" Brad asked.

A warning instinct tingled at the back of his neck. "What do you mean?"

"I mean…why did you two get divorced?" Brad eyed him, his expression smooth and poker-calm.

It stood to reason that his marital history would be common knowledge, and he wondered how he'd come out of that divorce in public opinion. Did they see the same hardened jerk that he was beginning to remember? Had there been any sympathy for Angelina?

Ben shook his head slowly. "I think I messed it up. I don't know what to say. Maybe learn from my mistakes."

Brad nodded. "Yeah. You kind of went outside the expected social circles there, didn't you?"

"Apparently," Ben agreed.

"A woman has to be used to the pressure," Brad said thoughtfully.

"Or I needed to protect her from it," Ben countered.

"Is that even possible?" Brad shook his

head and huffed out a laugh. "She can either swim or she can't. You know what I mean?"

Ben didn't answer that because no, he didn't know what Brad meant. He didn't fully understand any of this. But Ben did get a glimpse into the world that he came from. The expectations were high, and rather unfair, too. Had Angelina even wanted to fill those roles in a marriage with him?

And did he blame her if she didn't?

Ben put the last of the wood against the wall, and the side door opened again. A couple of Brad's buddies came outside in coats and boots.

"It's not as good as skiing, but it sure beats being cooped up in there," one of them said. "Want some help?"

Another gust of wind brought a blinding moment of snow, and Ben got another image in his mind of that horse, the cattle in the distance and his tough old grandfather with his bristly white mustache. And in that memory, that older man's gaze drilled into Ben with a recriminating look.

The family hadn't accepted Angelina, it would seem, but she was a better woman than anyone had ever guessed. At what point had Ben stopped following his heart?

CHAPTER EIGHT

ANGELINA WALKED BRISKLY back up the stairs from the basement where she'd been refueling the generator. There was always more work to be done, but it was doing nothing to distract her mind from that kiss. She sucked in a wavering breath. Damn it, Ben was still able to jostle her emotional balance these days. And before he'd lost his memory, he never would have acted on the simmering emotions between them.

What was worse was that she'd kissed him back. It was like thirteen years had slipped away, and she was making up with her husband after a fight all over again. She could remember those passionate fights, and the equally passionate reconciliations—what a relief it had been for both of them to slide back into each other's arms. But she wasn't his wife anymore, and she was happier now on the other side of their marriage. She was a better woman now.

And yet, Angelina had fallen right back into his arms.

She strode down the hallway toward her office and when she got inside, she stopped, putting her hand on the lambskin coat that lay over the back of the visitor's chair.

Why hadn't she told him about the papers? She could just hand them over and let him see exactly what she knew. Would that rattle his memory?

But she was enjoying this a little too much—the Benjamin King who was as charming and sweet as he'd been when she'd met him all those years ago. Before anything had come between them. Maybe she liked being the center of his world, the only woman he remembered.

It was a secret pleasure, although a very dangerous one. Because Ben was not just a man; he was the family that came with him, the responsibilities that loomed over him, and the expectations that came pinned to him. He had a good heart—but that heart hardly had a chance.

Angelina moved the coat, folded it with the soft crinkle of paper inside and set it on top of a filing cabinet instead. Then she sank into her office chair. To think she'd started feeling ready to find a serious relationship again. She leaned back and took some deep breaths the way her therapist had taught her years ago.

In and out. Feel your fingertips, feel your toes. Feel the way your lungs expand. Deep breaths...

She looked up at a tap on her door, half expecting to see Ben, but it wasn't him. Dr. Thomas stood there, his laptop in one arm. His blue plaid shirt was tucked into his saggy dress pants, which were held up with a worn belt. He looked every inch the overworked doctor, even now.

"Hi, Warren," she said. "What can I do for you?"

"I was just going to say hello. The young energy out there is exhausting, but it looks like this might not be a good time?" he asked.

"No, it's fine." She smiled and leaned forward. "Come on in. I could use a friendly face."

Warren came into her office and placed his laptop on her desk, then sat down in the visitor's chair opposite her.

"How is your memoir coming along?" Angelina asked.

"Not as well as I'd hoped, honestly," he replied. "Writing a book is harder than you'd think."

"I bet." She smiled at that.

"You want to tell a story," Warren said, "but stories never go in a straight line the way you think they will. Especially not in real life. I keep getting distracted with little tangents here and there...and then I worry that my memory of them won't be the same as someone else's memory of an event, and I think, am I lying? Will I be accused of lying later on?"

"I suppose everyone remembers things differently," she said. "That doesn't make you a liar, it means you have your own perspective."

"I'm a doctor. I work in science."

"And I'm a businesswoman," she said with a small smile. "I work in people."

"I like that—" He waggled a finger at her. "You see, I'm not quite so pithy as you are. But perhaps I'll use that, if you don't mind."

"Feel free." She angled her head to one side. "How far have you gotten in your story?"

"I've reached our wedding," Warren said, and sadness flickered behind his steady gaze. "And I'm remembering how much I loved her."

A wedding…the same thing that Angelina had been remembering lately, too.

"What's your ex-wife's name?" she asked.

"Louise." He sighed. "And she was a beautiful bride. When I proposed, she was twenty-two, and I was twenty-four. By my twenty-fifth birthday, I was a married man. I adored her."

"What happened?" she asked.

"Work. Busyness. She supported me through med school, and then there was my residency, which took up every spare minute. We had the kids—and I thought it was good because Louise could focus on them and she wouldn't be so lonely."

"I don't imagine that worked very well," Angelina replied.

"No, it didn't. Imagine that." Warren shook his head ruefully. "Back then, I got some terrible relationship advice from other men. And doctors have egos like you wouldn't believe, so for a long while I honestly thought being a doctor in and of itself was enough for me to bring to the table."

Angelina chuckled. "Louise set you straight on that?"

"Oh, yes," he said. "Repeatedly. I'm not sure I really got the message, though, because a little less than a year ago, I discovered that Louise was having an affair."

Angelina froze. "Oh, Warren…"

"He's a neighbor," he went on. "He used to stop and admire my wife's gardening in the front yard." He pressed his lips together, his eyes turning flinty. "And if you would just give me ten minutes alone with him…"

"I bet…"

"Anyway, when I was working those long hours, he was moving in on my wife. I caught her when I came home unexpectedly a few months before I retired, and she had made some intimate little breakfast for her and Claude."

"Oh my gosh!" she said. "What did you do?"

"I demanded that Claude get out of my house," he said with a shrug. "And I asked her what this was about. She didn't deny it. She told me everything. She said she and Claude had been seeing each other for years, and that she wanted a divorce." He sucked in a slow breath, then exhaled. "And here I am, vacationing alone, and writing a memoir for my children to see who their father really was. Because at this point, I have no idea what their mother told them, and to add insult to injury, my own children seem to like their mother's boyfriend."

"If it helps, I dislike him on principle," Angelina replied.

"Thank you." Warren smiled wanly. "I appreciate that. Apparently, he's more likable than I am."

"I find that hard to believe."

"He compliments everyone. Sits around and listens to them. He remembers their birthdays and anniversaries, and my son told me that he makes Louise happy." Warren pursed his lips.

"Was Claude married at the time?" she asked.

"Divorced," Warren replied. "Properly single."

"Can I ask you something?" Angelina asked, and he nodded. "Were you faithful to Louise? I know it's gut-wrenching to be cheated on, but if you were doing the same thing—"

"I was faithful." Warren's voice firmed. "I was busy. I didn't have any romance on the side, and I imagined that my wife understood that all my hard work was for her and the kids."

"I see... Sorry to have asked that."

"No, that's a good question. Do you have some paper?"

She slid a notepad toward him and he picked up a pen and wrote something down.

"That's the sort of thing I need to include more overtly, because if you ask it, so will my grandchildren one day. I want to be clear about that."

"Do you still love her?" Angelina asked.

Warren looked up, folding the piece of paper. "I took vows with her. I had children with her. I built my life with her."

"But do you *love* her?" she pressed.

"I never stopped," he replied quietly, and his words sank down into her gut. She knew that feeling all too well, loving an ex she'd rather forget. Ben didn't deserve that space in her heart, and yet she'd never been able to completely evict him.

"So what about our Benjamin King?" Warren asked. "Do you still love *him*?"

"I try very hard not to," she said, smiling faintly.

"You're being cagey," Warren said with a low laugh. "But I'll tell you this. I've seen the way Ben's been looking at you."

Angelina tried to hide her curiosity, but by

the smile that crinkled up the corners of Warren's eyes, she didn't think she'd managed it.

"How does he look at me?" she asked.

"He watches you like he's utterly in awe of you," Warren replied. "And I can't say I blame him."

"You're a smooth talker yourself, Warren."

"It's true, though," he replied. "You're a very impressive and, dare I say, intimidating woman."

"You don't seem terribly intimidated," she replied.

"But I have the doctor's ego, you'll recall," he said. "We think we're gods. We're prone to it."

Angelina laughed and shook her head. "Well, I'll admit that I've grown a lot over the last fifteen years. I'm no longer a bookkeeper who wants to see the world. I own a little piece of it, myself. And I love this place. It's… It becomes a part of you."

"Hmm." Warren nodded. "And if our Mr. King were to fall in love with you again?"

"He has memories to come back still," she said. "I think that will take care of it."

"Memories and emotions are chemically linked in the human brain," Warren said thoughtfully. "But you might not remember things quite the same way he does."

"Perspective," she said ruefully. "Very nice how you brought that back on me."

Warren laughed. "I'm sorry. I don't mean to meddle in your love life, Ms. Cunningham. It isn't my place."

Angelina sighed. "We didn't work out. I wasn't the sophisticated woman he needed."

"What about now?" Warren asked. "You hold your own, I assure you."

Angelina was silent for a moment. "In order to become the woman I am today, I had to struggle through a lot of tough times, learning as I went. And I wouldn't be me if Ben King hadn't let me down so phenomenally. I wasn't good enough for him as I was. The woman I was at heart…" She pressed a hand against her chest. "I was too far beneath his needs, when it came right down to it. So if after he's put me through everything that he did, if that process is what made me into the woman who is now good enough for him? He doesn't deserve me."

Angelina's hand trembled, and she curled it into a fist and dropped it down to her lap.

"What if he's grown, too?" Warren asked. "I don't know if he has, I'm only putting it out there. There are more ways to improve oneself with age. What if he's gotten deeper, wiser, a little more self-aware? What if he became someone better equipped for marriage?"

Angelina cocked her head to one side. "Did you grow?"

"I think I've grown the most over the last year," he said. "Is that fair to my family? Not at all. But life isn't fair very often. That's a little bit of old-timer advice for you. I can't think of very many times when life is truly fair to anyone."

"I hate that you make so much sense," she said with a rueful smile.

Warren chuckled. "You deserve the very best, my dear. And don't you forget it."

His words were so unexpectedly fatherly that Angelina's eyes misted. Back when she'd just gotten married, her own father had given her similar advice.

Warren picked up his laptop. "Well, I'd better get back to writing. You've given me something to think about."

"Likewise," she replied. "I'll see you at lunch."

After he'd gone, Angelina sat in the dim room, illuminated only by the pale light coming through the windows, and she let out a slow breath.

Marriage was complicated, difficult and, even when it was finished, it didn't feel entirely over. Warren was right about the fairness of life, too. Angelina's grandmother certainly hadn't deserved her lot in life. She'd married a man she adored after a whirlwind three-month courtship, and then been trapped in an abusive marriage. Angelina had particularly identified with that short but intense courtship. She'd been vulnerable to the same heady pull of romance—a family weakness, perhaps?

Angelina's grandmother had married again, and her second husband died in his late fifties due to an undiagnosed heart problem. Some people faced more heartbreak than seemed at all fair. And then there were people who hardly seemed worthy of their good fortune, everything always going their way. She thought of the King family. It didn't matter who Karl King railroaded—their family still prospered.

Angelina looked over at Ben's coat. She was the next one to be pressured into doing things for the King family's benefit.

Angrily, she checked her email on her

phone. She wouldn't have anything new because cell service and internet were both down, but it was habit. This was how she dealt with unresolved feelings these days—she threw herself into work.

But at the top of her inbox was an email that must have come in just before the cell service knocked out, from her good friend Belle Villeneuve. Belle was a new mom with a ten-month-old baby daughter, and they were already planning a first birthday party for Ashley with all the trimmings here at the lodge. Belle was one of the close friends who helped her keep moving forward with a good perspective. If she'd had access to phone and internet, she'd have called in the Second Chance Dinner Club for advice. What to do when Angelina started falling in love with her ex-husband all over again? *Someone* needed to snap her back into reality.

Angelina opened the email:

Angelina, you must be busy. I tried calling you again, but the lines seem to be temporarily down. Gotta love these storms. Here's hoping an email gets through! We need to have another dinner with all the girls. I miss you all!

Maybe it's for the best that we haven't yet, though, because I've got news—which was why I called—and I need to keep it a secret from everyone…except you, of course. I need your help to pull it off. Phillip and I were wondering if we could make a little tweak to Ashley's first birthday party. We want to make it into a surprise wedding, too. A surprise for our guests, at least. You'll have to be sworn to secrecy…

Another wedding. Angelina couldn't help but smile. It had taken a lot of work for Belle and Phillip to get to this point, and she was genuinely happy for them. Belle had been another woman who had gone through more than her fair share of heartbreak, even with Phillip! And the cards had been stacked in Belle's favor with her model beauty. Ironically enough, it was her perfectly symmetrical good looks that made Phillip so insecure about his ability to keep her, but Belle knew who she wanted and the life she wanted—a beautiful, ordinary life with a good man.

Angelina read the last of the email— Belle's hopes for her wedding day were entirely doable.

And you have to tell me what's happening over there to stress you out. Call me when you can!

They did need a Second Chance Club dinner, to remind each other that life was still beautiful, that happiness was still possible. And when one of them started falling back in love with an ex-husband, who better to help her stay grounded?

BEN COULD HEAR the thunk of wood being loaded up against the side of the building as he took off his winter clothes and rubbed his cold hands together.

He was leaving the last of the woodpile to the younger men. His mind was fixed on Angelina anyway.

When Ben had kissed Angelina earlier, he'd meant it. He might not have a lot of memories to back it up, but that kiss had been utterly sincere. And she'd responded. She'd leaned into him, tipped her face upward and kissed him back. He and Angelina seemed to know how to do this—there was no fumbling, no awkwardness. She knew his kiss, and on some instinctive level, he knew hers. What was that—muscle memory? He had a feeling that Angelina sank deeper than muscle, though. She was a part of him in a way he couldn't explain.

His memory was coming back, but there was a whole lot of time that had passed between his memories and the present. That was the tough part—she remembered things that held her back, and Ben could only remember that one fight. But an argument wasn't enough to end a relationship. Angelina remembered the rest of it, and he was still emotionally stuck at a point where he still had some hope.

"I'm an idiot," he muttered to himself, but he couldn't help but grin. It might have been wrong on every single level, but that kiss had felt like a victory, still.

Wood thunked against the building again. It would go a lot faster with several young men hauling and stacking. Plus it would give the college kids something to do.

He headed into the fireside room and tossed a few more pieces of wood onto the dying fire. He sat there, toasting his legs next to the flames for a few minutes before he heard the side door open and the voices of the young men coming back inside.

Job complete, it would seem.

"…like that movie…" one young man was saying.

"I know! I was just telling Matt the same thing!"

Then deep, male laughter.

"So that's Benjamin King."

Ben couldn't tell who had said it, but it grabbed his attention.

"I don't get why he's here."

"He had an accident."

"Yeah, so some billionaire decides to drive up the side of a mountain in the blizzard of the decade, and crashes his truck outside his ex-wife's resort."

"Ex-wife?"

"He's not a billionaire yet. His grandfather is still alive, as is his father. That's family money, not his personal fortune…"

"He's got enough in his own name that he's a multimillionaire—"

"Semantics—"

There was a brief argument over whether or not he deserved the title of billionaire before someone else said, "The owner—Angelina Cunningham. She's his ex-wife." One of the young men seemed to be answering the person who'd asked about Angie. "They had this incredibly short marriage ages ago. It was so short most people have forgotten about it."

"Wasn't it annulled?" one asked.

"No, it was a divorce."

"So, I'm thinking him showing up here all battered from an accident is a little less coincidental than it seems. Are they seeing each other again?"

"No idea, but they don't seem to be sharing a room."

"They could be hiding it. Isn't he engaged to someone else?"

"You can't really know what the King family is up to. Secrets, drama, nondisclosure agreements…"

"Their lawyers are faster than gunslingers. I suggest you pretend you didn't see anything. If the Kings have something going on here, they will crush you if you mess with it."

"That's the truth…"

The voices moved up the staircase. Ben let out a slow breath, his heart hammering. That was the family he came from… Was it jealousy from these college students, perhaps? Or was there some truth to it?

The description of his family sent a chill up his spine. His father had warned him that there were people to be wary of, who'd do just about anything to get their hands on the kind of money that the Kings had.

"Who am I?" he murmured.

And who were they as a family? Because that seemed to reflect rather heavily upon him, too.

Ben headed out of the employee lounge and down the hallway once more. Angelina appeared at the top of the basement stairs. She stood tall, her back straight, and she had an air about her that was almost regal. Her glossy blond waves fell behind her shoulders, and she paused when she heard his footsteps.

"Lunch is being served," Angelina said before he had a chance to say anything. Dismissing him? After that kiss, maybe he'd done more damage that he'd realized.

"Angie, look, I think we should talk," he said. "Angie—"

She froze, eyeing him.

Was she scared of him now? Or scared of his family? How much of her kindness to him had been inspired by her feelings for him, and how much had been a reaction to what his family could do if she didn't?

"I'll come with you," he said.

She angled her head to the side in acceptance, and Ben followed her down the stairs.

"So what's the problem?" she asked, glancing over her shoulder.

"First of all, I'm glad I kissed you," he said.

"That's how you start?"

He grinned at her back. Yes, this was exactly how he wanted to start—with some honesty.

"I don't remember everything that you do," he said. "But Angie, I know what's simmering between us right now, and this is real."

"This is *not* real." She turned around at the bottom of the stairs.

"Then what is it?" he asked.

"The same problem we always had—we work on a chemical level, but that's all."

"We do work on a chemical level," he agreed, and he caught her hand.

Angelina tugged it free. "Ben, I won't take advantage of you."

"Take advantage of *me*?" He blinked at her.

"When you remember everything, you'll know what I'm talking about," she replied.

"Okay…" He licked his lips. "I've got a question for you."

Angelina met his gaze, her eyebrows raised expectantly.

"Did I make you sign anything?" he asked.

Angelina didn't move, but her expression

turned to one of caution again. "Do you remember something you wanted me to sign?"

"No, I don't remember anything, but I overheard a conversation about me and my family, and they said that my family is known for our nondisclosure agreements. I was just wondering if you'd been made to sign one after our divorce."

"Oh, that." She shrugged.

"So…yes?" he asked.

"Yes, of course," she replied. "You didn't make me sign a prenuptial agreement, which made everyone in your family apoplectic. But when we divorced, before you signed the deed for this property over to me, you had me sign a nondisclosure agreement, where I wouldn't tell anyone details from our relationship, or about your family, your financial situation, business ventures, or anything that might impact the family reputation."

Ben felt the strength seep out of him. "I did?"

It was all so sterile, so locked down and dominating.

"Well, you and your gaggle of lawyers," she said.

"And you were okay with that?" he asked.

"I…" She sighed. "I understood it, Ben.

You were willing to help me start over with far more than I had to begin with, and you hadn't protected yourself in our marriage. So I understood."

"Did you stand by it?" he asked.

"Yes," she replied. "I was able to tell the truth in the strictest possible way—I could say that I wasn't the woman you needed. I didn't want to tell anyone about our fights, or the more personal aspects of our relationship as it ended. That didn't feel therapeutic to me, anyway."

"And my family—they left you alone after that?" he asked.

"More or less. I didn't give them any reason to come calling," she replied.

"Did they intimidate you?" he asked.

Angelina laughed bitterly. "Ben, you'll come to remember one of these days that your family intimidates everyone."

She turned then and headed toward the room with the growling generator. She opened the door of the huge metal box and looked at the listed instructions on the inside of the door for a moment.

"Was there anything else my family asked of you?"

"No," she replied as she undid the screw

top of the fuel opening. "Your father shook my hand, thanked me for my time and said that if anyone tried to interview me or offered me money for information about you, I was to contact him and he'd take care of it. That was all."

She lifted the red fuel container, and her arms trembled under the weight of it. Ben stepped forward and took it from her, then poured fuel carefully into the generator's tank until a light came on indicating that the tank was now full.

"Did anyone ask for information about us?" Ben asked.

She nodded. "There were a couple of reporters, and I called your father, and they went away."

"Were there any other requirements of you?" he asked.

"No." She shook her head. "I could live my life, grow my business, get married again... anything I wanted to do, so long as I didn't comment on the Kings."

"Get married again," he said.

She smiled faintly. "It'll happen one of these days, Ben. I've been holding off, and that's not your fault. You certainly moved on. But I've been more careful this time around."

"Are you saying you're ready to find someone?" he asked.

She nodded. "Yes, I am. I'd like to have someone who wants to build a life with me. I want someone to go to bed with and wake up to. And I want someone I can trust with my life."

An image rose in his mind of her bedroom—that neat bed, the framed pictures on her dresser... Apparently, there was a time when he was the answer to her hopes. What would it be like to have her turn to him again?

"That sounds really nice," he agreed softly.

"The problem is," she said, meeting his gaze, "and I've never told a single soul this before... But when I do find a good man to marry, I'm going to find myself in the same situation you were in—in love with someone, and with so much to lose if the marriage fails."

Ben frowned. "You're thinking about a prenuptial agreement, aren't you?"

"Yes." She shrugged. "You see what you've done to me? You gave me the step up to find some actual success, and I'm changing."

She smiled, then, a bright, glittering smile that nearly took his breath away.

"What a jerk I am," he said with a low laugh.

"It's the bitter irony of life," she replied. "I'll never have the high ground again in quite the same way. I'll have to do what you weren't tough enough to do when I married you—ask someone I love to sign a piece of paper stating what we'd do if we divorced."

Ben swallowed. "I can see why I couldn't bring myself to ask it of you."

"It would have been incredibly difficult," she agreed. "We were so young and idealistic—we'd never get divorced. Not us." She smiled ruefully. "And if you'd asked me to sign, that would have tipped me off to your family's money, and you didn't want me to know about that. If I knew about the money, and if you'd asked for that prenup, I think it would have made me stop and think."

"About whether I was worth it?" he asked.

"Just if I knew what I was getting into," she replied, her voice softening. "Anyway, when I do find the right guy, I'm going to have to ask him to sign. There's no way around it. I have too much to lose now."

Ben looked at her sadly. "Before me, you never would have even considered that."

"Before you, I didn't have a resort," she

said. "There's a silver lining to having nothing to lose—an innocence that you don't appreciate in the moment. I suppose I'm sympathizing with your position more now than I ever did in the past."

Angelina might understand his position… but he didn't completely understand it. Of all the things he'd learned about himself and his family, he didn't like what he saw.

"Maybe you should keep that idealized high ground and expect better," he said.

In this gray area that seemed to surround his family's money, Ben could only feel a sense of heaviness. Whatever his family's money had done for him, it hadn't made him happy.

"Oh, I do expect better," she said with a humorless laugh. "Don't worry about that."

Ben smiled ruefully. "I guess that's a good thing."

Angelina angled her head toward the door. "Come on. Let's get upstairs to lunch. I don't know about you, but I'm hungry."

Those words reverberated through his mind, and this time, the memory that surfaced wasn't a shard but a whole memory—connected to the wizened face of his grandfather, and to this very lodge. His breath caught.

Let's get in there, Ben. I don't know about you, but I'm hungry. The voice in his memory was low and gravelly.

"Angie—" He put out his hand and caught her sleeve, almost afraid to move. "I remember this lodge."

CHAPTER NINE

GRANDDAD LED THE *way up the lodge steps. It was a warm day—warm enough that sweat trickled between Ben's shoulder blades. He pulled open the big, heavy door, and inside the lodge could be heard the sound of conversation and laughter. The smell of fish and chips filled the place, and Ben's stomach rumbled.*

"Mr. King!" A man wearing jeans and a flannel shirt came over and shook his grandfather's hand. "Good to see you. What can I get you today? I'll get the kitchen started on it ASAP." He pronounced it ay-sap, two syllables.

"Are you busy? Ben and I can wait," Granddad said.

"Not too busy for you," the man said with a grin, and he thumped Ben on the shoulder with a meaty hand. "Fish and chips, like usual?"

"You know me, Sam," Granddad said, re-

turning the grin. "And a Coke for Ben here, and a light beer for me."

"Coming up."

They never paid, because Granddad owned the lodge and the land that it stood on. But Granddad always left a generous tip on the scratched table next to their empty plates.

"That's because waitstaff make most of their money off of tips," Granddad said. "And there are people who live on much less than our family does, Ben. Losing a tip could mean missing a meal for some people. Don't ever be negligent and let someone go hungry because you forgot to have some cash on you."

These people intrigued Ben. They were "ordinary people" who didn't have much money, who drove beaten-up old cars and who didn't fill up their tanks all the way when they went to the gas station. That part had never quite made sense to Ben—why not just fill it up? Dribbling in gas a little at a time didn't cost any less.

"That's because they don't have enough money on them to fill it all the way," Granddad explained. "So they put in what they can, and when they have more money, they put in more."

210 SNOWBOUND WITH HER MOUNTAIN COWBOY

"Could you pay for their gas sometimes?"
Ben asked.

"You've got too big of a heart, Benjamin. It would offend a workingman to have some rich old guy like me pay for his gas. A man pays his own way. You don't insult him by treating him like he's poor."

"But what if he is poor?"

"Then he doesn't like the reminder. What you can do for a man is pay him decently for his work. That's the way out. And you can leave a generous tip—that's how you pay it forward."

These were ordinary people who came to the lodge, and Granddad liked to mingle with them. He liked to hear their stories and laugh at their jokes about fishing or Chevy trucks...

"Ben?" Angelina's expression was strained. "What do you remember?"

"This lodge," Ben breathed. "My grand-dad used to bring me here for fish and chips."

It was coming back—a flood of memory. But nothing recent, just memories of child-hood times here at the lodge—canoeing out on that lake, and getting reprimanded for not wearing a life jacket.

"That lake doesn't care who you are, young man! You could be the king of England,

and it would still swallow you up. There's un-derground springs that feed that lake, and a powerful current that can drag down the most powerful of swimmers if you end up in just the right spot. A life jacket will save you, Benja-min King, and the next time you try and im-press some girl with acting tough, I will drag you off by your ear in front of her!"

"This was a special place for my grand-father," Ben said. "He used it to... I don't know...connect with the common man, so to speak."

"Common man." Angelina's tone was dry.

Ben sucked in a stabilizing breath, then headed past Angelina toward the hallway that lead back upstairs. This lodge was coming back to him—the lodge he remembered from his childhood, but it was like seeing double with the lodge from his memory lying on top of the present one as gently as a shadow.

He took the stairs two at a time until he got back to the foyer, and he looked over the immaculate hardwood floor. But back when Ben was young, this floor had been gouged and scratched. There were no rugs or mir-rors, no Chippendale side tables or chandelier lighting. There'd been antlers on the walls, and signs that had mildly inappropriate jokes on them about men needing their space and leaving the wives at home. There'd been the smell of greasy cooking in the air, the memory of which made Ben hungry. And there was the sound of scraping chairs and rough male laughter.

Not all the men here at the lodge were course and loud. Some sat quietly, looking out at the lake chewing on toothpicks.

Men came out this way to hunt, and they'd tell each other stories about the "the big one" they couldn't bring themselves to shoot, or some idiot city slicker who came out to try his hand at hunting who shot himself in the foot or just about got himself eaten by a bear.

Some told sadder stories, about wives who left them and about bosses who didn't appreciate them. Most talked about politics and the politicians who promised the world and never delivered. But in this lodge, while they couldn't fix any of it, they could at least talk about it to other men who understood their frustration. As a boy, Ben had found their talks depressing, but there was a part of him that responded to it. There was something about the testosterone that had soaked into the very walls of this place. These were men, talking like men.

Ben heard Angelina's footsteps behind him, and then he felt the soft tickle of her sweater against his arm. He reached back and caught her hand. It was instinctive, and Angelina didn't pull away. Her soft, cool fingers sat in that meaty spot on his palm and they stood there for a few beats in silence.

"Yeah, I remember this place…" he murmured.

"Do you remember signing it over to me?" she asked.

He shook his head. "No, I remember visiting here when I was a kid with my grandfather, and how he taught me about tipping your waiter and how regular people lived. It was eye-opening to me."

"What did he say about…regular people?" she asked.

"Oh, that some people couldn't afford the stuff I took for granted, or they had to save up for it." Ben's gaze moved over the polished wooden walls. They'd been yellower back when he was a boy. Angelina must have had them refinished. "He explained that some people lived one paycheck to the next—that if they missed a check, they wouldn't pay their bills and they'd get their power shut off, or their phones canceled, or…"

He didn't finish the thought, because when he looked back at Angelina, he found her gaze locked on him.

"If your grandfather understood regular people so well, what did he have against me?" she asked.

Right. She was one of those regular people that Ben had found so interesting. There was a reason why he'd been willing to marry her so quickly—he'd always held a secret longing for a regular girl who wouldn't be saddled with all the complications of money and position.

"I don't remember," he admitted softly.

"Because your grandfather told me that I was some little gold digger trying to get my hands on the King money," Angelina said. "And he figured I should just go home to California and let our marriage be annulled."

Annulled...that was something one of the college students had mentioned, too.

Ben frowned. "When was this?"

"Six months in," she replied.

"Wow." He sighed. "Look, the stuff I'm starting to remember—my grandfather doesn't seem horrible. He seems... I don't know, human. But he actually said that to you?"

"Yes," she replied, and she pulled her hand free of his. His palm felt cold where her fingers had been, and his stomach sank.

"What did I do about it?" he asked.

"You talked to him, and came home and told me that he was an old man and the family made allowances for him. He was losing it a bit."

Ben was silent for a moment, the memories still slipping back as softly as ghosts—faces he hadn't seen in decades, sounds, smells…

"This place meant something to me," Ben said, his voice tight as he let his gaze move over the foyer. "It was… I don't know. This lodge was part of me learning who I was, and what I owed the world around me."

It was a part of him learning that people who had less than he did had an awful lot to offer the world. It had rattled some of his inherited snobbishness loose.

"I had no idea this place meant anything to you. You never told me that. Why would you sign this place over to me?" Angelina asked.

Ben looked down at her and sighed. Why would he take a place so intimately connected with his own childhood and give it away? There was only one explanation that made sense. "I must have really loved you."

Angelina's mouth opened as if she was about to say something, then she dropped her gaze.

"That's all I can sleuth out," Ben admitted. "I must have loved you deeply. Your happiness must have meant more to me than my own history here. Even after we broke up."

Angelina was silent for a moment. "We did love each other, Ben. That I can't deny. What we had was beyond anything I've ever experienced. But we didn't last."

"Last or not, you're the first one I remembered." She was the one in his mind, and it wasn't just the fact that she was here. He'd been coming to this lodge—determined to get here. There was more to it—he knew it on a bone level.

"Ben, there is one thing I know about you," Angelina said. "You always have a Plan B. And it always benefits the Kings."

Ben felt his irritation start to rise. That was her response to how much he'd loved her? She said his family intimidated everyone, and yet he remembered a grandfather who taught him about respecting those who had less than they did. It didn't add up.

"Did I cheat on you?" Ben demanded.

"No."

"Did I ask anything of you when we got married? Did you have anything I needed besides just having you in my life?"

She was silent for a beat. "No."

"So in spite of all of that, you think I gave this lodge to you for some reason, to take advantage?" he asked incredulously. "Is that actually easier to believe than me loving you? I might not remember my history, but I think I know what I've got in here—" he thumped his chest "—and I'm not some manipulative jerk. I don't want to win at all costs. I've been nothing but honest with you. I just want to remember...and remembering you brought me some comfort. So maybe *you're* the one who has some skewed image of me that isn't fair! Maybe I'm not the jerk you think I am. Isn't that a possibility? That *you* could have been wrong?"

"Ben, I'm sorry if I—"

"Maybe I just loved you!"

Angelina was so close to him that he could have reached out and pulled her into his arms. She was a breath away from him, and just as he lifted his hand to touch hers, the dining room door opened behind them. Ben turned to see Brad and Elizabeth coming out of the dining room. Brad had a hand on Elizabeth's shoulder, and they sauntered toward the staircase.

Angelina took a step away from him and smiled in the young people's direction.

"Did you have a good lunch?" Angelina asked, and her professional demeanor was back—cool as the snow outside. He wasn't the one who hid what was happening inside of him—she was the expert there. Ben's heart was hammering in his chest.

Brad looked at him with mild curiosity, and Ben met his gaze with a drilling one of his own. He wanted answers from Angelina, not an interruption from this kid. For the first time since arriving here, he was willing to bet that he was the one being manipulated. She knew more than she was letting on. He was giving her everything he knew, and she was holding back.

"The meal was great, thanks," Elizabeth said. "You have a really good turkey soup."

"Thank you. I'll pass that along to the chef," Angelina replied.

Angelina was the boss here, and her authority was almost palpable. She waited until the couple had started up the staircase, then she turned back and met his gaze.

"You need to see something," Angelina said

curtly, then turned on her heel and headed in the direction of her office.

Angelina was the one in control, completely capable of keeping her emotions locked down. Whether he had memories here or not, he was on *her* turf.

"Come on," Angelina said over her shoulder, and without a better option in front of him, he followed her.

ANGELINA FISHED HER keys out of her pocket and unlocked her office door. There was no more putting this off. Ben needed to know what she knew—and maybe she was hoping that it would jostle something loose for him. He'd come here for a reason.

"Come in," Angelina said, and she went in first. "Close the door, if you don't mind. I think you'd rather keep this private."

"Keep *what* private?" He shut the door harder than necessary and crossed his arms over his chest.

"Do you remember why you came to my resort?" she asked.

"I know as much as I did ten minutes ago!" Ben snapped. "I don't know why I'm here. I'm guessing I came to see you, but it would seem I was misguided."

Angelina got the coat from the top of her filing cabinet and passed it over to him.

"Are you asking me to leave?" he asked.

"In this storm?" She sighed. "No, I'm not kicking you out. Check the inside pocket."

He did as she asked him and pulled out the envelope. She watched his expression, noting that he looked genuinely surprised to see it.

"Do you remember anything about that?" she asked.

Ben opened it and flicked through the pages, then came back to the first one and read for a moment. "This is—" His eyes widened. "This is an offer to buy this resort."

"Yes." She leaned back against her desk and waited for him to process the information.

"Why are we trying to buy it?" he asked. "Did you ask for this?"

"No, this isn't coming from me," she replied.

"How long have you known about this?" he asked.

"Since you arrived and I…snooped." She felt some heat in her cheeks. "I'm not proud of that."

Ben took a closer look at the documents. "There is no dollar amount here, just a blank space. Maybe this is what my father was talking about when he said not to sign anything."

"Maybe," she agreed. "But it would appear that you were on your way to see me for a specific purpose."

"I didn't know." He looked up at her, his gaze clouded. "You have to believe me about that. I had no idea."

His face was pale, and he scrutinized the pages again.

"I do believe you," she replied. "It's not like you to do this."

Ben really was the ideal ex-husband—her grandmother's advice had guided her that far.

"An attempt to buy you out of your divorce settlement?" Ben said incredulously. "Yeah, I'm glad this doesn't seem like me. This is pretty underhanded."

So it shocked him, too.

"Do you know why your family would want to do this?" she asked. "Besides the fact that I've built this place into a profitable resort?"

"No." Ben rubbed a hand over his forehead, and when his fingers touched the bandage, he let his hand drop. "But if I came dashing over here just before a snowstorm with the papers in my pocket, I must have been on board."

Angelina felt tears prickle in her eyes and she blinked, looking away. "Do you know what this place means to *me*?" Angelina's voice caught. "I know it meant something to you—having those childhood memories attached to this lodge—but you willingly signed it over. It was your idea. I wanted a three-story Victorian-style house in town that I could turn into a bed-and-breakfast. You're the one who suggested this lodge. The land was worth more, you said, and I'd get a better loan leveraged against it for the work I'd have to do to make it into a resort instead of an old hunting lodge."

"It was *my* idea..." he murmured.

"Do you remember that?"

He shook his head again. "But I think I believe you."

"This resort has become a part of me." Angelina leaned forward. "I didn't know what I was capable of until I turned my attention to renovating and reimagining this space. I had this idea of a luxurious yet rustic getaway that would allow guests to enjoy this unspoiled mountain lake while staying in complete comfort. There's something healing about Blue Lake—it's so pure and clean. And the process of renovating everything...

it was rejuvenating for me on a very personal level. I grew here—I started out as an uncertain divorcee who'd lost the love of her life, and I climbed my way up to being a confident businesswoman who is well respected. You might have learned some life lessons here but, Ben, I literally became the woman I am inside these walls."

"I can appreciate that."

"I've been able to give back, too," Angelina plunged on. "I told you about my dinner club friends. I started that club purposefully. I had this casual friend—a bank manager— whose husband had come out as gay after thirty-five years of marriage, and she was just crushed. She was this shell of herself, and everyone was whispering about her and talking, and… I invited her for dinner, and I told her that we'd make a habit of it. We'd get together every few weeks and we'd talk. I wanted this resort to be healing for more than just me. I wanted to prove that there was life—real, true, happy life—beyond heartbreak."

"That's the picture in your suite—you and the women at the table," he said.

That photo was a treasured memento. They needed an updated picture that included their newest member, Taryn, but that picture reminded her of the early days.

"That's us. We grew over the years—we were careful about who we invited to join us because this dinner club wasn't just for women who were starting over. It was for women who wanted to build each other up. That's a rare quality, but an important one."

Angelina thought back to those first few dinners, just two women, and then three... then four and five. She used to look forward to those shared meals like they were actual food for her soul. To laugh and talk with women who not only understood, but who were determined to grow from the pain, to hold each other higher, even when it hurt.

"You were all divorced?" Ben asked.

"Yes," Angelina replied. "Some had cheating spouses, and some had just realized they were tired of being pushed into a corner. But the thing we all had in common was a determination that it wouldn't suck the joy out of our lives forever. We might have been divorced, heartbroken and starting over, but we were worth a good dinner and a nice bottle of wine."

"Did I push you into a corner?" he asked, his voice low.

Ben had been different. The other women were able to point to obvious, terrible, glaring flaws in their spouses. She didn't have that luxury.

"No," she said. "We just weren't right for each other."

He nodded and dropped his gaze.

"Ben, the point I'm trying to make is that this resort isn't just a financial investment," Angelina went on. "Your family buys and sells properties for the profit, and I can appreciate that. But I've invested more than money here—this resort has years of my life, and relationships that matter to me. It's given me a voice and a vision and an identity."

"A job should never be your identity," he said. "That's dangerous. Don't ask how I know it—I don't remember. But I'm sure that it's true."

"This place isn't a *job*," she said. "It's... This resort is my *home*. I'm not interested in selling."

"That's fair," he said with a nod. "I have no reason to talk you into it. This is brand-new for me, too."

"Your family isn't going to like it," she said. "Once your father sets his sights on a piece of property to acquire, he's hyper focused until he gets it."

"No one can make you sign this!" He tapped the document against his palm.

"Apparently, you thought you could," she said bluntly.

Ben exhaled slowly. "It looks that way. But maybe I underestimated what this place meant to you."

"It would seem," she said dryly. "But here's the thing. Your memories are all going to come back to you. You never could see what I could see in your family. To you they will *never* be a threat. Unless you count what they can do to a marriage they don't approve of."

"And you see something different in them," he said.

"I see the power of their attorneys," Angelina said quietly. "I see the laser focus of their will when they want something, and the sheer weight of their money. They can bankrupt someone just by dragging them through court for long enough. They can strong-arm competition. They can turn public opinion against a company—and they've done it. For us little guys, your family is incredibly dangerous, especially when they set their sights on something we have that they want."

"You think my family would intimidate you into selling?" he asked, his brow furrowing.

"I think you were confident you could get me to sell for a reason," she said.

Ben never could see what his family was capable of. He excused them. He explained their quirks. He ignored their demands when they didn't suit him, but they'd gotten their way in the end.

"Angie, I don't know what to say." He crossed the space between them and caught her hand in his. "I don't know what this offer to buy your property is about, but I admit that it looks shady."

"It is definitely shady," she said.

His expression was conflicted. But he pulled her closer and touched her cheek with the backs of his fingers.

"This place is yours," he said earnestly. "If you aren't willing to sell, then you aren't. Period. And if my family wants to try and bully you into it, then I'll stand between you. You have my word."

"Really?" Angelina's heart skipped in her chest.

"Yeah. Of course. There's right and there's

wrong. I'm not going to be part of bullying you into anything. Trust me on that."

This was the old Ben, the one she'd fallen in love with all those years ago—the champion of the underdog, the noble knight when she'd needed him most. But how much would he change when the rest of his memories returned?

"Angie, look," he said. "Was I ever a good man?"

"Yes. Of course."

"Then if you can trust nothing else right now, please trust that. I'm not going to take advantage of you. I'm not going to try and take this place away from you. I promise."

Angelina met his gaze, and she saw such tenderness glittering there that her breath caught.

"I'm not a jerk, Angie," he whispered. "I know that much."

But that offer to purchase in his pocket suggested otherwise.

Angelina should be pulling back, but this was the Ben she'd lost somewhere along the line in that first year of their marriage. This was the man who'd swept her off her feet, who'd touched a place in her heart that no man had ever gotten close to again. This was the man she'd vowed to love and cherish until death did them part.

Angelina put a hand on his chest, feeling the steady, comforting beat of his heart, and Ben leaned down, his lips a breath away from hers. She knew she shouldn't do it, but she lifted her face upward and their lips came together. She might never see this kind, noble version of the man she'd married ever again.

Maybe it was a goodbye. Or maybe it was just weakness, but she leaned into his embrace and kissed him. He gathered her up in his arms, taking over from there. His hands slid down to her waist as he pulled her close. Their heartbeats reverberated against each other, and the faint stubble on his face tickled her face.

When she leaned back, feeling a little bleary and weak in the knees, she looked up into Ben's familiar face.

"I'm going to take care of you," Ben said, his voice low and deep, and she wanted to believe it so badly that she felt tears prickle in her eyes. She stepped back out of his arms.

"I've got to stop doing that," she said, sucking in a stabilizing breath.

"So you keep saying," he said, then he sobered. "I'm serious, though. You can trust me, Angie."

"You should go to lunch," she said with a small smile.

An inviting little smile curled up one side of his lips. "Are you coming?"

She shook her head. "In a few minutes."

This time she was asking him to leave. She needed her balance back. Ben picked up his coat, the envelope in one hand, and turned toward the door. Angelina sank back against the desk, her heart pattering in her chest.

"Angie?" He paused at the doorway and looked back.

"Hmm?"

"I'm a better man than you think," he said. "It's important to me that you know that."

Ben held her gaze until she nodded, and then he disappeared out the door. She exhaled. But what happened when the rest of his memory returned? Would he be keeping those promises to protect her? Or would she be back on her own?

CHAPTER TEN

ANGELINA RUBBED HER hands over her face. That had been stupid. Kissing Ben? It didn't matter if she'd been thinking about him for the past few days, or if the kiss had fulfilled some deep, heartbroken longing inside of her.

Whatever had drawn them together all those years ago was still simmering between them. Having him here with hardly a memory of their doomed marriage was harder than she'd thought it would be.

"What I need is a dinner with my friends," she murmured aloud.

Belle Villeneuve, Gayle Pickard, Renata Spivovitch, Melanie McTavish, Jen Bryant and Taryn Brooks were as close to family as it was possible to get without actually being related, and they were the straight-talking women who lifted each other up and kept each other accountable. Angelina had been there for each of the women in turn, and it seemed that her turn was fast approaching when she'd be leaning on them, too…

What would they tell her? Gayle would be practical and point out that the King family was not to be trifled with. Renata would be more rebellious, and she'd say that Ben might be a man with a fat wallet, but a man all the same. Belle would agree with Renata and tell Angelina to get herself a "regular man" with a big heart, like she had. As tough as things had been with Phillip, Belle was in love with him. Melanie would ask Angelina if she was still in love with Ben, and Jen would likely want to know, too.

Angelina would have to admit the truth, of course. And then they'd all look at her with mutual sympathy and tell her that they'd love her no matter what she chose, and then proceed to argue good-naturedly about whether or not Ben was worth it.

It would be comforting…as that process was for all of the women in the group when they needed it. They'd talk it out, look at it from different angles. Her friends would share their opinions, and in the process, she'd get a better idea of what she needed. Because right now, she could feel her very well-thought-out resolve crumbling.

The goal of their gatherings wasn't to bounce themselves back into new marriages. This group was about support and understanding, about living life to the fullest without regrets. And maybe she was hoping that the other women would reassure her that she wasn't the biggest idiot on the planet for kissing her ex-husband.

Angelina came out of her office and headed toward the employee lounge. A whisk of frigid air whipped down the hallway, causing Angelina to look more closely. Was the side door open?

She picked up her pace, and when she got to the door, she pushed it open far enough to look outside. There was a fresh pile of wood along the side of the building, already capped with snow. The flakes blew, cutting off Angelina's view, but when the wind suddenly changed direction, she spotted a flash of color. Someone was out there—was that Elizabeth?

She was hardly visible since she was in a white sweater, but her dark hair stood out against the blast. She was cradling something in her arms and she was visibly shivering.

"Elizabeth!" Angelina called. "Are you okay?"

Elizabeth came toward her and when the snow blocked their view again, Angelina held her breath until the young woman came into sight once more.

"What are you doing? I told you to stay inside! Do you have any idea what happens when people get caught out there—"

But Angelina stopped as Elizabeth pushed past her and into the warmth of the lodge. Her lips were already white with cold, and she was trembling.

"Is anyone else out there?" Angelina opened the door again, scanning for any signs of color or movement.

"No, just me," Elizabeth breathed. "I'm sorry—I saw… Here—"

Elizabeth turned into the employee lounge and when she got to the couch, she sank down into it and opened her arms. Crouched in her embrace was a small white rabbit, its eyes wide with fear and trembling with shock. There was a red smear of blood down one side of the rabbit's body.

"I saw it out the window," Elizabeth said. "A hawk came down from the trees and grabbed the rabbit, but it fought hard. I've never seen a rabbit fight like that! And the hawk dropped it and flew off, but the rabbit was hurt. So I ran downstairs to see if I could get to the rabbit before the hawk came back." Elizabeth nodded toward some towels in a basket. "Could you lend me a towel? I need to cover her head, so she calms down. Rabbits can die of shock."

Angelina grabbed a towel, and Elizabeth created a little burrow for it on the couch cushion.

"I know it's not convenient," Elizabeth said apologetically. "But I couldn't let her just die."

"It's okay," Angelina replied. "I understand. How badly is she hurt, though?"

"There's not too much blood," Elizabeth replied. She lifted the towel. "It looks like she got scratched. If we keep her warm and fed, when the storm is over we can release her."

Elizabeth seemed different than she'd looked before, more confident and in control. There was a new sparkle in her eye, too, that Angelina hadn't seen yet in her. Elizabeth pulled her hair away from her face and reached under the towel, wincing as she parted the rabbit's fur for a closer look.

"Yeah, it's a bad scratch," Elizabeth said. "It'll heal."

Angelina smiled. "You're good with animals."

"My sister is a vet, remember?" Elizabeth replied. "I trailed after her for years, rescuing animals with her."

Elizabeth looked around. "Is there a box with a lid, or even flaps that we could close?"

"Here—" Angelina pulled down a box of outdoor gloves and emptied it onto the table, then brought it over.

Together, they arranged some towels on the bottom, and Elizabeth lowered the rabbit inside, keeping her covered. Then they carefully closed the flaps.

"If we get her some lettuce or carrot to nibble on, that will give her enough moisture, as well," Elizabeth said.

"You love this," Angelina said.

"Animals? I do. I'm a little jealous of my sister. She actually wants me to come out to help her at her vet practice when I graduate—you know, like a bit of a gap year while I figure out what I want to do."

"Sounds like a good idea," Angelina replied. "You'd probably enjoy it."

"Brad and I have other plans," Elizabeth replied. "He wants me to go with him and his parents on a Europe trip, and then he's starting law school, and…" She pressed her lips together.

"What?" Angelina asked.

"All of that kind of rested on Brad asking me to marry him, though. If I had a wedding to plan, and future in-laws to get to know, I'd be busy. But he hasn't asked."

"You won't travel with them unless you're engaged?" Angelina asked.

"I won't plan a future with him unless he's willing to marry me," she replied. "A trip? Maybe. But what about when we got back? What then?"

Angelina nodded. "I get it."

"Brad needs a politician's wife." Elizabeth looked down at her hands. Her white sweater had a little bit of blood on the sleeve, and she plucked at it. "You support your man no matter what, and together, you rise. That's how it works. Unless he's changing his mind about me."

It wasn't right to meddle in the romantic affairs of a guest, but there was something in this young woman's face that felt so familiar.

"I have a group of girlfriends who get together for dinner with me once every month or so," Angelina said. "We learn a lot from each other. One of those women, Belle, worked as a professional model for a few years. She was on all sorts of catwalks in

Paris and all over the world. She ended up marrying her agent."

"Oh?" Elizabeth looked up.

"But he was awful to her. He wanted to keep her skinny, and he wanted to keep her under control. A woman can only handle that for so long—"

"Oh, Brad isn't controlling," Elizabeth said quickly.

"Don't worry," Angelina said, sinking into a chair. "This is about Belle, not you."

"Okay…" Elizabeth laughed self-consciously and pulled out another chair to sit down.

"So anyway, Belle decided that she wanted to find a regular guy. She was used to the powerful types—the rich men, the ones who could afford to give her a really good life. But she said they ended up treating her like another acquisition. She might as well have been a Lamborghini. She wanted to find a sweet man who would love her for who she was. She met one here in Mountain Springs, a teacher. And she fell for him."

"Did she marry him?" Elizabeth asked.

"They're going to get married soon," Angelina replied. "It wasn't an easy relationship, though. He was intimidated by her. I mean, you have to see Belle to understand. She's absolutely stunning. She can silence a room just by walking into it."

"Yeah?" Elizabeth smiled faintly. "Wouldn't that be nice."

"Belle would be the first one to tell you that you're beautiful," Angelina said. "She's like that—she makes anyone sitting next to her feel like they're just as gorgeous as she is. She'd also be the first one to tell you that you deserve someone who lets you be who you are, lets you shine in your own right, be that with a man who has a lot to give you financially, or if that's with a guy who doesn't make quite so much."

"Brad isn't at his best this trip," Elizabeth said quietly.

"He was probably at his best the first six months you were together," Angelina replied. "And you're chasing that high."

Elizabeth opened her mouth, then shut it.

"And, sweetie, I'm doing the same thing," Angelina said softly. "We keep making mistakes. But sometimes it helps to have someone point it out. That's something I've learned over the years."

That was the beauty of their dinner club—straight-talking friends were more valuable than most people realized.

"So you think I should find some regular guy and give Brad up?" Elizabeth asked.

Right about now, Angelina should take that advice, too. She should find a decent, hard-working man who loved her if she wanted to settle down. The glamorous life that the King family led was never hers to begin with, and she wasn't drawn to the money or the power. She was drawn to the "regular guy" inside Ben—the sweet man who wanted to protect her. But that wasn't the whole man. She was no wiser than the young woman in front of her, was she?

"No, I don't think you should just exchange him for another man," Angelina said. "I think you should find something you love and chase that…and then wait and see if Brad can handle you when you're actually happy."

Because Angelina had just now seen Elizabeth with a sparkle in her eye when she was working with this injured rabbit.

Suddenly there was hum and buzz, and then the lights popped on and the microwave clock started flashing 12:00. Angelina felt a rush of relief.

"We have power back!" she said.

"Oh, thank goodness!" Elizabeth stood up, blinking in the sudden light.

Angelina smiled. "Let's get some fresh lettuce and carrot for the rabbit, shall we?"

From above, Angelina heard some hoots and celebration.

"Come on, admit it," Angelina said. "The best part of your trip so far has been rescuing the rabbit."

"Actually…" Elizabeth paused at the door. "The best part of my trip has been meeting you."

Angelina's throat tightened with emotion. "That's sweet…"

"You are truly inspirational, Ms. Cunningham." There was a blip from Elizabeth's pocket and she pulled out her phone. "Oh, look! We've got cell service back, too!"

Angelina smiled, trying to hide an unexpected wave of emotion. The sad part was, give this vibrant young woman ten years with a man like Brad, and she'd make an excellent addition to the Second Chance Dinner Club—divorced, frustrated, crushed and needing to find herself all over again. And Angelina didn't wish that on anyone.

If an older woman had sat Angelina down on the cruise ship and told her to be careful, she wouldn't have listened, either. Because youth believed that life could turn out differently, if one just loved hard enough, and believed deeply enough. Apparently, a woman old enough to know better wasn't immune to her own heart's desires, either, because when Angelina thought about finding some "regular guy," her heart still balked a little bit.

"Damn it…" Angelina muttered.

She pulled her cell phone out of her pocket. Their little snow globe was back in contact with the rest of the world.

LUNCH HAD BEEN a bowl of soup and a grilled cheese sandwich. The food was good, but Ben's mind wasn't on eating. Those papers in his coat pocket felt heavy with recriminations. He'd come out here to buy this property—the papers were proof enough of that fact, and he was still running the information through his head, trying to see where it fit.

The electricity and cell service were both back—people were making calls and checking messages, and it looked like life was starting to come back to normal…or closer to normal, at least, because the snow was still coming down out there. It was time for a few answers of his own.

He flicked through his phone's contacts until he got to his father's number, and he dialed it. The phone rang twice, and a man's deep voice picked up.

"Son? That you?"

"It's me," Ben said. "Is this my father?"

There was a pause. "So your memory isn't back, I take it?"

"It's coming along," Ben admitted. "I'm remembering a lot more."

"Do you know why you're there?" There was wariness in Karl's tone.

"There were some papers in my coat," Ben replied. "I'm supposed to buy this resort."

"Yes. Exactly." A relieved sigh. "Have you done it?"

"No, I haven't," Ben said curtly. "This resort was Angelina's divorce settlement. She's grown it into a popular tourist spot, and frankly, it's impressive. I'm not asking her to sell this place."

"Yes, yes," Karl said, sounding tired. "We've been over this. But if she's been this successful with an old lodge, she can do it with some other place."

"I don't imagine there are a lot of mountain lakes just waiting for a hotel," Ben said. "I'm thinking zoning, environmental protection measures and access from main highways… Something just came back—the fact that this lodge was already built meant that she could renovate without going through all that red tape."

"You're sounding more like yourself again."

Ben was… Some of this was jogging loose. "And I seem to recall that this lodge was losing the family money on a yearly basis. Cheap beer and cheaper food wasn't enough to even pay the utilities as well as the staff. I don't know why we held on to this place as long as we did if we weren't going to make it pay for itself."

"You could have done that, if you really wanted to," Karl replied.

"Apparently, Angelina was the one with the vision for the place," Ben replied.

"And she did an admirable job. She's got more business savvy than I gave her credit for, I'll admit to that. That's why I think she'll be just fine starting over with another property of her choice."

"Why *should* she start over?" Ben asked, lowering his voice.

He moved over toward the windows, further from the doorway where he might be overheard.

"What does it matter?" Karl replied. "We're

willing to pay whatever she wants for it. I mean, within reason. That's why you were adamant that you be the one to talk to her. I highly suspect you wanted to fleece your grandfather in the deal and give Angelina far more than the place is even worth."

Ben frowned. "You think?"

"You don't?" Karl barked out a laugh. "Look, she did the work, and we're asking her to give it up and go start over somewhere else. You wanted to make sure that there were no lawyers taking advantage of her, so you went to make the deal yourself."

"And if I offered her some absurd amount and she took it?" Ben asked.

"I'd be annoyed if the amount was too high, but we'd honor it," Karl replied. "Besides, I trust you. You'd go as high as you needed to in order to make the deal. You have a good sense of these things."

Ben's mind was spinning, new bits of memory whipping through his head and connecting. He'd been trying to get to the lodge before the storm hit because he didn't want to give his father and grandfather a chance to change their minds. He didn't trust that they'd stick to it if he didn't have signatures in place, and he wanted to make sure that Angelina got as much money as possible for all she'd been through. Otherwise, Karl would find some other way to push her out.

"I was coming here to talk her into selling this place," Ben said, his voice firming. "And this would have been good for her..."

"Better with you in the mix, that's for sure," Karl said with a raspy laugh. "So now that you remember, are you going to get the deal made?"

Ben looked out into the falling snow, biting the inside of his cheek. He was silent for a moment, and then said, "I can't."

"Why not?" Karl demanded.

"She found the papers, so it isn't exactly a surprise to her now that you want this property," Ben said. "But more than that, she told me what this place means to her."

"I'm sure enough money will help change her mind," his father replied.

"I doubt it," Ben replied. "This place is personal to her."

"How personal could it be?" his father asked dryly. "This property belonged to our family for decades."

Ben hardly thought his father would understand it, but Ben did. She'd healed here, and she'd grown phenomenally. She'd found some deeper meaning to her life, and a connection to the wilderness around her. Ben had broken her heart, and at this resort, she'd rediscovered the resiliency of her own spirit.

"I promised her that I wouldn't ask her to sell," Ben said. "I gave her my word."

"Your grandfather is determined to get this place back," Karl said. "If she makes the deal with you, it's easier for her. You used to know that."

Ben turned and looked around the fireside room—the gilt-framed watercolor paintings, the deeply polished log walls. The overstuffed chairs looked to be scattered around the room at random, angled toward windows, or in little circles for conversation, but there was reason and pattern to it. Brass reading lamps glowed warm over the backs of a few chairs now that the electricity was back, and the overall effect was soothing, charming, elegant.

Angelina had made more than a vacation spot—she'd created an expression of herself.

"Why not just leave her alone?" Ben asked. "She signed the nondisclosure agreement. She's not giving any trouble. I don't see why this matters so much."

"Because your grandfather wants it back!" Karl sounded irritated. "Besides, the value is starting to rise for this property, and it's worth the investment."

"Dad, I dare say that the investment in this place isn't rising because of a few renovations. The investment is in *her*."

"Then she'll be fine elsewhere, won't she?" Karl replied curtly. "You're going in circles."

Ben sighed. His father wasn't going to be swayed.

"Here's the thing," Karl said. "I know you always had a soft place for Angelina, and heaven knows I can see why. But she's never going to get more for this property than what we're offering. Ever. Especially if you're the one making sure she gets everything that you feel she deserves. No one else is going to look at her emotional contribution to this place. So you can refuse to talk to her about this, or you can help her wring every last penny she can out of us. That's up to you."

"Dad, I'm not trying to screw the family here, either," he said with a sigh.

"I know," Karl replied. "Ben, I trust you. This is your legacy and your inheritance. You've always put the family first, and I appreciate that. But I can also appreciate it if you feel like you need to give her a little extra here. Maybe she's even owed it. We can afford to be generous. Just how generous, that's your call."

So Ben wasn't some heartless millionaire out to get her, after all. His family might be hard to derail, but they were giving him the opportunity to make this as positive for Angelina as possible.

"Son, I know you'll always love her," Karl said, his voice softening. "I get it. There are some women who get into your heart, and it isn't logical. That's Angelina for you. I'm trying to respect that. Angelina won't trust me or the lawyers. But she might trust you. We're doing our best to do well by her, son. We really are."

Was his father a little softer and gentler than he let on normally? It would seem he had some decency deep down. And if Angelina sold this place now, while his family was willing to part with a good deal more than the property was worth because of their own sense of responsibility toward her, then this might be incredibly good timing for Angelina to sell. Besides, if his grandfather was really so bent on getting this property back for whatever reason, the next efforts to acquire it might not be sweetened like this one.

"Thank you," Ben said. "I'll talk to her

again and see what she says. But I can't promise anything."

"Understood. At least your own conscience will be clear. You'll know you tried."

"And your conscience, too," Ben said.

"Yes, but I hardly expect you to care about mine," Karl said. "I'm in a difficult position. My father wants this property back for personal reasons, and my son signed the land over to his ex-wife in good faith that it would help her restart her life."

"Yeah, I can appreciate that," Ben agreed. "Is there anything else I should know?"

"About the deal? Not really. As for the rest of your memory, I'd like you to talk to our doctor and see what he thinks about your recovery, but that's about it."

"Fair enough," Ben replied. "You can get him to call me now that the cell service is back up."

"I'll do that," Karl said. "Is there anything else you need, son? Anything I can help you out with?"

Ben sifted through his fragmented memories. There were a few that still hung out there alone and unexplained.

"Yeah," Ben said slowly. "I have this memory of a woman—she was cleaning something off my cheek. She was bending down and smiling at me, and she licked her thumb and cleaned my face off... I don't know who she is."

"What color was her hair?" Karl asked.

"Brown. Cut kind of chin length..."

"That was one of your nannies," Karl said. "Cynthia, I think. Your mother wouldn't have licked her thumb, for one, and she was a beautiful blonde."

"Could you email some pictures of my mother?" Ben asked. "And you, too—you know, just a few family photos to jog my memory? I don't like the idea of remembering a nanny and not my own mother."

"Uh—" His father faltered for a moment. "Yes, of course. I'll dig up some old albums. I'll text them to you."

"Thanks. I'll talk to you later."

Ben hung up, relieved that more of his memory was clicking back into place. He could feel more of himself connecting again. A talk with his father had been just the jolt he'd needed to bring back some more detail and remind him of who he was, and the family that had created him...but he wasn't going to be able to stand quite so firmly on his resolutions as he wanted to. Ben wanted to be the man who stood between Angelina had his family's whims, but sometimes a man wasn't going to be big enough to be the protection he wanted to be.

He turned back toward the room and spotted Warren standing in the doorway eyeing him thoughtfully.

"How are you feeling, Ben?" Warren asked.

"Uh—fine," Ben said. "I'm remembering more."

"You look like it," Warren said.

"Oh?" Ben asked. What did a man with memories look like?

"You look more sure of yourself," Warren replied. "A little more weighed down, too."

Both of those statements were accurate, but he'd also lost some of his innocence as his memories returned. He was a King—that meant more than he'd realized.

"At least I know who I am again."

For whatever that was worth.

CHAPTER ELEVEN

FOR BEING WITHOUT internet or phone for several days, Angelina was surprised at how few emails were waiting for her once she logged back into her computer. Most of the day-to-day questions would be fielded by Noah Brooks, her general manager, and he would have taken care of things from home.

Angelina called Noah to check in, then phoned Karl King.

"Ben seems to be doing pretty well," Angelina said. "Reception is back, so you can contact him and judge for yourself."

"Yes, I've spoken with him already," Karl replied. "There was something he wanted to talk to you about. Maybe you could seek him out."

Right. Did Karl know that she knew about the plan to buy her out? She leaned back in her chair.

"Mr. King, I'm going to level with you,"

she said. "I know that you want to buy my resort."

"Talk to Ben. Please."

"If you think our history will make me more pliable with Ben—"

"Nothing further from the truth. But if I hammer a deal out with you here and now, he isn't going to forgive me."

"You're not understanding me," she said. "I'm not selling."

Karl's voice was calm and unchanged. "Talk to Ben, Angie."

Angelina rolled her eyes up to the ceiling. "Fine. I'll talk to him. But I'm not selling."

"Just talk to him. Call if you need anything more." Then Karl hung up.

Angelina clenched her teeth. The Kings were always the same. They had plans, and they worked those plans, no matter what anyone else said. A no right now meant nothing to Karl. It was just the opening negotiation for that man. But Angelina didn't have a price.

She knew she needed to call Belle back, but right now she didn't think she had it in her to celebrate secret wedding plans. She would soon, but right now, she needed something else… Angelina dialed Gayle Pickard's number.

"Angelina? I've been watching the news about how hard that storm hit the lake area. How are you doing?"

"I'm not too bad, actually," Angelina replied. "But I needed to talk to a friend."

"What's going on?" Gayle asked, her tone softening.

"You wouldn't believe who landed on my doorstep."

"Who?"

"My ex-husband." Angelina told the story as succinctly as possible, leaving out some pertinent details like the shared kisses, and ending with "...so he's here."

"My goodness, Angelina..." Gayle breathed out a sigh. "And you're not okay, are you?"

"I thought I was over him, Gayle," Angelina said. "It's been thirteen years since that divorce! Thirteen years! But having him here, without his memory..." She cast about in her mind, looking for a way to describe it. "He's like he was on the cruise—just Ben, no family connections tugging at him, no demands being made on him. Just Ben and his innate nobility."

"You're falling in love with him again," Gayle said.

"I don't know... I'm definitely feeling

something, but I should know better. Please remind me why this won't work."

"Because his family will always come first," Gayle said simply.

"Always…" Angelina looked up at the ceiling. "There's a young woman—one of the guests who decided to ride out the storm. She reminds me a lot of myself back then. She's got this boyfriend from a pretty well-off family and he's got political aspirations. She's a definite afterthought for him."

"Were you an afterthought with Ben?" Gayle asked.

"No… He loved me. I know that. I just didn't know what I was getting myself into. This girl—she has no idea. And *someone* will end up marrying this guy! I mean, it isn't my place to try and steer her away from him. It's obviously my own issues with Ben that make some college student's romance feel so personal." Angelina leaned forward and rested her elbows on her desk. "But I'm remembering what I was like all those years ago, and Gayle, you wouldn't have recognized me."

"I bet I would," Gayle countered.

"I doubt it," Angelina replied. "I was bright-eyed and ambitious. I thought that a good heart would be rewarded. I married Ben fully believing that our love could carry us through anything…"

"There's nothing wrong with that," Gayle said softly.

"I *needed him*, Gayle." This was the part that was so hard to admit. "I relied on his love for me. With him and his loyalty, I was whole. Without the kind of love I needed, it was like being hollowed out."

"That's called being in love with him," Gayle said. "And it's always a risk. Now, I'm going to say something you don't want to hear, but I'm saying it in love."

There was silence for a beat. "Okay," Angelina said. "Give it to me."

"You need to find someone you can be vulnerable with again," Gayle said. "You've seen most of us move on into romantic relationships, getting married again, and you've held out. It wasn't because of a lack of options. I think you're afraid of needing a man again."

"Ben is still dangerous for me," Angelina said.

"I didn't say Ben, did I?" Gayle asked. "You need to trust *someone*…some regular, sweet man who will worship you. Someone who will know just how far you are above him and live the rest of his life in gratitude."

"I'm not sure I can do that," Angelina replied.

"Then some fantastic duke!" Gayle laughed. "Sweetie, I'm almost old enough to be your mother, and I managed to move on again after Stu came out of the closet. It was hard to trust again, but do you know what made it worth it?"

"What?" Angelina asked.

"Being loved," Gayle said. "There is something about having a man at the breakfast table who thinks you are amazing, just as you are. I want you to find that."

"Do you know what I need?" Angelina asked. "I need a Second Chance Club dinner—all of us together with a really good bottle of wine. That's what I need."

"We're due for a nice dinner," Gayle agreed. "And we can see what the other girls have to say about this. I think you'll be outnumbered in this. We'd all like to see you open yourself up again. Obviously, a man won't solve your problems—we all know better than that. But the right one might help you destress a little bit, and put a smile on your face. You deserve that."

"Maybe so." Angelina smiled. "Thanks,

Gayle. I knew a chat with you would help me settle my thoughts."

"Glad to help," Gayle said. "So...where does this leave you and Ben?"

"I don't know where it leaves Ben," Angelina replied, "but it leaves me with my feet solidly on the ground."

"Glad to hear it."

"I'd better go," Angelina said. "I have to get some lunch, and then I'm going to be shoveling snow."

"Have fun," Gayle said. "Should I call the girls and find a night that works?"

"Please!" Angelina replied. "I appreciate it."

Angelina had to admit that she did feel better. There was something very grounding about a group of friends who knew her so well. They'd keep her accountable and wouldn't let her go do something stupid...or at least not very stupid. Apparently, they all wanted to see her enjoy some romance again.

She'd said she was ready for that, hadn't she? Ben had a way of derailing her attempts to move on without even trying.

Angelina tucked her phone into her pocket and headed out of her office, locking it behind her. Karl wanted her to talk to Ben, and maybe she should. She'd listen to the pitch, and then give her answer. Whatever the price the Kings were offering, Angelina wasn't selling. It was high time they didn't get their way for once.

Angelina glanced into the fireside room and the dining room, but didn't find Ben, so she headed up the stairs toward his suite.

Angelina's knock was answered a moment later. Ben stood in the doorway with his phone in one hand. He'd taken off his sweater and was wearing a white undershirt with his jeans, a relaxed look that she hadn't seen in a long time.

"Hi," she said. "I talked to your dad."

Ben nodded. "Come in?"

Angelina brushed past him and came into the room. The bed was made and a faint smell of bleach that indicated the cleaning staff had already been through came from the bathroom.

"So what did he say?" Ben asked.

"He asked me to come talk to you," she replied. "I told him that I'm not interested in selling, but he just kept repeating that I needed to talk to you. So that's what I'm doing. Let's get this out of the way."

Ben pulled a chair around for her, and Angelina took a seat. Then he sank onto the edge of the bed.

"I asked my father about that memory," he said quietly, "the one with the woman wiping my face when I was a boy. And you were right. It was a nanny. My father said my mother would never have licked her finger to clean my face."

His dark gaze clouded. "I don't remember her... That feels really wrong."

Angelina's heart gave a squeeze. He hadn't remembered his mother yet? "Your mother suffered from depression, Ben."

"She did?" He stilled.

"Yes. I didn't think it was my place to talk about her since I never met her. I only know what you told me. She passed when you were a teenager, but she could be very emotionally distant—not that it was her fault. From what I understand, she just had a lot of other things going on in her mind. That's why the nannies were such a big part of your life."

"Oh..." He nodded. "I don't remember that."

For a moment they were both silent, then Angelina said, "Are you going to save us both the time and just tell your father I'm not selling?"

Ben shook his head. "It's a little complicated, actually…"

Her heart sank. Here it was… Ben was siding with his family. It shouldn't surprise her, but it stung all the same.

"Can't you just tell them no, and let it be?" she asked, feeling tired. "You know my answer. You know why."

"I wasn't lying when I said I wanted to protect you," he said. "I do. But there's more to the situation."

It had always been the same—Ben making promises, and then breaking them for his family. Not without remorse, and never without explanation, but breaking them nonetheless. The same line that he'd used over and over again that year of marriage had been that things were complicated. But she was no longer a hopeful young wife.

"There is nothing complicated here," she said frankly. "There are some rich men who want their way with property that doesn't belong to them. From where I stand, it's pretty simple."

"That might be partly true," Ben agreed. "But there's more to it. Angie, when I came dashing out here to try and catch you ahead of that storm, it was because I wanted to help you. This wasn't selfish on my part."

"Help me?" Angelina tried to tamp down the anger that rose up inside of her, but she couldn't do it. "You came out here to try and buy this place out from under me because it was all about what would make *me* happy?"

Had he listened to anything she'd tried to tell him? Did he even care what she felt about this place, or was this going to be about the Kings wanting their way again?

"You're smart, talented and good with business," Ben said quietly. "You're so much more than anyone gave you credit for—me included. You can start over."

"I don't *want* to start over." She couldn't help the ice in her tone.

Ben's expression remained solemn, and he didn't even blink.

"Angie, I really think you should consider it. Just from a business perspective."

BEN WATCHED ANGELINA'S FACE, waiting for some eruption of emotion, but she met his gaze icily. And in the back of his mind, he had that memory of the argument they'd had early in their marriage, where he'd said something cruel and gotten that same frozen response before she crumpled into tears. His heartbeat sped up, and he had the urge to take it back, to tell her to stand her ground, to give her what she wanted to hear. But he knew better, and avoiding this confrontation now wasn't going to change the lengths his family was willing to go to.

"What happened to backing me up?" Angelina asked.

There weren't going to be any tears here. This Angelina was stronger, older and she needed less from him.

"This is a chance for you to make a lot of money," he said, "more than you'd ever make selling this place later. It's worth hearing me out."

"You remember more," she said.

"Yeah…" He sighed. "A lot more has come back."

"Is this personal?" she asked. "Are you angry? Was there a grudge that I didn't know about?"

"Yes, it's personal," he said, leaning forward. "But this isn't about a grudge. I promise you that. My grandfather and my father are determined to get this land back."

"Who cares?" She spread her hands. "They

want a lot of things in life and most of them they get. Money can't buy everything."

"I know." Ben leaned forward. "And I agree with that. But hear me out. I know this place is personal for you, but if you looked at this from a purely financial perspective for a moment—"

"Purely financial," she said dryly. "Is anything purely financial?"

"Let me talk." His own frustration was rising. He didn't ask to be stuck in the middle of this, but he was. "I forgot how eloquent you get when you're angry. I can't argue with you about the finer points of my family's dysfunction, all right? But I think this is important. And at the very least, you need all the information that I can give you. You can't argue that!"

She pressed her lips together. "Fine. Explain it."

Ben could see the way her expression had changed—closed off, hardened. He was breaking his word that he wouldn't ask her to sell. He was letting her down, and he hated that. He wanted to be the guy who helped her, not someone who pushed her into a corner.

"I don't know why my grandfather wants this property back," Ben said. Her expression grew less impressed, and he plunged on. "Whatever his reasons, he's willing to do just about anything to get it."

"Is that a threat?"

"No." Ben sighed. "My dad says he understands that I—" He paused. He was going too far admitting this, but maybe it was better to say it out loud. "He understands that I still feel…a lot…for you. There are some women that come and go from your life with hardly a footprint. And then there's the kind of woman who is your first memory when you start recovering from amnesia."

Ben met her gaze pleadingly. Did she understand what she was to him?

"I'm not trying to manipulate you with that," he added quickly. "I promise. But my dad knows that for me, you're that woman. And he also appreciates that you've been cooperative. You really impressed him over the years."

"Ironic," she said. "I wasn't impressive enough when I was married to you."

"I'm not defending him." Ben pressed his lips together. "But the thing is, there is a combination that works in your favor right now."

"Which is?" Her gaze locked onto his.

"First of all, my father seems to be feeling

nostalgic. Secondly, my grandfather has decided that he wants this property more than anything else. He's absolutely stuck on it. Thirdly, my dad doesn't want to screw you over. Call it fear of karma or whatever you want, he wants to make sure that our family's treatment of you remains fair."

"And you believe that?" she asked.

"They've put the entire deal into my hands."

Angelina let out a slow breath. He could tell that she was listening now, her combative posture easing as she uncrossed her arms.

"That means I can give you whatever I want for this place, and they'll sign off on it," he concluded.

"What makes them so willing to overpay?" she asked.

"I don't know," he admitted, scrubbing a hand through his hair.

"What if they aren't actually offering to overpay?" She crossed her legs. "What if they want this place because they know something that I don't—like the true value of the land?"

"I don't think that's the case." Ben shook his head.

"Why not?" Angelina asked. "Why else

would the King family suddenly be overcome with generosity…for me, of all people?"

Ben couldn't help but feel a stab at those words. Was this Angelina's personal bitterness toward the family, or was it a broader attitude that people around here had toward them? He wished he knew. But as he probed his scarred memory, all he seemed to come up with was that image of his grandfather in a cowboy hat, staring him down reproachfully. Granddad wanted this.

"I've been told about a possible connection between Blue Lake and the WWII Camp Hale training facility. Apparently, it's possible that there were a few training marches out to the lake, and if there is a historical connection, the value of this property might go up significantly."

"I didn't know about that," he said.

"Well, now you do."

"My father didn't mention it, either," Ben said. "We have money, but that doesn't make us monsters, plotting to take advantage of every business owner we stumble across. We're *people*."

Angelina angled her head to one side. "Your family has a reputation for getting what they want. The little guy seldom stands a chance."

"We pay fairly," he countered.

"Maybe."

"I intend to pay fairly."

"It's not always about money," she replied softly.

Ben sighed. "I'm just telling you what I know, okay? They're willing to pay a lot for this property. And if there is a connection to Camp Hale, I'll make sure that's taken into account. I don't want to see you taken advantage of. That's why I'm here, apparently—to make sure you aren't."

"And what would I do if I sold?" she asked. "If I sold and gave up everything I've worked for here, what am I supposed to do then?"

"You've got more going for you than you seem to realize…" Ben shrugged. "I guess do it again, but with more money behind you."

"Just do it again… As a businessman, you should know that some of this is pure luck. Just because someone has done it once doesn't mean it will all come together a second time in the same way. You need more than a beautiful building and a scenic location, you need tourist traffic and timing. Everything came together for Mountain Springs

Resort, but it isn't something that happens just by willing it."

"You don't think you can make over another place?" Ben asked.

Angelina rubbed her hands over her eyes. "I don't know. I don't *want* to start over."

She dropped her hands and met his gaze. "Is it possible that they just want to get rid of me?"

"My father told me expressly that he appreciated how cooperative you've been."

"And if I agreed to this, I would be cooperating again." Her tone was dry. "How lovely."

"I think he was being genuine, not manipulating you to go along with this," he replied.

"And how generous are you willing to be?"

"Very." He felt a wave of relief to say it. "I care about your feelings, okay?"

"I need specifics, Ben." She whispered, but there was a change in her tone. It was harder. She was considering this.

"Okay, well, I'm willing to take into account any debt you might need to pay off, the actual value of the property right now and if there is a connection to Camp Hale. Plus, I think you deserve some extra on top of that to make starting over worth your while," he said. "That would be…a lot."

"You do realize that if I take the money, I'll have to go elsewhere…maybe even a different state," she said.

Ben swallowed. "You could stay in Colorado," he countered. "There are more locations in the Rockies here—"

"None quite so perfect as Blue Lake," she replied. "I wouldn't want to take a step down from this. I need to find something better. That won't happen in Colorado."

"I have to admit," Ben said quietly, "I don't like the idea of you leaving. You're a part of things."

"I hold you back," she countered. "Hilaria would say so, at least."

"Hilaria wasn't right for me," he replied.

"Hilaria was *perfect* for the heir to a fortune." Angelina sighed and leaned back. "She knew the job of being a King wife, and she could move through those social circles easily. She could help you grow your family's position. Hilaria is ideal—you're just too stubborn to see it."

How could Angelina pretend that she wasn't miles above Hilaria in every way? She was toying with him now, and he knew it.

"Hilaria wasn't right for *me*," he repeated.

"I'm more than the money I came from, Angelina!"

"You are!" she agreed, and her eyes flashed. "But you also have a unique set of needs when it comes to finding a wife, and Hilaria ticked those boxes nicely."

Except for the one that mattered.

"I can remember her now," Ben said. "Our relationship, the proposal, how pleased everyone was. But she wasn't perfect."

"No woman is, Ben."

"She wasn't *you*!" The words were out before he could think better of them, and Angelina caught her breath.

"Angie, maybe I am still hung up on you," he admitted. "And Hilaria wasn't the one to shake me free of you. No matter how much everyone, including you, thought she should."

"Who you dated or married wasn't my business," Angelina countered.

"Did you want to see me fail?" he asked.

"Of course not!" she retorted. "I wished you well!"

"That—" He jabbed a finger at her. "That is a lie. Because if you truly wished me well, you would have told me not to marry her. I came to you and told you what I was planning, and you just looked at me with that cool, collected expression of yours, and *congratulated* me."

"You wanted me to talk you out of it?" Angelina shook her head. "As your former wife? That was my job? Then I'd just be your bitter ex trying to ruin your happiness. Hilaria was perfect on paper, and if she wasn't perfect for your heart, then it was your business to figure it out. Besides—" Her voice broke. "Do you think it's going to be easy for me when you do find the perfect fit for you?"

"We've been playing this game back and forth for a while," he said. "We keep coming back to each other."

"But nothing has changed, has it?" she asked. "Even if I could match the social demands you live with, I don't want to."

He felt his throat tighten at those words. Maybe he needed to hear it out loud. He caught her hand and brought it up to his lips. He pressed a kiss against her fingers.

"No woman is going to match you," he said, his voice tight.

"And I'm not ever going to be your perfect society wife." She tugged her hand free. "Where does that leave you, Ben?"

"Where does it leave *you*?" he countered.

Angelina blinked, emotion flitting across

her face, and he could tell that he'd finally shaken that icy shell of hers.

"It leaves me refusing to find a good man," she said. "I've been holding back, too. I'm in my prime, and I can't bring myself to move on. That's not right… It's time that I found someone to share my life with. We both need to find someone who can make us happy."

Like Hilaria? Any woman he met was going to be the same—wonderful in many ways, but not Angelina. No one had warned him that a first wife could lodge in a man's heart like that.

"Does that mean you're considering the offer?" he asked at last.

"Maybe," Angelina said. "But before I consider it, I need two things from you. The first is a dollar amount, broken down into those categories you mentioned, including the value if there is a connection to Camp Hale. I'd have to discuss it with my lawyer."

"And the second?" Ben asked.

"The second is maybe even more important than the first," she said slowly. "I want to know why your grandfather wants this property back so badly. I need an explanation that makes sense. And I need the truth. Without that, I won't even consider it."

Ben nodded. "Okay."

Angelina met his gaze and he could see the pain in her eyes. Was he really trying to talk her into leaving?

"I want to know why, too," he added. "I'll feel better knowing the whole story."

Angelina smiled faintly. "What happens if the reason is that they just wanted to get rid of me?"

Honestly, right now, that wouldn't shock him. Maybe she was right, and this whole thing was about shaking Ben's heart loose so that he could move on.

"I'll tell you that," Ben replied. "I'm not keeping secrets, Angie. I'm being completely honest with you."

Angelina rose to her feet. "Okay. So, get some answers, and we'll see."

Did he want her to leave Mountain Springs? This resort wouldn't be half so successful under different management, and he knew it. Angelina brought something to this place that no one else could.

He'd never move on in his own life with Angelina here, either. He could see that now.

It would have to be her choice. He couldn't hold her here and be the reason she gave up some real, lasting happiness, either. Ben was determined that he wouldn't be one of the Kings who got his way at other people's expense, especially Angelina's.

CHAPTER TWELVE

AFTER THEIR BREAKUP, but before any papers were signed, Angelina had sat in her parents' California kitchen with a mug of tea in front of her and her heart in shreds. One year was all it had taken for her hopes and dreams to be dashed. One year.

Her mother's answer had been to feed her—cookies, toast, leftover roast beef, anything that came within reach. Her father's response had been silence. He'd just sat there in the chair opposite her, his hands folded on the table in front of him.

"What do I do?" Angelina had asked hopelessly.

"You carry on," her mother had said, sliding another plate of buttered toast in front of Angelina. "You're young still, Angelina. You have your whole life ahead of you."

"I still love him…" she'd confessed.

"Well, turn that love into hatred, my dear," her mother had said passionately. "Because it's over—and he'll move on. So you'd better, too. He used you, and then he allowed his family to treat you like garbage. I didn't raise you to accept that kind of treatment from anyone."

"He asked what I wanted," Angelina had said, her voice thick. "And I didn't know what to ask for."

"Money," her mother had said fervently. "I know you're in pain right now and that cash won't help with a broken heart, but trust me, my girl, it will help you put your life back together. You ask for money. Ben can afford it."

"No…" For the first time, her father broke his silence. "That's not what she should do."

"If you have better advice," her mother had said, offended.

"She should ask for property," he'd said.

"Why?" Angelina had asked woodenly.

"Because back before you married him, your big dream was to open a bed-and-breakfast," he'd said. "Well, you might have a broken heart, but you can still have your business. And that will support you for a lifetime. Invest in your own future, Angelina. This is painful, but it's not the end of you."

Angelina had taken her father's advice, and when she next sat down with her soon-to-be ex-husband, she'd told him that she knew what she wanted. How little she'd known then what a big part of her this piece of property would become.

And now, Ben was offering her the money she hadn't asked for back then—a replacement for everything she'd built, for the healing atmosphere of this place, for the memories here. It might make financial sense, and if she sat down with an advisor, they might tell her to jump at it. But there was something inside of her that resisted. Mountain Springs Resort was more than a financial investment, and it always would be. The fact that the Kings would overpay for it was proof enough.

After dinner was served that evening, Angelina headed down toward the employee lounge to check on their rabbit patient. Her mind had been on Ben's offer all day. She'd been right that the return of his memory would change things, but she wasn't prepared for feeling that heartbreak all over again. For a little while, she'd had the old Ben back, and losing that sweet man was just as hard this time around.

As Angelina approached the lounge, the door opened and Elizabeth came out.

"Hi," Angelina said, but then she saw Elizabeth's red-rimmed eyes and she slowed. "Are you okay?"

"Yeah... I just...um...made a little pen for the rabbit. She's staying pretty still, but rabbits do well with more freedom." She blinked quickly.

"Elizabeth," Angelina said softly. "You're crying."

"Maybe a bit." She sucked in a breath. "It's going to sound stupid, though."

"Try me," Angelina said with a small smile.

"I called my mom." Elizabeth wrapped her arms around her middle. "And I had to explain that Brad had brought his buddies on this trip, and that he hasn't even hinted at an engagement. And that was...hard."

"I'm sorry," Angelina murmured. "And it isn't stupid. It's entirely understandable."

"He's not going to ever propose, is he?" Elizabeth asked.

"I don't know," Angelina said.

"He hasn't exactly been doting this trip."

"To be fair, he's come to find you a couple of times," Angelina replied. "And you looked pretty cozy when I saw you coming out of the dining room the other day."

"I know how to keep up appearances." Elizabeth shrugged. "I really wanted the engagement ring. I know it sounds so shallow, but that mattered to me. I have these friends who are all getting married and they keep asking me what the holdup is with Brad. And they give advice about how to get him to propose."

"Like what?" Angelina asked with a wry smile.

"Oh, leaving ads for engagement rings where he'll find them, and watching movies with him that end in romantic engagements and telling him I won't do certain things until he makes a commitment. I had one friend who wouldn't travel with her husband until they were engaged, and he really wanted to take her to Paris, so he proposed, and then took her. I already tried that with that trip with his family to Europe. It hasn't worked yet."

"I don't think manipulating a man into an engagement is the kind of relationship you want," Angelina said. "Just a guess."

"It isn't," Elizabeth agreed. "But I do want to get married and start a family. I want to start that part of my life. I'm ready for it."

"You're young," Angelina said softly.

"Maybe I am, but I'm still ready!" Elizabeth shook her head. "I don't have to have huge career ambitions, you know. I can want to make a life out of loving the ones who belong to me. There's nothing wrong with that."

"Of course, there isn't," Angelina agreed.

"But I imagined marrying someone a little more eager to marry me," she added.

Angelina chuckled. "There is that."

"What should I do?" Elizabeth asked.

Angelina's smile slipped. "Sweetie, I can't really give advice."

"You have an opinion," Elizabeth pressed. "I just want to hear it. What's your honest advice?"

Dare Angelina give it? It didn't make good business sense to meddle, but Elizabeth looked up at her with such pleading.

Angelina blew out a breath. "Okay, I'll probably regret this, but I'll give it. Go find something that makes you happy—not a man, something else. A career, a hobby, an ideal, a mission, a project… Create a life that makes you happy in and of itself."

Elizabeth was silent for a moment, then she asked, "What about Brad?"

"Dump him."

Elizabeth blinked. "What?"

The girl's doe-eyed look was exactly why

Angelina had held back. Elizabeth wanted some secret to change Brad, but there wasn't one. Brad had to choose who he wanted to be, and if Elizabeth didn't like it, she had a choice to make.

As if on cue, Brad and a couple of buddies came out of the fireside room laughing raucously at something on one of their phones. Brad saw Elizabeth down the hallway.

"Betsy, can you grab us something to eat and bring it upstairs?" Brad called.

"Sure, Brad!" Elizabeth called, a trifle too brightly.

Was this the life this young woman really wanted? And should it matter to Angelina? How many women made choices that Angelina wouldn't make? It wasn't her place to judge. She was forty-three and very, very single right now. If Elizabeth wanted marriage and children that badly, she shouldn't pattern her life after Angelina's.

"I should get going," Elizabeth said and walked away without a goodbye. Angelina followed a little more slowly. Once upon a time she'd been young and hopeful, too. Maybe Elizabeth was willing to jump through hoops for Brad, but Angelina hadn't been any wiser at that age. She'd married a man she met on a cruise after two weeks of knowing him.

Wisdom came with age…and some tough experiences.

"Penny for your thoughts?"

Angelina startled when she saw Warren standing at the entrance to the fireside room, his hands plunged into his pockets.

"Hi, Warren," Angelina said with a smile. "Just remembering being that young."

"They're babies still," Warren said. "At least from my vantage point."

"What do you think of that couple?" Angelina asked. "Brad and Elizabeth…or Betsy, as he calls her."

"Oh, they're classic," Warren said. "I've seen it a lot. She's smarter than him, but he's got more money behind him. If he marries her, he'll feel mildly intimidated by her and try to even the balance by making her feel badly about aging. She'll start jogging, even though she hates it. He'll run for Congress."

Angelina sighed. "I can see it happening."

"We all start somewhere, don't we?" Warren asked. "Even if we end up miserable and regretting our choices."

"I suppose so," she agreed.

Where had Angelina started? Was it as the independent woman who decided to go on that cruise alone when her friend hadn't been able to come with her? Was it falling in love with Ben? Was it her dogged determination to be the wife he needed, even though it went against everything she wanted? Was it her commitment to this resort, even though she knew that staying so close to Ben was holding her back from truly embracing the next half of her life?

At what point would she look back and say, "That was it. That was the pivotal point that changed everything..."

"You okay?" Warren asked.

Angelina pulled herself out of her thoughts. She'd built this life—every piece she was so proud of, and she had to take some personal responsibility for the very heartbreak that she couldn't quite heal from. She had no one to blame but herself. Not even Ben, or his family. This life was of her own making.

"Oh, yes, I'm fine." Angelina shot him a smile. "I should go get some work done. You have a good night."

Angelina was holding on to everything she'd built. But just like Elizabeth, who was sticking with a relationship and didn't want to give it up after all that work, was Angelina holding on to something she should be letting go of?

BEN SAT BY the window in his suite, flicking through email on his phone. There were a few new ones. Most seemed work related. There was another email from Hilaria telling him that she was done trying to win him back, and if he wanted to find her, she was going to be spending some time in New York.

Things were coming back now. He knew what her veiled threat meant. Hilaria was going to be working the social circles in New York, schmoozing with her friends, going to some fashion shows and putting out her feelers for other bachelors with enough money to interest her.

Ben sighed. He wasn't interested in stopping her, even though he knew that was what she was hoping he'd do. He'd meant it when he broke off their engagement three months ago, and it was a testament to just how much Hilaria was losing that she'd hung on this long trying to convince him to come back. But it wasn't the emotional connection that was so important to her, he was sure. Hilaria wanted an equal match, a husband who came from the same wealth that she did. She cared about him, he knew, but if he lost all that money and the lifestyle, would Hilaria still want him back? Would she be fighting for a future with him if he was an ordinary guy? He doubted it.

Call him old-fashioned, but he wanted a woman who was with him for better reason than that.

He flicked a couple emails into his junk folder, and then stopped at a familiar name. George King. It was from his grandfather.

Ben, I do hope you are recovering. And while I want that property, don't do anything stupid.

What would Granddad consider stupid? Getting back together with his ex-wife, perhaps? Giving her a more generous offer than she knew she could get? And suddenly an image came shooting into his mind of a lined old cowboy with a bristly white mustache sticking one boot into a stirrup and swinging up onto a horse's back.

Granddad had refused to stay off the land. He had employees for this, but at least one day a week he used to saddle up and check the property lines… That was when he was young enough to still ride, though.

It was coming back together, clicking into place. This was his family, and there was a heavy burden that came with them. There was obligation, responsibility, integrity and just a bit of judgment… It wasn't bad—it was a good thing to stand firm on something, but his grandfather was standing a little too firm on getting this property back, and he didn't make sense.

Ben picked up his phone and flicked through his contacts until he reached his grandfather's number.

"Benjamin. About time," his grandfather said when he picked up.

"Hi, Granddad," Ben replied, putting the phone onto speaker. "How are you?"

"I'm old, and I'm irritable," George said. "How about you? How much is rattling around in that brain of yours? Your father says you have a general idea of what's going on."

Ben's phone pinged, and he looked down to see some photos his father had texted to him. He touched the first one—a blonde woman with mournful eyes and a small, rosebud mouth. His mother…a whisper of memory was coming back now, but he had to get some answers from his grandfather first.

"Here's the thing, Granddad," Ben said. "I need to understand why this property is so important for you to get back."

"No, you don't," George retorted. "You just need to do as you're told."

Was he some errand boy? But his grandfather had always been a difficult sort of character.

"I'm not asking her to sell or making any deals with her until I understand your reasons," Ben said. "I have to be able to live with myself after this."

"And you don't trust me?"

Ben sighed. He wasn't going to just duck his head and do as he was told. Not this time.

"I just don't get it," Ben said. "Why do you want this property back? Is it because she's made something of it? Is it the connection to Camp Hale? Do you have building plans?"

"No, not that." George sighed. "And while the connection to Camp Hale does pique my interest, it isn't really that. Look, some things are private, Ben. I'm sure you can appreciate that. A man has…regrets. And this one I'd like to make right."

"By taking my ex-wife's divorce settlement away from her?" Ben asked sardonically.

"We'd pay her!" George said. "Stop being

so dramatic. We aren't robbing the woman. Besides, getting her out of here would be good for you, too, my boy. She's soured you toward other women."

"This is about Hilaria?" Ben frowned.

"Hilaria would have done nicely," George replied. "She'd have been a perfectly acceptable wife for you. And after thirteen years, she's the closest you've come to getting married again after Angelina. That makes her special."

"I don't love her," Ben replied. There was another woman lodged in his heart, and there was absolutely no competition. Even if that wasn't good for him, it was a fact. "So this is about getting me farther away from Angelina?"

"So nitpicky." George heaved a loud sigh. "But no, she's not the reason, either. That would have been a helpful little bonus, but I want the property back for myself."

"You agreed to sign it over to Angelina without hesitation when we were signing our divorce papers," Ben said. "What changed?"

"It wasn't without hesitation, but I did agree," George said. "Ben, I have personal history there."

"Granddad, I can't keep this twenty-question

game going here! You either tell me why you want this property, or I tell Angelina that she should hold on to it. And that would be my honest advice to her. It's obviously worth more than I know."

"You can't just cooperate?" George asked sharply.

"No!"

For a moment, Ben thought his grandfather might hang up on him, but he didn't.

"I'm not proud of this," George said quietly. "And this is something I haven't even told your father because it would hurt him deeply."

"What is it?" Ben asked, softening his own tone, too.

"Your grandmother was a lot like Hilaria," George said slowly. "She was smart, beautiful and knew how to work a social scene like no one else. She got a governor elected with the power of her dinner parties alone. But she wasn't the first woman I fell for."

"Who was?" Ben asked.

"Her name was Eleanor. She was smart, too, but she was also brave and witty and such a risk taker. She was also from some middle-class family that my father would never even entertain as good enough for me.

But I loved her anyway. What can I say? I adored her, and I figured I'd get my father to warm up to the idea of marrying her eventually, if I held out long enough and didn't marry some other debutante..."

"Quite the rebel," Ben said ruefully.

"Oh, yes. You'd hardly have recognized me," George said. "But then Eleanor got pregnant, and I thought that would be enough to get my father to agree to a wedding. He still refused. It was a huge drama in our family, all behind closed doors, of course. I battled them for months. I used to come out to Blue Lake with Eleanor—that was long before the lodge was ever built, and that lake was a serene spot where the rest of the world couldn't touch us. Including my family."

"What happened to the baby?" Ben asked.

"My daughter died." George's voice sounded tight. "Eleanor was almost five months along when she lost the baby. It happened out there at the lake. I tried to get her back to a hospital, but she delivered the tiny thing prematurely in the back of my car. We were both heartbroken. We didn't know what to do. She'd been hiding the pregnancy from her family, and..." There was silence. "We buried our daughter under the pines by the lake together."

Ben felt a lump rise in his throat. "I'm sorry…"

"The Second World War was raging," George went on. "America had just gotten involved. They'd started Camp Hale for mountain training and that was a very big deal here in Colorado. But they needed pilots."

"Did you enlist?" Ben asked.

"Me? No, but Eleanor did. They took very few women, but Eleanor was something special. She had been learning to fly with one of my friends on a lark, and she had a knack for it. They accepted her—shockingly. I'd prayed they wouldn't. I stayed here and helped my father build factories that made ammunition. We made a lot of money during the war, but I never quite forgot the shame of having been the man who stayed home while Eleanor enlisted. I begged her not to. It wasn't safe. That was not a place for a woman! She didn't care anymore. Losing our daughter did something to her—killed something inside of her—and she joined up and finished learning to fly. It was a short course—I'm shocked they let those pilots take off with so little training. She died when her plane was shot down over the ocean."

Ben swallowed hard. "You lost them both."

"I did." George cleared his throat. "I had no more fight in me. My father introduced me to a lovely debutante, and I did what everyone expected of me and proposed. It wasn't a bad thing—your grandmother was a wonderful woman. She was more than I deserved, that's for sure. And I loved her too much to hurt her with my past. So I did my best to push those memories away when your grandmother was still alive. You wanted to sign that property over to Angelina, and your grandmother felt it was a noble thing to do. She had sympathized with Angelina's situation—thrown into the fray, as she'd been. I never told your grandmother about Eleanor. She was my secret, and my heartbreak, and she wasn't exactly a part of our family tree."

"I suppose not," Ben agreed.

"But my daughter—" George's voice caught. "She's buried out there. And she's part of *my* family. She's my child. And over the years I've been thinking of her more and more."

"Where is she buried?" Ben asked.

"On the edge of the lake, out past the trails," George replied. "I feel like I could find the exact spot, if I could just get out there."

Ben let out a slow breath. "You don't need

to own the property to visit the place where she was buried."

"I need to keep her in the family, and this is my way of doing it. I want to keep that property in King hands. It matters to me." George sounded tired. "So, is that reason enough for you to cooperate with my wishes and buy back that property, Benjamin?"

"I can understand why it means so much to you," Ben said quietly. "I can talk to her, at least."

"Thank you," the old man replied.

"I have to tell her the reason, though," Ben said. "That's one of her stipulations. She has to know why."

There was silence on the other end.

"Granddad, she's stood by the nondisclosure agreement so far. We could have her sign another one if that makes you feel better, but she has to hear the story or she won't sign. I know her."

"Fine," George said gruffly. "But don't just throw money away, either, okay?"

"I'm not going to promise that," Ben said. "She's my Eleanor. And if I can give her an easier life, I will."

"Stubborn," George muttered. "But I do understand the sentiment, probably better

than your father does. So...don't go overboard, but do what you need to."

George didn't wait for a goodbye, he just
hung up, and Ben dropped his phone down
to his lap. There had been another woman
before his grandmother...a woman who had
stuck in George's heart. If a man was lucky
in life, there was one who'd touch a place that
no one else would ever get to.

Ben picked up his phone and went back
to the photos his father had texted to him.
There were pictures of his mother dressed
in formal wear, her hair done in 80s curls.
There were pictures of her with Ben standing proudly next to her. The memories were
coming back—his mother's laughter, even the
sound of her voice raised when she was angry.
His mother's hands were a special memory,
too, how the heavy diamond rings were loose
around her fingers. Ben used to like to fiddle
with them. And then there was a photo that
gave Ben pause...

It was a picture of his father and mother
together—one they'd taken alone. His mother
was wearing a riding helmet, and she was
kissing his father's cheek. It was the look in
Karl's eyes at that kiss that Ben recognized.

It was love—pure, unfiltered and washing

over both of them. Ben's parents had been madly in love with each other. Even with their personal faults and limitations, Karl had married the one who filled his heart.

"Good for you, Mom and Dad," Ben said quietly.

It wasn't impossible, it would seem. Two people could find each other and make each other happy.

There was one woman for Ben who'd touched his heart in such an unexpected way that he'd married her within two weeks. When Ben was an old man, would he be remembering Angelina, his sleep disturbed by the things he hadn't made right?

CHAPTER THIRTEEN

ANGELINA AWOKE THE next morning five minutes before her alarm. Through a gap in the curtains, she could see the golden morning sunlight peeking over the mountains, soft and comforting. She let her eyes shut once more. She'd been dreaming about California—a sandy beach near her childhood home, the smell of sunscreen and the far-off call of some gulls. She'd been walking along the beach with her grandmother, and they'd been picking up shells as they walked. They weren't talking, but they'd exchange smiles, and Angelina found herself flipping between being a little girl smiling up into her grandmother's face and being a grown woman, looking to Grandma Cunningham for some sort of answer, some sort of wisdom... Angelina could almost get the feeling of the dream back if she lay still, but even with the faint scent of salt still etched in her mind, that beach wasn't home anymore. It was only a place to visit.

Last night she'd chatted on the phone with her mom and dad, assuring them that all was well and that a blizzard was nothing too terribly out of the ordinary here in the Colorado Rockies. In response to that, her father had read online news articles to her that called it the storm of the century.

"Dad, it's okay. This lodge has withstood storms for fifty years. It's solid. I'll be fine. I promise."

"You should come back for a visit, Angelina," he'd said. "You could use some sun, I'm sure."

"That's a good idea. I'll schedule some time off this spring and come see you guys. I think I could use a little sun, too."

She could use some comfort, too, and a reminder that a future was possible apart from Ben King. That was what this resort was supposed to be, too, but somehow these past few days were blurring too many lines. Ben was supposed to be a part of her past, not entangled in her future.

That was probably what had prompted the dream. California represented a different phase in her life, where she was born and where she'd grown up and gone to school—a life her parents had bestowed upon her. But her life here in Colorado was about what she'd earned through hard work and heartbreak. Colorado was the home she'd earned. Blue Lake had seeped into her soul.

Angelina sat up, looking back toward that gap in the curtains again—she had seen sunlight! It took her until now to realize it. She pushed back her covers, shivering in the chilly morning air, and grabbed her bathrobe. Out the window, the snowfall had stopped, and a thick blanket of white covered everything. The mountain lake was covered almost to its center, to the dark patch that showed where it wasn't quite frozen.

But the blizzard was past. Birds twittered, and Angelina spotted a white rabbit hopping along close by the building, leaving a trail of prints behind it. An eddy of wind whipped up a swirl of snow, glistening like diamonds in the air before it drifted back down.

"It's over," she murmured. She hadn't realized quite how heavy the stress of that storm had been, but having those howling winds and blinding snow past was a relief.

Angelina turned away from the window, flicking the curtains shut all the way so that she could get dressed.

The storm was over, but there would still

be a lot of physical work digging the snow away from the doors and starting on some paths around the building, so she wouldn't get back into her business casual attire just yet. She grabbed a pair of jeans and a dove-gray knit sweater. She combed her hair and pulled it up away from her face with a clip, and then sat down to put on a bit of makeup. It was then that her gaze fell on that perfume atomizer...the one she'd stopped using.

New scent, new you. Or something like that... She'd needed the change, but she missed the scent of Chanel No. 5.

Angelina picked it up and spritzed some scent into the air. The soft floral vanilla aroma wafted around her. Funny all the memories attached to a perfume—her teen-age years, her time in college, her early years as a bookkeeper when she'd come back to her little one-bedroom apartment, so proud of putting her life together. Her first solo vacation had been on that cruise. It wouldn't be her last vacation alone—she'd gone to London and Paris on her own, and visited Prague, too. But that cruise was by far her most memorable vacation. Her young hopes and dreams felt like they all combined in that scent.

This would always be a special fragrance

for Angelina, but she wasn't sure if she'd ever wear it again. She wasn't the same woman she was back then. There was no going backward. Maybe that was a good thing to remember with Ben, too. She couldn't slip back to the past, even for a few days. It didn't work that way.

Angelina finished dressing. She made her bed and straightened up, then headed out of her suite, locking it behind her. There was a lot to do today.

She started in the kitchen and made sure everything was ready for breakfast orders when the guests came down. They were running low on supplies, so they'd be serving hash brown patties, pancakes and some tinned fruit. Restocking would be a relief. Warren was out in his spot by the window, his computer in front of him. He was dressed in pair of baggy corduroy pants and a worn brown sweater over a button-up shirt, a cup of coffee next to him. The older man looked thoughtful and a little melancholy.

When Angelina reached his table, he looked up with a smile that didn't reach his eyes.

"How are you this morning?" Angelina asked.

"Oh, alive and well," he said.

"Can I have a seat?" she asked.

"Sure." He gestured to the chair opposite him.

"You look sad, Warren," she said, sitting down. Was that too honest? Maybe. But she didn't have the energy for more these days.

"Do you know how much Louise crops up in my story?" he asked.

"A fair bit?" she guessed.

"I keep trying to write around her—prove that she wasn't part of everything that I did, but she keeps coming back up in the story. She's there every step of the way—raising our children, keeping the house in working order, remembering special dates and anniversaries for extended family, and putting together those birthday parties for the kids. She was in the background of every accomplishment I had, holding my home life together."

It would seem that Warren had discovered exactly how much his wife had done for him just a little too late.

"I'm not much of a writer," Warren said after a moment.

"I don't know—you seem to be doing the hard work," she said.

"This memoir has no shape," he said. "It's

just meandering stories that keep coming back to the one woman I'm trying to avoid talking about."

Angelina nodded. "Writing a book isn't as easy as it looks, I suppose."

"No, it isn't." He exhaled a sigh. "I think I need to see it on paper. On a computer screen, it all just blends together."

"How many pages is it?" she asked.

"About a hundred," he replied. "I thought I had more to say than this. I envisioned a thousand-page tome. But no, I'm coming in at ninety-six pages so far. And that includes a page of dedications, and really big breaks between chapters."

Angelina chuckled. "I don't think the length is the important part."

"Ah, but a greater length would have made me feel more important." He waggled a finger with an amused look on his face.

She imagined the elusive Louise laughing at this man's jokes.

"We do offer fax and printing services here at the resort at a reasonable cost, if you'd like to print it off."

"That might help," Warren replied, sobering. "I'm starting to worry that I look like a fool in this story. Just a silly old man trying to explain away his own mistakes." Warren closed his laptop. "I'm sorry to unload that on you. Old men are supposed to have figured it all out. But we haven't."

"You aren't that old, Warren," Angelina said with a faint smile.

"Tell my back and my knees." He winked, then he sighed, his humor fading. "But printing it wouldn't be too much trouble? I'm sure you have work to do."

"No trouble at all," Angelina replied. "I'm happy to help."

From down the road, Angelina heard a familiar grind and growl. She and Warren both turned toward the window, and down the drive they spotted the large yellow snowplow as it crept up the road, snow billowing off to the side. They must have been plowing all night to get this far up the mountain this morning.

Cars would be able to make it through now, as would a tow truck to haul Ben's truck out of the ditch and to take Ben King back to his life, back to his family, and to the comfort he was accustomed to.

"You should be happier than that to see the plows," Warren said.

"I should," Angelina agreed quietly. She didn't have it in her to even force a smile.

Ben was going to leave, and if all went according to his plans, she'd end up in the same place she had been at their divorce—in a room with a group of lawyers and papers for her to sign. The very thought made her want to cry.

THE DINING ROOM was busy with the college students, and Ben scanned the room, looking for Angelina. There were a couple of staff members eating breakfast, but Ben didn't spot her. Through a window, he could see another snowplow coming up behind the first one, a tag team effort to clear the stretch of road.

Ben headed toward Angelina's office. He had a feeling he might find her there. Her door was shut, and he knocked softly.

"Yes?" Angelina called.

Ben pushed open the door. Angelina was at her desk putting some papers together. She looked up, those blue eyes meeting his with mild surprise.

"Ben... I thought you'd be Warren." She pulled out an envelope and slid the thick ream of papers into it.

"No, just me." Ben closed the door behind him. "I wanted to talk to you before I call a tow truck and figure out a way home."

Angelina rose from her chair and came around the desk, meeting his gaze expectantly.

"I talked to my grandfather," he said, "and he told me why he wants this property so badly. But it's sensitive."

"Does that mean you won't tell me?" she asked.

"No, that means I need you to promise not to tell anyone."

"I've already signed a nondisclosure agreement, Ben," she said softly, and he smiled at the ruefulness in her tone.

"That's what I told my grandfather," he replied. "It's not about the money this time. And I agree that normally with my family it would be. But my grandfather is getting older and he's at the stage of life where he lives in his memories a lot. He's got a few regrets."

"Don't we all," she murmured.

So Ben told her the story of George and Eleanor, of their forbidden love, their secret baby and the deep regret that George had lived with ever after. It was strange—telling the story seemed to solidify it in his own mind, and his relationships with his family started to make more sense. The family money was both a blessing and a curse—holding them back from paths they'd rather take. It gave them opportunities that other people could only dream about, and at the same time it clipped their wings. It was a frustration that went back as many generations as the money had. That land represented more than a burial ground for a baby girl no one was supposed to know about. A man's innocence and his ideals were buried here, too. It was the place that kept calling to him, telling him that he'd failed.

"And your grandfather wants to own the land where his daughter is buried," Angelina said when Ben had stopped speaking.

"Yes. That's what it amounts to."

Angelina was silent for a moment. "And you're asking me to sell it."

"No," Ben said, shaking his head. But was he? "I don't know. I mean… I think I just need you to understand that we're human. We mess up, we try to make things better. The land matters to my grandfather, but how you see us is what matters to *me*."

Couldn't she recognize that he was the

same man who loved her? But that money tethered them, too. They had to grow it for future generations, and it made relationships a little more difficult when a man didn't know if someone was just being friendly or if they were trying to get something.

"No, the King family is not just filled with flawed, but regular people," Angelina replied, taking a step back. "Your family is wealthier than anything a regular person could ever hope to experience. Ever. Regular people worry about regular things. They worry about paying their bills, and about planning for retirement. They worry about their kids, and about what kind of world will be left to them. The Kings? The Kings meddle in the affairs of regular people and buy them off!"

"That's not what this is... This is about my grandfather's guilt from a mistake older than we are—" Ben sighed. "My grandfather did mention that he thought you and I were holding each other back. He said that he understands loving a woman, especially after his situation with Eleanor, but he did think that some space would be good for us."

"I see."

"Just to be completely transparent here,"

Ben said. "I told you I'd give you all the information, and now I have."

Angelina met his gaze earnestly. "Now, I need you to keep being completely honest with me," she said. "And I want you to tell me if you think this is really about his guilt over his baby girl."

"It's what he told me," Ben replied.

"That doesn't let you off the hook, Ben!" Her gaze flashed fire. "I want to know what you believe deep in your heart about this situation. I want to know what your gut is telling you. Is this what the buyout is really about?"

"What do you want me to say?" Ben demanded. "I can't read minds! I'm giving you an offer you are absolutely allowed to refuse! I'm giving you all the information. I'm not trying to manipulate you! I'm just trying to do things the honest way. I have no idea if my family is holding back information on me, but I'm not holding anything back from you. You're right—they're a force to be reckoned with, and my ninety-seven-year-old grandfather is still calling shots! He will until his last breath—you can be guaranteed of that. So all I can do is give you the information that I've got." Ben's hands were shaking with the strength of his emotions, and he searched her face, looking for some sign that she understood what he was trying to do here. He wasn't a monster! "Do you want the money? Do you want to start fresh with more money than you started with here? Or do you want to stay here? That's what this is about."

"What do you want?" Angelina's voice trembled. "Do you want me to leave, Ben? I'm not saying what I'll choose, but this is what matters to me. When you have all the information in front of *you*, what do *you* want?"

"It's not my choice to make—"

"No, it's mine," Angelina agreed. "But if you could weigh in—" She put a hand up. "Never mind. That's answer enough."

Ben didn't know how to say it all—he never had. This was the problem. What he felt for her, what he wanted for them—he'd never been able to show her the depth of it. So he pulled her into his arms and lowered his lips over hers. He kissed her long and deep, and he felt her relax against him. This attraction, this passion, had always made sense between them. But his kiss was more than that. When he pulled back, he looked down into her eyes.

"I want you to stay…" he breathed.

Ben loved her again. Or he loved her still… Angelina Cunningham tugged at him in a way no other woman could, and even if she could never love him again, he couldn't help but speak the truth.

"I love you," he said. "And I don't want you to leave."

CHAPTER FOURTEEN

ANGELINA LOOKED UP at Ben, his breath tickling her lips. She could make out the fine lines around his eyes, the sprinkling of gray through the stubble on his face. And yet, even after all these years, he was the same old Ben.

"Don't tell me that you feel nothing," he pleaded. "For once in the last decade, let's just tell each other the unvarnished truth. I know you feel something between us—I know that!"

"We always did." Angelina pulled out of his arms and took a cautious step away from him. "That never stopped. It wasn't the problem."

"Do you love me?" he asked.

"Why do you want me to say it?" Angelina felt tears mist her eyes. "After all these years, after all we've learned about exactly why we don't work—"

"Do you love me?" he repeated, his voice low.

"What does it matter how I feel now?" She

looked into his face, searching for why he was doing this. "During our marriage, I told you over and over again what I was feeling and what I wanted. I wanted you to choose me once in a while over the meeting, or the dinner party, or whatever advice was being tossed my way about how I should better conduct myself. I told you when you hurt me, I told you when I wanted some time alone, just you and me. I was very open then, and what good was it?"

"So tell me now! We're both different people now. We're older, and hopefully a lot wiser. I've learned to listen better, too." Ben caught her hand and held it firmly. His dark gaze probed hers. "And be honest, because I just was! I love you. I have for years. I fell in love with you again when I could hardly remember you. You're in my blood, Angie. You're in my bones! I love you. So tell me straight—cut out the professional crap. What do you feel for *me*?"

She felt adrift and filled with longing at the same time. She felt like she was constantly fighting back the memories of the one man she'd married, and it never worked. He was there, in her thoughts, in her memories, in her dreams. Ben was always there, and no matter how much she lectured herself about moving on, she couldn't set him free, either. She was so busy trying to help others put their lives back together that she hardly stopped to look at her own life. Her heart was hopelessly entangled with this man.

"I love you, too…" she breathed.

Ben dipped his head down and kissed her again, but she broke it off this time, pulling back.

"Let's do something about it!" Ben whispered. "I love you, you love me…"

"That's never changed," she said. "We always did love each other. But you're still the same man inheriting the same fortune. And I'm still not a socialite."

"You can hold you own—" he started.

"I don't *want* to hold my own!" she retorted, shaking her head. "Ben, that's the thing! I shouldn't have to be a warrior in my own marriage. I should be able to feel safe, secure, able to let my guard down. I can't take that pressure anymore."

"What about being a warrior *for* your marriage?" he asked.

"I shouldn't have to!" Her voice shook. It was tempting. He was appealing to that competitive, determined core inside of her. "Ben, it's exhausting. It drains a woman dry to be constantly on her guard, looking for attacks, looking for ways to help you get the upper hand. I will never be acceptable to your family, and if you want proof of that, they are offering me a ridiculous amount of money to just go away right now. Yes, it's more complicated, but it's part of it. You were brought up with this, and you've had years more training in it. It comes as second nature to you. But I'm not the same."

"I think you're tougher than you think," he said.

"I might be," Angelina agreed. "I'm certainly proving myself competent in areas I never thought I'd be quite this good! I'm good at building up a business, and I've earned people's respect. And there is a big difference between a woman in her twenties and a woman in her forties. But I haven't just gotten stronger these last thirteen years, I've gotten softer, too. I've learned more about who I am as a woman, and what I need. What's not negotiable. I've gotten more self-aware, and I've learned how to take better care of myself as well as my friends."

"So have I," Ben said quietly.

"Have you?" She felt the crack in her heart

spread just a little further. "Because you haven't told me about that."

"I need the real thing," Ben said. "I don't want a woman who knows how to move in those social circles, but who I'm not completely in love with. This isn't a job application! I need honest, real, full love. I can't make do with halfway."

As if a halfway kind of love was even possible with him. Ben was the kind of man who was too easy to fall in love with, too easy to give up her heart to. And Angelina was just too fragile for the world he navigated.

"It might be easier if you could," she said, her voice catching.

"It would be," Ben agreed. "But I'm looking for a life partner, not a business partner. And it isn't worth it if I'm not completely head over heels in love...like I am with you."

"You want the kind of love we had, but you need it in a different package. I disappoint you, and there is nothing more painful than seeing that happen. I'm quite the catch for the right man, Ben. I don't need to be where I'm never enough."

"You're enough for me," he whispered.

"No," she said, shaking her head. "Because you're more than this..." She put her hand in the center of his chest. "You're a King. You've got responsibilities, expectations, people who are depending on you. You aren't just the man with the heart. You're the man with the inheritance. And that changes everything."

"I can't help it," he said. "Do you want me to give it up?"

"You can't give up something you were born to," she said. "Even if you gave up the money, you would still be a King. You have a family, and while I'll never be enough for them, they are everything to you. I know that. You are who you are. And I'm not enough to make up for your entire family and the businesses you run. I'm *one person*, Ben."

"So there's no solution for us," he said. "Love each other as we do, there's no way for it to work."

Angelina's heart clenched, and she wished she could say that it would, that they'd make it work, that they'd wrestle the world into the shape that they needed it to be…but the world wasn't quite that pliable. And hearts could only take so much.

Angelina took a handful of his shirt and tugged Ben down toward her. His lips met hers with such longing and sadness that it nearly broke her. She loved him…oh, how she loved him, but that wasn't enough when tangling with a family like the Kings.

Eleanor had learned that generations ago. Hilaria was learning that even now. And Angelina had already learned the lesson, but apparently needed to refresh it one more time. These King men might be easy to love, but they were hard to stay married to. Money might be a tool, a blessing for some, and even an advantage, but it was a solid wall between a woman and the heart she longed to hold.

Ben pulled back, and he looked down into her eyes sadly. "Are you going to give us a chance?"

She shook her head. "I already did, Ben. It didn't work."

"Does that mean you're leaving?" he asked, his voice wooden.

Would she stand in another room with King lawyers? Would she take a big, fat check and walk away to make things easier for them?

"No." She swallowed. "I'm not. I built this place, and it won't be the same starting over somewhere else. I've created something out of heartbreak, and that combination is both painful and deeply beautiful. I'm not giving it up. I paid too dearly for it."

"Money isn't everything," he whispered.

"It never was," she said.

Ben wiped his eyes and if he stayed just a moment longer, she would have gone right back into his arms. But he swallowed hard and moved toward the door. This was it— this was the final goodbye they'd both needed and had both been too afraid to ask for. And it hurt just as much as she'd feared it would.

"Ben?" Angelina said.

Ben turned, his eyes filled with misery.

"The next time you decide to marry someone," she said, her voice catching. "Don't ask me for my blessing, okay?"

"You wouldn't give it?"

"My heart can't take it." A hot tear leaked down her cheek, and for a moment it looked like Ben would come back and pull her back into his arms.

But he didn't. He let himself out of the office and closed the door gently behind him.

It was then that Angelina sank into a chair and the tears began to flow. She covered her face with her hands and her shoulders shook with the force of them. This wasn't supposed to happen—she wasn't supposed to fall in love with Ben all over again, and it wasn't supposed to hurt just as much as it had the first time.

A TOW TRUCK pulled into the freshly plowed parking lot, Ben's truck hooked up behind. A couple of resort employees were digging snow out from around the vehicles in Employee Parking. Late-morning sunlight sparkled on the stretch of new-fallen snow.

His memory was back now, or most of it from what he could tell. He woke up with a multitude of memories in his head—pulling a red wagon down a sidewalk as a little boy, waiting for the chauffeur to pick him up from middle school, the smell of orange peels and pencil shavings from his second-grade classroom… It had all come back in a jumbled mess, but when he reached out and grabbed a memory, it fell into place with the others, and connected to more details. It was all making sense now. No more holes or gaps.

He remembered his mother, his nannies and that one groundskeeper who used to show him how to properly plant the spring flowers. He remembered high school dances, college parties, girls he'd dated, friends who had slipped away as their lives went in different directions. He remembered Hilaria and how hopeful his family was that she'd "stick."

But more than any other woman who had touched his heart, Ben remembered falling in love with Angelina. He remembered the wedding, and his obstinate belief that their future would be bright and would prove to his snobbish family just how wrong they were about women who didn't come from money. He remembered the frustration he felt as his marriage crumbled, the terrible advice he'd received from friends and family alike, and the ultimate heart-shattering moment when he signed those divorce papers.

Remembering how he'd scratched his signature at the bottom of those papers, the grief welled up inside of him all over again, as if the divorce were happening again. But this time, he was sitting on the edge of his unmade bed in the upstairs suite of Mountain Springs Resort. He'd finally let it all out—the grief of what he'd lost yet again. Why couldn't he make things work with this woman? Because it wasn't an option to stop loving her. He might have fooled himself before in that respect, but he was wiser now. Angelina wasn't going to stop being a bone-deep part of him.

Maybe he had more in common with Granddad than he thought—the kind of regrets that were hard to put to rest, no matter how much time slipped by.

Warren had insisted upon taking another look at him before he left, and he'd seemed pleased with how Ben had recovered. So that was that—he was better. Except he almost wished that he weren't, that he could forget some of the pain he'd rediscovered. It might be easier to deal with one heartbreak over Angelina instead of a span of years where he'd ached continually.

The tow truck driver pulled up next to Ben and undid the passenger-side window. He leaned over and raised his voice to be heard.

"I can give you a lift back to town, if you want," the driver called.

Ben shook off his wandering thoughts. He had a life to get back to, and accepting the ride would be quicker than waiting for a cab. Ben looked over his shoulder toward the lodge, but he couldn't make out anyone in the windows. Was Angelina there? Did she even realize he was leaving?

He'd use the excuse of thanking her to call her later. Hearing her voice again was a small bittersweet pleasure to look forward to. But they'd said all they could for now, and he needed to get his emotions back under control, because his throat felt thick, and he just needed to get away from this resort, away from the reminders of everything he'd lost.

"Thanks," Ben said. "I appreciate it."

He got up into the passenger side of the truck, and the driver pulled forward.

"I'm Corey," the driver said.

"Ben King." Ben gave him a nod.

"My wife and I have a weekend booked at the resort next month," Corey said. "We've heard good things, but we've never seen the rooms there. What's it like?"

"Really nice," Ben said. "Angie—the owner has done a great job with it."

"Yeah, we heard that," Corey replied. "I tried booking a room as a surprise for my wife last Valentine's Day, and I couldn't get one. The best I could do was bring her for dinner. She was so disappointed. I ended up getting her jewelry instead."

"Hmm. Sounds nice." Ben looked out the window as the man chatted on.

"Anyway, this year, I'm getting the room for us for her birthday weekend. The whole weekend! Am I ever glad the snowstorm didn't wait. I've got the whole package—in-room massages, room service meals, and if the snow sticks, we might be able to do this private sleigh ride…but I think that starts in December. So I might be out of luck…"

A husband making plans for his wife. It was sweet, really, and what Ben wouldn't give right now to be able to do the same thing. Just not for any woman—there was only one in his heart, and he'd messed that up years ago.

"How long have you been married?" Ben asked.

"Three years," Corey replied. "So we're still newlyweds."

Newlyweds… Ben had been married and divorced in one year, and this man had managed to outlast him. But then, so many couples did. Ben had gone over the marriage in his head countless times, and sometimes he thought he hadn't explained things well enough to Angelina, and other times he wondered if he'd been the idiot who hadn't told his father to back off for the sake of his own marriage. Over the years, the family would have adjusted…

But still, when he lay in bed at night, he remembered the way her golden hair used to shine on the pillow next to him, how her perfume used to linger on the silky skin of her neck. There was no getting her out of his system—not completely. A very powerful part of him wanted to head straight back to that lodge and pull Angelina back into his arms. They belonged together—Ben belonged with her.

But some mistakes couldn't be fixed.

"So, three years in," Ben said. "What's your advice to couples on staying happily married?"

"Oh, I don't know," Corey said. "The first year or so was pretty hard. I still thought I could hang out with the guys after work, and…yeah, that's not a good plan with a wife at home. But I guess it comes down to relying on each other. I mean, we don't have much, but Shelley's fantastic with money, like, you give her a hundred bucks and a well-stocked kitchen, and she'll give you Christmas, you know? She was the one who encouraged me to buy my own tow truck. We're paying it off slowly, but I can work my own hours now, and pick up extra work. But she's the one who gave me the idea."

"What does Shelley do?" Ben asked.

"She's working at a daycare, which is actually perfect, because she's pregnant, and when the baby comes, the daycare place will let her bring the baby to work with her after her maternity leave. And they won't charge her for it, either. It's a really great setup. She applied to work there because she's got a friend who told her about their policy."

Just two regular people who loved each other working things out with the tiniest fraction of the financial comfort that Ben enjoyed. And somehow, these people were happier.

"But you asked my advice to other couples, right?" Corey said. "I think my advice would be, work really hard and make sure you book ahead if you want a room at the Mountain Springs Resort." Corey chuckled to himself. "She's going to love it…she really will."

Ben's phone pinged and he looked down to see a text from Angelina.

Did you leave?

His heart skipped a beat. He hated texting—he had no idea what she was thinking. Was she glad to have him gone, or disappointed? There was no way to tell. Did she miss him? He texted back.

Yeah, I thought I'd head out. I'm sorry.

He was sorry for everything—for letting her down in their marriage, for not being enough now. He was sorry for holding her back, for offering to buy the place she poured her blood and sweat into. He was sorry for the pressure his family put onto both of them, and for not having been strong enough to tell them to give him space when it mattered.

Angelina didn't reply, so Ben added, I wanted to thank you for taking care of me. You didn't have to do all that.

Yes, I did, she texted back.

I'm still grateful, he replied.

It's okay.

And I miss you, he typed, but then he back-spaced and deleted that.

"Lots of cars and trucks hit the ditch in this storm," Corey was saying. "Lucky you ended up in front of the resort. Your truck looks pretty banged up."

"It flipped," Ben said.

"Yeah, I was going to say—it looks like it'll take a fair amount of work. You want to go to the dealership, right?"

"That's right."

"I've got a buddy who works there—he's the head mechanic..." Corey talked on about his connections at the dealership, and Ben looked out the window, his phone still in his hand.

It was all said, right? They hadn't worked in the past, and nothing had substantively changed between them to make it work now. His family was a unique burden. They were intense, overinvolved in his life, and demanding of his time and his priorities.

Was this the life he wanted to live? Did he want to make the family business his top priority for the rest of his days? Was he supposed to find a woman who knew how to live with the burdens he was used to, and just make the best of it? Plenty of women would be glad to take it on, except for the one who filled his heart.

Ben looked down at his phone again, and he started typing.

I miss you. That's not going to stop.

It was honest. He pressed Send. Whatever— he wasn't going to try to save face with her. He was going to err on the side of honesty. He should have told her how he still felt a long time ago. What was he afraid of—that she'd laugh at him? She loved him, too.

"Corey, let me ask you something," Ben said.

"Sure."

"What makes your wife know that she can trust you?" Ben asked. Because maybe this workingman had a secret that Ben could learn from.

"I can't afford a divorce!" Corey said, belting out a laugh. "Or a mistress for that matter. She cleaned me out with the engagement ring and the wedding! She's it. She knows that. It's ride or die."

Ben chuckled. There was a certain freedom to having less—he could see that. People depended on each other more when they didn't have quite so many options to fall back on. Maybe they appreciated each other more, too.

Ben knew what he'd lost with that divorce—absolutely everything that mattered.

They rode in comfortable silence for the last twenty minutes, and when they got into town, Ben felt like Mountain Springs Resort was still tugging him back. It was that same feeling he'd had stumbling toward the lodge through the gusting wind and falling snow... He belonged there. He could feel it deep inside, and it had nothing to do with his family's desires for the property. This was about Angelina, and only Angelina.

Except it wouldn't be so simple to convince her to take a risk on him again. He couldn't change who he was, could he? He was a King, and even if he gave up the money, he couldn't give up his family. As he felt so obliged to explain, he wasn't heartless. He loved them.

His phone pinged just as Corey pulled up in front of the dealership.

"Thanks for the ride," Ben said, pulling out his wallet to pay. "And here's a tip for being so prompt. I appreciate it."

He'd included a generous tip. Regular guys had regular bills to pay, and this man had a wife to impress for her birthday. Maybe he could make that a little bit easier.

"No problem. Thanks a lot." Corey accepted the cash with a smile. "Here's my card. If you ever need a tow, I'm the one to call."

"You bet." Ben gave him a nod, and they both got out so that Corey could unhook the truck.

Ben looked down at his phone, then. It was a text from Angelina.

I miss you, too.

CHAPTER FIFTEEN

ANGELINA'S GENERAL MANAGER, Noah, was back, as were the rest of the staff and guests. The lodge was bustling, and Angelina stood by the fireside room doorway, her arms crossed. Mountain Springs Resort had become the spot for people to celebrate their happy times together, and it normally felt good to see all this humanity and happiness in one place. Except she still felt wrung out from the goodbye she'd said yesterday, and she wasn't sure how to even process it. She missed Ben so much. It was like all that time of healing had slipped out from under her and she was right back to the place of sadness that she'd been in right after her divorce.

Except it was different this time. She was no longer the naive young ex-wife. She was now a woman with life experience, and some wisdom, and she'd still gone and fallen back in love with Ben. It was like loving him was inevitable—she couldn't avoid it, even when she knew better.

Angelina had reserved a table by the window—the Second Chance Dinner Club was meeting up. Angelina wanted to see her friends and get some moral support, but she wasn't feeling social now. This was going to hurt for a long time, and even the dinner club wasn't going to change that.

The college students were checking out, and Angelina watched as the young men carried their bags outside. Brad was paying at the front desk. Elizabeth came down the stairs, her bag in one hand, and when she spotted Angelina, she came in her direction.

"I released the rabbit this morning," Elizabeth said with a smile. "She's healed up."

"I'm glad to hear it," Angelina replied. "I checked on her last night, and she'd eaten the carrot and cabbage."

"She was eating and pooping—signs of a healthy rabbit," Elizabeth replied with a smile. "I texted my sister and asked her advice. I sent her a video of the rabbit, and she agreed that she seemed healed up nicely, so we've got an official opinion there, too."

"You come well connected," Angelina said with a smile. "I hope you enjoyed your stay."

"Not as much as I was hoping, but that wasn't about the resort," Elizabeth said, and her chin quivered.

Angelina felt a surge of sympathy for the young woman. She'd been longing for something wonderful, and that seemed truly far away right now.

"I'm sorry," Angelina said. "I know you won't believe me right now, but you are so young. You have a lot of time."

Elizabeth looked over to where Brad stood, then lowered her voice. "I found an engagement ring in the bottom of Brad's bag."

Angelina looked over at Elizabeth in surprise. "Really?"

"And I took a peek at it."

"What's it like?"

"The rock is…pretty big," Elizabeth said. "I'd guess three carats. A princess cut solitaire set in white gold. It's absolutely beautiful."

"It sounds like it," Angelina said. So maybe her trip had improved after all, and the young Elizabeth would become Brad's supportive Betsy. She wished she could feel happier for her. "Congratulations."

"Don't congratulate me yet," Elizabeth replied. "He hasn't given it to me."

"He brought it with him, though…" Angelina said.

"He might still have plans to give it to me. Or not." Elizabeth sighed. "I'd be lying if I said I wasn't excited when I saw it, but I don't know if I could accept it now."

Angelina looked at the young woman in surprise. "Really? I didn't expect that."

"Your advice was that I should do something that made me happy and see if Brad liked me happy, and I'm going to do that. When I graduate in May, I'm going to work with my sister at her veterinary clinic. When I talked to her about the rabbit I asked what she thought, and she said she needs the help."

"That sounds like a great plan," Angelina said. "Are you excited?"

A smile spread over Elizabeth's face. "I am. I'm looking forward to it. I love working with animals."

"Have you told Brad?"

"I'll tell him when we're alone," she replied. "We had a lot of people around us these last few days."

That was an understatement.

"Are you going to tell him you saw the ring?" Angelina asked.

"Yeah," Elizabeth replied seriously. "I don't

want to play games, or keep secrets. We can either be straight with each other, or not. This is my life we're talking about, and possibly the rest of it. But this is where I stand. I need to find something I love to do and clear my head a bit. Brad can't be my career or my hobby, either. If he's going to be my husband, I have to know we're both in it for the right reasons. You know?"

"I do," Angelina agreed. "That's mature of you to realize all of that."

"You helped." Elizabeth smiled. "Thank you for being willing to tell me your honest opinion. I needed to hear it."

For whatever it was worth. It looked like Elizabeth was sticking it out with him, and this shouldn't matter to Angelina at all... Brad finished paying and he looked around, then spotted Elizabeth. He beckoned to her.

"I'd better get going," Elizabeth said. "Can I give you a hug?"

Angelina wrapped her arms around the young woman and gave her a squeeze. "Take care of yourself, Elizabeth."

"Thank you. You, too."

Angelina released her and watched as Elizabeth carried her bag over to where Brad was waiting for her. He didn't offer to carry her bag, or take her hand, and Brad's gaze followed another woman's figure as she walked past. Angelina saw Elizabeth's expression as she looked up at her boyfriend—not angry, or hurt or incensed—all of which would have been perfectly warranted. It was a sudden realization—Elizabeth had just seen a blaze of reality…an image of what marriage would be like with that man, perhaps?

"What?" Brad said irritably.

"Nothing." Elizabeth adjusted her bag to her other hand, but there was a new fire in her eyes that hadn't been there before.

Brad's head swiveled toward the other woman once more, and then he headed for the door, chatting and laughing with his buddies. But Angelina knew that look. Elizabeth looked over her shoulder and met Angelina's gaze just as she reached the door, and she smiled faintly. If Angelina was a betting woman, she'd say that by the time they got back to Denver, Elizabeth would have taken Angelina's advice and she'd be single again. That gorgeous ring in the bottom of a duffel bag wasn't going to be enough to keep her now.

Good, Angelina thought. *You deserve better.*

Brad and Elizabeth went out the big front

doors, and Gayle Prichard passed them as she came inside. Gayle's silver hair was cut in a chin length bob, and she was dressed in a long mauve woolen coat. Angelina couldn't help but smile at the sight of her friend.

It was time to have a meal with the girls and start the process of getting her balance back. But this time, it was going to be harder…so much harder…and she'd need all the support her friends could give.

ANGELINA SLIPPED INTO the seat next to Gayle. This would be a lunch date, and they didn't have a lot of time, but it would be good to see everyone again. The table Angelina had reserved was in the back corner with a view of the frozen lake, sunlight reflecting off the glittering snow.

"So how was the storm up here?" Gayle asked. "Matthew and I spent an hour this morning digging out the car! The plows were going through town continually to keep the roads clear. It was crazy."

"Well, we survived," Angelina said.

"But what I really want to know about is Ben," Gayle said. "What happened? Is he still here?"

"No, he left," Angelina said, and she cleared

her throat against the lump that rose inside of it. "He…uh…he and I love each other, but it'll never work."

"Oh, sweetie," Gayle said softly.

The very endearment Angelina had been using with Elizabeth. Sometimes it was nice to be the younger, less experienced woman at a table.

Jen Bryant arrived then with Renata and Belle in tow. The three women took their seats, exchanging hellos as they settled in. Melanie arrived a couple of minutes later with a bright smile.

"Is Taryn going to make it?" Jen asked.

"Yes, she's coming," Angelina replied. "She's in her office right now."

Taryn was the marketing specialist for the resort, and was married to Noah, Angelina's general manager.

"It's so nice to get together again," Belle said. "It's been ages. Now, since I've got you all face-to-face, you're coming to Ashley's first birthday party, aren't you?"

"We wouldn't miss it, Belle," Renata said.

"Of course," Gayle replied. "It'll be the first time I go to a child's party where there's a semiformal dress code, though."

"Oh, the party is more for me and Phillip,"

Belle said with a laugh, her gaze flickering just for a second toward Angelina. "Ashley will never remember it, but if we're all dressed up, at least we'll get some great pictures. Plus, Phillip and I are hiring a photographer. So dress up and come take advantage of that."

So Belle was going to stick to this being a surprise wedding for her and Phillip, it seemed. Angelina couldn't help but smile. It would be fun, and it was nice to be on the inside of that secret.

"It's a great idea," Jen agreed. "Nick and I haven't had any formal pictures of us with Drew since the wedding. Time flies."

"Does it ever..." Melanie said. "I'd love to get some pictures of our dinner club together, too. The last one I have is of the five of us that one night—the picture the waiter took, remember?"

"And Taryn wasn't in that picture," Belle said. "So you see? Not so crazy, is it?"

"This is a good idea!" Gayle agreed.

Taryn arrived then and took her seat. She was plump with a second pregnancy, and she was glowing. She cast a smile around the table.

"Sorry to make you all wait," she said. "I just had to finish up a couple of things."

They all caught Taryn up on the birthday dress code, and chatted for a few more minutes about babies and birthday cakes. When they'd exhausted that, the conversation came back around again.

"So who has news?" Jen asked with a smile. "I don't really have anything but I'm here all geared up to be supportive. So let's dish!"

"Actually," Gayle said quietly. "I think we need to devote this lunch to Angelina."

All eyes turned toward Angelina, and she felt her cheeks heat. She was normally on the supporting end of these meals, and it was hard to switch places—humbling.

"What's going on?" Renata asked.

"Everything okay?" Belle echoed at the same time.

"Well…it's a long story, but Ben ended up at the resort during the storm," Angelina said.

"Ben? Who is that?" Taryn asked.

"Her ex-husband," Jen replied. "Ben King, of the King family. Anything with the King name on it in Colorado, that's them."

"And then some!" Belle added. "So what happened? Why was he here?"

Angelina told the story with many interruptions from her friends, who were explaining details to Taryn or asking more questions. When she was finished, the women were silent, their gazes fixed on her with sympathy.

"And that's it," Angelina said.

"Is it, though?" Gayle asked. "You love him, Angelina. That has to count for something! And he loves you… Is this really just over?"

"He's the same man he was before," Angelina replied. "A little older, but still under the sway of his family, who are just as determined as ever to control things. I'm old enough to know what I can handle and what I can't."

"What do they do that makes it so hard to stay with Ben?" Taryn asked.

"I can't talk about it, legally speaking," Angelina replied. "But it's difficult. That's about all I can say."

Taryn gave the others a quizzical look.

"Nondisclosure agreements," Melanie said by explanation. "It's how big expensive divorces work."

"Ah." Taryn nodded. "I'm sorry."

"I'm not the only one who realized that her first marriage wasn't the right match," Angelina replied. "But I do have the added bonus of still being in love with him. It would be easier if he were just a regular guy, not a man with an inheritance and a family reputation."

"You might be the only woman I know who sees a man's incredible wealth as a problem," Belle said with a sad smile.

Angelina shrugged faintly. "It's not as rosy as it looks."

"It's kind of ironic," Taryn said quietly. "My ex-husband's family loved me. They thought I was just wonderful and that Glen couldn't do better. When I found out that Glen was cheating on me, I talked to his mother. I knew I was leaving Glen, and I was more worried about breaking his mother's heart than his. His mother thought I was the most wonderful daughter-in-law to walk the planet, and his father used to pick me up doughnuts from this local shop and drop them by the house about once a week, just because he thought I could use a treat. His brother and sister used to call me just to chat. I had all sorts of family support, but family wasn't enough to hold us together. It certainly wasn't enough to keep my husband's love."

Angelina met the other woman's gaze

thoughtfully. "How did they react to the divorce?"

"Tears, pleading with me to change my mind, pleading with him to stop being an idiot and focus on the wife he had... When they realized that Glen was determined to stay with his girlfriend, they just about cut him off completely they were so upset with him."

"Wow," Belle murmured. "That's really nice."

"It was," Taryn replied. "But an extended family can't hold a married couple together, no matter how hard they try. It isn't possible. But now I've got a man who loves me heart and soul, and it has nothing to do with duty. He just loves me. And I feel more secure now than I ever did with an entire family one hundred percent on my side."

Angelina nodded. "It was the opposite with Ben. He adored me, and they loathed me."

She didn't doubt Ben's love for a moment. She was intimidated by his family, and by the pressure of their expectations, and by extension, Ben's expectations, too. But his love? He'd have shut it off long ago, if that was even possible. Neither of them seemed to be able to control their feelings for each other.

"How crazy am I?" Angelina asked. "I'm serious. I want tough love here. What do you all think? Am I right in trying to get over Ben? Or am I giving up something really amazing out of fear?"

"You were his first memory," Renata said quietly.

"And he couldn't bring himself to marry another woman because she wasn't you," Jen added. "That's really something."

"A family is complicated," Taryn said. "But maybe there's a way to deal with them. It's been thirteen years, and they couldn't get him married off to anyone else. Maybe they've grown a little, too."

Had they? George King seemed to be facing his own regrets right now... It was hard to admit, but the Kings weren't terrible people, just more than Angelina could handle on her own, and that scared her. She was normally the strong one, just not strong enough to face that lot day in and day out for the rest of her life.

"My ex's kids never did accept me one hundred percent until after the divorce," Melanie said. "That was the point when they realized everything I'd been doing for them."

"Ironic," Belle said.

They all murmured their agreement.

"What about you, Gayle?" Angelina asked. "What do you think? Don't be gentle—tell me straight."

"Oh, sweetie," Gayle said with a misty smile. "I think you're scared to death, and I just want to give you a hug."

"I really saw this going the other way—all of you encouraging me to kick him to the curb and keep my head up," Angelina admitted.

The women exchanged looks, but Gayle's gaze stayed fixed on Angelina.

"You're scared," Gayle said softly. "We all understand fear, don't we?"

The other women nodded.

"And I think the best things in life require a leap of faith," Gayle went on. "Maybe there's a way. I'm not saying that you can go back to the way things were, but there might be a way to make things different for the future. A love like that…it's not common, trust me."

"She's right," Belle said with a shake of her head. "Sometimes you have to really work hard to find your path."

"My ex moved on with Tiffany pretty seamlessly," Jen said. "I don't know…to have a man who pined that long? It's quite romantic."

Angelina let out a slow breath. This really had not gone according to plan, but they were right. She was scared, but there was no getting over Ben. He was sheltered inside of her heart, and she couldn't evict him. He'd always be the one she compared every man against...

...and what if there was a way to make it work with the only man she'd ever loved this deeply? But if there was a solution, she couldn't see it. Love didn't always win in the end.

The waiter came up then with a notepad and a smile.

"Let's order," Angelina said.

It was good to get together with friends, to get her feet back under her. Whatever happened, she'd have her friends to get her through it. Life would go on. The pain would lessen. Wasn't this what they kept telling each new member of the group? It got better with some fine dining, some nice wine and some solid friendship.

Angelina's gaze moved out toward the lake, and in the back of her mind there was the story of a baby girl born too early and buried on this very land beside the lakeshore somewhere...

Love wasn't easy on any of the generations. It was complicated, messy and sometimes filled with regret. Even if Angelina never was able to have her heart's desire, she didn't want to mar the memory of a tiny girl who deserved to be remembered.

BEN OPENED HIS truck's window and pushed the buzzer on his father's intercom at the gates of his Denver home. There was a pause, then the security guard's voice came through.

"Can I help you?"

"This is Ben," he said. "I'm here to see my grandfather, if he's around."

"Sure thing, Mr. King. Drive on through."

The gate opened, and Ben pulled through and drove up the winding drive toward the house. It was familiar, and when he parked in front of the house, he looked up at the brickwork and the antique design thoughtfully.

His family had lived this way for generations—a cut above the rest, he'd been taught. Somehow, they'd thought they deserved this life of abundance, just by virtue of their DNA. His grandfather had tried to teach him otherwise, but the message had still gotten through—the King family was special. There were different rules that applied to them. They had weightier responsibilities than other people. And yet here he was envious of a tow truck driver whose wife was having a birthday.

Ben got out of his truck and the middle-aged housekeeper, Irina, had the door open for him when he came up the steps.

"Good afternoon, Mr. King," Irina said with a smile. "It's nice to see you again. How are you?"

Ben touched the bandage on his head. "In one piece still. Thanks for asking. Where is my grandfather?"

"In the library," she replied.

"Thanks. I'll go find him."

Ben headed through the house toward his grandfather's favorite room. The library was stocked with thousands of books, and George had always been an avid reader. Now that his horseback riding days were behind him, he was turning more to the library than ever before.

Ben knocked once on the door and then pushed it open. George sat in his wheelchair at the far end of the room by a window. His white mustache was just as bristly as ever, but he was much slenderer than in Ben's recovered memories.

"Hi, Granddad," Ben said.

George looked up. "Oh, good. You're back. How are you feeling?"

"I'm healing up," Ben said. "My memory is back."

George nodded and smiled. "I'm glad. We were all worried. Having you snowed in up the mountain was downright scary." George nodded toward a chair. "Come have a seat."

"I was in good hands. Angelina took good care of me," Ben replied.

"I knew she would. She's a decent woman."

That was high praise coming from his gruff grandfather.

"How did it go?" George asked. "The offer, I mean. Did she take you up on it? Is she willing to sell?"

"No," Ben replied.

George sighed, pursing his lips so that his mustache bristled even more. "Do I need to talk to her? Is it a matter of hard feelings between the two of you?"

"No, it's not that," Ben replied. "The thing is, she doesn't want the money."

George squinted, then leaned back in his wheelchair. "Everyone wants the money. You could offer her more, you know. I mean, I didn't want you to go overboard, but if she needs more to sweeten the deal—"

"Offering more would insult her," Ben said. "Besides, I pretty much offered to give her anything she wanted and then more on top of it. I wasn't trying to save you any money at all—no offense."

"Really," George said dryly.

"She doesn't want the money, Granddad. She built that place up. She created something beautiful out of something painful. She's not interested in selling. It's that simple."

George nodded slowly. "So she wants to do things the hard way…"

The hard way. That was a threat, and Ben's blood simmered up in anger. Just to get his way? Just to set another sin to rest, he'd commit a new one? This was what happened time and time again with their family. They expected people to bend to their wishes, to soothe their feelings. His grandfather was the one who'd made the mistake, and now he was asking Angelina to bend over backward so that he could find some internal peace? George was willing to force her hand to make up for his youthful weakness?

This was what his family did—and he'd

always excused them. He defended them because he loved them. But it was wrong, and he wasn't accepting this behavior anymore! This pattern stopped with him.

"Granddad, I'm going to be really clear," Ben said, his voice growing hard. "If you try to manipulate, threaten or otherwise mess with Angelina's happiness, I'm going to come for you."

"What?" George barked out a laugh.

"I went along with your plans for the family business all this time out of respect for what *you* built, but that stops now," Ben retorted. "Mountain Springs Resort no longer belongs to this family, and it's off the table. I'm sorry that you have some painful memories associated with that land, but there won't be any strong-arming going on here."

George sighed. "She should sell it back. It's the right thing to do."

The right thing to do had sailed years ago. They'd all messed up, making mistake after mistake, and Ben was no different. He'd let the love of his life go because he couldn't separate his family from his marriage.

"And what if this is just business?" Ben asked. "What if this is about a woman's desire to build her brand? Have you ever sold a successful business back to the person you purchased it from for sentiment's sake? She'd be stupid to do it."

"It's stupid for her to pass on the kind of money we're willing to give her!" George shot back.

"It's her business," Ben said. "You have to respect it."

"It's never just business with Angelina Cunningham, and you know it," George said, softening his tone. "You love each other. That never stopped."

"So you'd take advantage of her feelings for me?" Ben snapped.

"Yes." George shrugged. "A little bit. But I like her. She's got spunk, and a good brain."

"You didn't like her when I was married to her," Ben replied.

"I thought she was a gold digger. I didn't believe that she had no idea who you were," George said. "I thought she was there to take you for everything she could. But she's impressed me. She's a decent ex-wife."

"She impressed you enough to try and get her out of the state?" Ben asked.

"Hey, you're the one incapable of moving on with your life if she's anywhere nearby," George said. "This isn't about her. It's about you! You're the heir. You're one who has to steer this ship after your father and I go. I thought you'd be better off if she was farther away, but maybe I'm wrong. Maybe she's the one you'll lie awake and think about when you're an old man like me." George was silent for a moment. "If you love her, do something about it. If you don't, then find someone else. It's pretty simple. But you've got to move forward, one way or another."

"It was the family pressure that drove us apart," Ben said.

"*My* pressure?" George asked.

"Some of it," Ben replied. "A new couple needs support, not criticism. And Angelina didn't deserve the treatment she got."

George's expression softened. "I'm sorry about that. We were rather hard on her. If that were Hilaria, she'd have stood up to us."

"Hilaria had your undivided support, and is considerably older than Angelina was," Ben said. "And just for argument's sake, if she had been Hilaria, I'd have been able to move on. Angelina's different."

George met his gaze. "Look, my greatest regret in life is being a coward. I didn't enlist because I was afraid for my safety. The war was still going strong when I turned eighteen in 1944, and I knew better men than me who'd gone off to fight, but I was scared to go. And then I didn't marry Eleanor because I was afraid of my family's censure. I didn't tell anyone about my daughter because I was afraid of their judgment. I was a coward. I tried to make up for that over the years, but it's the truth." George rubbed a hand over his chin. "So let me give you a piece of advice from an old man who knows. Don't live with regrets, Ben. Even if it means angering your family."

Ben smiled faintly at his grandfather's language. "My regrets are one thing. The problem is, Angelina has already had her taste of this family. She knows what she's up against, and she doesn't want more of you."

"Then it might be too late," George replied. "I'm not about to die to suit her."

"Of course not," Ben said, but his mind was already spinning. "There might be a way to even the score, though."

"I'm not sure I like the sound of that," George retorted. "I enjoy having the upper hand."

Angelina had said that she understood prenuptial agreements now, because she'd need to use one if she didn't want to risk everything she'd worked for if she ever got married again... Was that a sad change in her mindset, or a good thing that she could finally appreciate his position a little bit? Maybe there was a way to prove to her that things would be different...a King way to do it.

"Granddad, I'm going to meet up with one of the family lawyers," Ben said, "and I'm going to have some papers drawn up. I need you to look the other way while I do it."

"Oh?" George's bushy eyebrows went up.

"I don't want regrets," Ben said. "I need to try this."

"Don't do anything stupid." George met his gaze seriously. "Love is one thing, but you have a family to consider, too, as well as your own financial future."

"I know that," Ben said. "You're just going to have to trust me on this one."

"Tell me what you're going to do," George said.

"No."

George's eyebrows went up. "No?"

"I'm a grown man, Granddad," Ben said, softening his tone. "I'm not a fool. I know what I'm doing, and I know my responsibilities to my family and the employees who depend upon us. I'm not going to ruin anyone."

His grandfather looked away, then nodded.

"Best of luck, my boy," he said gruffly. "Regrets are heavier than you'd think. Just make sure you aren't chasing something down that has no hope. Think it through."

Ben already had—for thirteen long years. He looked at the time on his phone. He could still make it to the lawyer's office before the end of the business day. Angelina would need more than his word that things would be different. She'd need proof.

Ben was going to provide it.

CHAPTER SIXTEEN

ANGELINA'S MORNING HAD been a busy one. She'd been texting a little bit with Ben, even though she knew this wasn't good for her emotionally. She should get over him—be strong. But Ben had always been her weakness, and when he texted some sweet little thing like Thinking of you. I wanted to come see you later...how could she not answer? So Ben was due to come by later on today, and she found herself looking up every time that front door opened and let in cold air.

But she couldn't make her days about anticipating Ben, either. In some ways she was no better than a woman Elizabeth's age. All of her experience wasn't doing her any good.

Angelina had dressed in a woolen pantsuit with a silk blouse underneath, and she paused to look into the fireside room.

Several guests were in the chairs by the windows, watching the lake. A pair of eagles were circling, and then dove down, drawing everyone's attention as the observers murmured their appreciation of the wildlife and the amazing view.

But over by the fireplace, Warren was crouched with his ream of memoir pages. One by one, he crumpled them and pushed them into the fire. Angelina went over to the fireplace and sat on the chair closest to the doctor.

"What are you doing?" she asked.

"Burning my work," he replied.

"Why?" she chuckled. "Is this a writer thing—self-doubt and all that?"

"Maybe," he said. "But it's permanent. I deleted it off my laptop, too."

"Oh." She sobered. "What's going on?"

He sighed, crumpling another page and pushing it into the flames, where it blackened and curled in on itself. Then he got up with a grunt and a wince and moved back to the chair next to Angelina.

"I realized something in writing my memoir," Warren said. "First of all, it's boring. No one cares about the day-to-day minutia of a Denver doctor."

"Your family sure will," she said.

Warren shrugged. "More importantly, I realized that it's the story of one woman... Everything leading up to her, and the life I had with her. I thought I could look at my life through a different lens if I wrote it out, and prove that my life was about more than Louise, but it isn't."

"I'm sure you've helped a lot of people," Angelina said softly.

"And I couldn't have done it without her taking care of my home and my children… taking care of me." Warren leaned forward and pushed another sheet into the flames. "She's the one I was supposed to retire with. I was supposed to grow old next to her, and look back on the life we built together."

Angelina felt a wave of sadness.

"I know the feeling, Warren."

Warren added another couple of sheets to the blaze, watching them as the flames licked up the words and crumpled them into gray ash.

"What will you do?" Angelina asked. "Go back to work?"

He looked over at her thoughtfully. "I'm retired."

"Yes, but I'm sure a doctor can find somewhere he's needed," she replied.

"Do you want to help me burn this?" he

asked, and he passed her a section. "It's cathartic. You might like it."

Angelina accepted the pages, took the top sheet and pushed it into the fire. It did feel nice—there was something so elemental about burning things. She and Ben used to put twigs in the fire when they camped together...

There it was again, the memories of Ben chasing her.

She put a few more pages into the fire, watching them catch flame and go up in a short blaze. Life was shorter than anyone liked to think. In her youth, life felt so very long, but the years slipped past without her ever realizing how fast they went. How long until she was Warren's age, with her own regrets?

"What are you going to do?" Angelina asked.

"I'm going to burn this manuscript, and then I'm going to pack my bag and go home," he replied quietly.

Angelina was silent, thinking. She put the last of her pages into the fire, and Warren did the same. Sparks and little gray bits of burned paper floated upward toward the chimney.

"It took a hundred pages of fruitless writing for me to see what my life was about," Warren said. "And I'm going to go back to my old house, and I'm going to ask Louise if there is any way she could love me again."

"Even after she cheated?" Angelina asked.

"Yes." He nodded soberly. "I didn't say it would be easy, but it's what I have to do. For years, I wasn't the husband she needed, and I'm going to make the rest of my life about making that up to her. If she'll have me."

"What about Claude?"

"I'm going to steal her back." A smile flickered at the older man's lips. "Two can play that game."

Angelina felt tears prick her eyes. "You love her."

"I do." Warren nodded. "There's no replacing her." He rose to his feet and looked down at Angelina thoughtfully. "What are you going to do?"

Angelina was younger than Warren was, and she knew that logically there were options ahead of her. She could find another man to love and determine to forget Ben. But determining and actually succeeding were two different things.

"I'm in love with my ex-husband," she said.

"I know," he replied.

"I'm not sure I can do anything about it, though," she said. "It's complicated."

"It always is," Warren replied. "Don't let it get away from you, though. The years pass faster than you think, and you don't change as much as you hope you will. You see an old man in front of you, and you aren't wrong, but I just feel like a regular man. My body might not cooperate as well as it used to, but there is no great wisdom waiting for you at this age. Make better choices than I did."

"I'll try," Angelina said.

"And work isn't quite so fulfilling on the other end as you think it will be." He winked. "That's the last of my unsolicited advice."

Angelina smiled. "I'm glad you came, Warren. And thank you for helping me with Ben's head injury during the storm. I don't know what I would have done without you."

"My pleasure," he said with a smile. "Now, I'd best go pack. I don't want to waste daylight."

Angelina gave him a nod of farewell, and Warren headed out of the room and disappeared into the foyer. Angelina looked back toward the fire.

Warren Thomas's life was all about one woman, when it came right down to it. And

Angelina's life ever since that fateful cruise was all about one man. She couldn't deny that, and somehow she seemed powerless to change it.

"Angie?" It was a different voice behind her, and she caught her breath. She turned, and her voice felt stuck in her throat.

Ben stood in the doorway in his lambskin coat, his black cowboy hat cocked up so that his face was fully visible.

"Do you think we could talk?" he asked.

BEN COULD FEEL the thick envelope inside his coat. It had taken two hours of back-and-forth with the lawyer before he'd finally consented to draw up the papers. It went against legal advice, but Ben didn't care. It was right—he could feel it.

He followed Angelina down the hallway. She nodded to the guy in the other office as she passed him, and she opened her office door and gestured for Ben to go inside first.

It was a power move. She was the one in control here, and at Mountain Springs Resort, she was the boss. Ben went into her office and waited while she shut the door. She paused with her hand on the knob, and he couldn't help but smile.

"Angie?" he said.

Angelina turned toward him, and she sucked in a wavering breath. "If this is about your grandfather's baby girl, I have an idea."

"Okay?" Ben said.

"I've been thinking it over, and I could build a little chapel out there by the water. Maybe your grandfather could give us an approximate location. It can be a place for people to meditate… I could dedicate it to his daughter. Maybe just use a first name so that only he would know who she was, but he'd still know that she'd been honored. I have no interest in embarrassing anyone at this late stage."

It was kind…more than kind, it was generous. This was the Angelina he loved—she was a truly good woman.

"You'd do that?" Ben asked.

"Of course," she said.

Ben touched his coat, and his earlier courage started to wane. Was he being crazy here to hope for another chance with her?

"Angie, I love you. And I need to say this, so just hear me out. I have loved you ever since I saw you the first time on that ship. I'm not getting over you, either, apparently. I tried for the better part of thirteen years, but there is no one else for me. I know what I want. I want a life with you."

Angelina started to shake her head, but he caught her hand.

"You love me, right?" he asked.

"Of course, I do," she said. "But your family—"

"I have a solution there," he said, and he pulled the envelope out of his coat.

"What's this?" she asked, accepting the envelope.

"Open it."

Angelina opened the flap and pulled out the documents. She scanned them, and as she did, her face grew paler. She looked up at him in surprise.

"Ben?"

"That's a prenuptial agreement," he said. "But if you look at the details of that agreement, it's heavily in your favor. If you're unhappy with me, or if my family makes you miserable, pull the trigger on that agreement. Divorce me again, and you'll get fifty percent of everything in my name. And this resort stays in your name regardless. I can't touch it."

"Ben..."

"Do you want to make it sixty percent?

Seventy?" he asked. "I'm happy to change the numbers, because we aren't going to need this. I'll make you happy—I promise you. But you said you'd need a prenup if you were going to get married again, and I understand. You have a lot to risk, but this is my proof that I'll live every single day of my life making you as happy as I possibly can. And this—" he reached out and tapped the pages "—this is going to keep my family in line, too. If they want to keep the fortune together, then they'll make sure they keep you happy, too."

"And if they just disinherit you?" she asked.

"Then we run the resort together," he said with a shrug. "It'll all stay in your name, and I'll sign anything you want to protect that. But I'm pretty sure they won't just write me out. We're more human than you think."

Angelina dropped the papers onto her desk and slipped into his arms. He pulled her close against him and buried his lips in her hair. *This* was home—in her arms. The ranch, the mansions...none of it came close to making him feel so complete as this woman did.

"I love you, too," she whispered.

"Will you marry me?" he asked quietly, resting his cheek against the top of her head.

She was silent, and he felt like his heart

stopped beating while he waited for her·answer. Then he felt her nod.

"Yes."

He held her close, relief flooding through him. This was what he needed—Angelina in his arms. He needed her as his wife, and when she looked up at him, Ben covered her lips with his.

This kiss was everything he'd tried to deny these past thirteen years, and it was his promise for every day of the future. He'd tried living without her—it wasn't worth the effort.

Angelina pulled back. "Are you sure about this?"

"Positive," he said.

"I want a wedding, then," she said. "The one we never had. I want my parents there, and your family, and our friends, and... I know exactly who my bridesmaids will be—"

"Don't worry about it," he said with a slow smile. "Angie, my family will be there. And they'll be happy, and well-behaved. They will treat you like their best friend, and they'll be incredibly supportive of our marriage. I can personally guarantee it."

They'd be on eggshells by the time he was finished with them. He'd make sure they understood exactly how much was at stake here—and what it would take to keep the King fortune intact. One happy woman—it really wasn't so hard.

"Really?" Angelina laughed softly. "You're very confident about this."

"We might need to make that seventy percent of everything in my name that goes to you just to be positive, but yes. Trust me. It's going to be different. I can't go another day without you, and you'll never have reason to use that prenup. Okay? It's you and me. That's a promise."

Tears welled in her eyes. "Oh, Ben… I love you."

He lowered his lips over hers once more. He'd marry her again, and he'd make her happy this time. He'd be hers, heart and soul. He had been all this time anyway. This would just make it official.

EPILOGUE

JUST BEFORE ANGELINA'S June wedding, she got a card in the mail from Elizabeth. She'd been wondering what had happened with the young woman, but of course, it wasn't her business to pry. Angelina had been right— Elizabeth had broken up with Brad on the drive back to Denver, and upon graduation, she'd taken her biology degree and joined her sister at her veterinary practice. She wanted to go on to veterinary school the next fall.

"I just want to thank you for showing me what a confident woman looks like," Elizabeth wrote. *"One day, I hope I can pay this forward and I'll encourage another younger woman like you did for me."*

That was the secret to a life well lived. Angelina had learned it the hard way, but that wisdom didn't have to be picked up with pain. If each woman reached down to a younger woman and gave her the benefit of her experience, the world would be a brighter place.

And when those encouraging women got together on a regular basis over dinner with a nice bottle of wine and a mutual determination to build each other up, it truly made all the difference.

Angelina didn't opt for traditional white for this wedding. Instead, she bought a pink ombré gown that started as the very lightest pink at the top and darkened to a deep coral at her feet. She wore her hair down with a glittering diamond clip holding her veil in place. Angelina had a feeling that her grandmother would have approved of both the dress and the husband. Ben had lived up to Grandma's standards at the very least—he'd made a considerate, kind and deeply decent ex-husband. Angelina was sure that somewhere, Grandma was happy for her.

The wedding ceremony was held outside in a park in town, and this time the seats were packed with friends and family. The vows were heartfelt, but Angelina hardly remembered them for the emotion of the moment. Ben stood in his tuxedo in front of all of the people they loved most, and he'd vowed to be hers. Angelina's parents sat proudly in the front row. Honestly, it had taken some time for her mother to make her peace with Ben again, but he'd been patient, and by the time the wedding rolled around, she'd welcomed him back into the family with the stipulation that if he broke her daughter's heart again, she'd strangle him herself. Ben had told her in all solemnity, *You'd have to get in line. My father might beat you to it.*

Angelina wasn't worried, though, because this time it would be different. The Kings were significantly more polite to her now, and Karl King had even given Angelina a wedding gift of an upgraded electrical generator for her lodge. It was the kind of gift that told Angelina that Karl had finally accepted her. It was a very King kind of present, and she'd given him a spontaneous hug.

"I thought it would be useful," Karl said gruffly. "And it's because…well, storms come, and I like how prepared you are. I want you to know that we're proud of all you've accomplished. Really proud."

Angelina was once more a King, but this time, she was also their equal. Money wasn't everything.

The wedding photos were taken down by the lake with Angelina and Ben surrounded by the soaring beauty of those mountains and the plunging depths of their love for each other. Family photos were taken, as well as one very special picture of Angelina and the women from her dinner club. They'd had a few group photos taken at Belle and Phillip's wedding earlier that year, but Angelina wanted one from her own. These women had gotten her this far—they'd buoyed each other up when they needed it most, and in every way that mattered, they were family.

The wedding reception was held at Mountain Springs Resort, of course, and when everyone arrived George had asked to be wheeled down to a particular spot by the lake, just past the trails. His granddaughter pushed him out there, and Angelina had watched him from a distance as he sat, his head bowed, paying honor to the baby girl he loved and lost.

The women from the dinner club all sat together with their men at one table in the back of the room, three shared bottles of champagne on the table, a litter of napkins and finger foods and smiles on their faces. Belle and Phillip only had eyes for each other. Gayle and Matthew were in animated conversation with Jen and Nick. Renata and her now-fiancé Sebastian seemed to be fielding phone calls from her children, and Taryn and

Noah were slow dancing to the soft music played by the live band. Melanie sat with a flute of champagne in one hand and Logan's arm draped around her as they listened to the music. Angelina sat with Ben and watched her friends, and her heart swelled with gratefulness for this generous group of women who had made the decision to live their lives to the fullest in the face of all the unfairness and pain that life could throw in their direction. They were her truest inspiration.

These friends had made such a difference in Angelina's life, and as she scanned the room, spotting her parents talking with Karl, George King dozing in his wheelchair, friends and family on both sides talking and eating, laughing and dancing, she reached over and took Ben's hand in hers.

"We did it," Ben whispered in her ear.

"Hmm?" She looked toward him and found his glittering gaze locked on her.

"We had a real wedding, and everyone behaved." Ben lifted her hand to his lips and pressed a kiss against her fingers. "I told you I could pull it off."

"Your grandfather told me that I bring some spunk to the family," Angelina said. "I'm going to take that as a compliment."

"It is a compliment." Ben squeezed her hand. "Trust me on that. It didn't even take that prenup to soften him up. He likes you. You've proven yourself to be a better person than they imagined. I'm the lucky one here."

"I love you, Ben," she said, and she leaned over to kiss his lips softly.

"I love you, too," he murmured. "You're the only one for me. You know that, right?"

"I do," she said, and she leaned her head against his shoulder.

"Dance with me." Ben stood and tugged her to her feet. "Just one more dance before we abandon everyone and I take you upstairs, Mrs. Cunningham-King."

Ben shot her an incorrigible look, and Angelina laughed. She gathered her long dress up into one hand and followed her husband out onto the dance floor, where Taryn and Noah were still dancing. Other couples followed as Ben swung Angelina into his arms, resting his cheek next to hers. Their heartbeats seemed to come into rhythm together as they moved to the instrumental version of a pop ballad. It didn't matter what song was playing so long as Angelina was in Ben's arms.

This place—this resort, the lake, the mountains that soared up around it—was healing. It was like some sort of ancient power came bubbling up from the underwater springs that fed the deep mountain lake. Angelina could never be convinced that there wasn't a sort of magic in this spot. But it was a magic that required the participation of honest hearts to bring it to fruition.

With her cheek against her husband's, she spun past her guests, and Ben pulled her close and slowed again. This was not the beginning of her life, but it was the start of a commitment that she would protect with every ounce of her being.

She looked out the window at the summer sun setting behind the mountain peaks. She felt a wave of gratefulness so deep that it felt like it pulsed with the very heartbeat of Mountain Springs. "Let's go start our life together," she whispered, tugging him toward the door.

Ben smiled in response. "Let's go."

* * * * *

Get 4 FREE REWARDS!

We'll send you 2 FREE Books plus 2 FREE Mystery Gifts.

Love Inspired Suspense books showcase how courage and optimism unite in stories of faith and love in the face of danger.

FREE Value Over $20

YES! Please send me 2 FREE Love Inspired Suspense novels and my 2 FREE mystery gifts (gifts are worth about $10 retail). After receiving them, if I don't wish to receive any more books, I can return the shipping statement marked "cancel." If I don't cancel, I will receive 6 brand-new novels every month and be billed just $5.24 each for the regular-print edition or $5.99 each for the larger-print edition in the U.S., or $5.74 each for the regular-print edition or $6.24 each for the larger-print edition in Canada. That's a savings of at least 13% off the cover price. It's quite a bargain! Shipping and handling is just 50¢ per book in the U.S. and $1.25 per book in Canada.* I understand that accepting the 2 free books and gifts places me under no obligation to buy anything. I can always return a shipment and cancel at any time. The free books and gifts are mine to keep no matter what I decide.

Choose one: ☐ **Love Inspired Suspense Regular-Print** (153/353 IDN GNWN) ☐ **Love Inspired Suspense Larger-Print** (107/307 IDN GNWN)

Name (please print)

Address   Apt. #

City   State/Province   Zip/Postal Code

Email: Please check this box ☐ if you would like to receive newsletters and promotional emails from Harlequin Enterprises ULC and its affiliates. You can unsubscribe anytime.

Mail to the **Harlequin Reader Service:**
IN U.S.A.: P.O. Box 1341, Buffalo, NY 14240-8531
IN CANADA: P.O. Box 603, Fort Erie, Ontario L2A 5X3

Want to try 2 free books from another series? Call 1-800-873-8635 or visit www.ReaderService.com.

*Terms and prices subject to change without notice. Prices do not include sales taxes, which will be charged (if applicable) based on your state or country of residence. Canadian residents will be charged applicable taxes. Offer not valid in Quebec. This offer is limited to one order per household. Books received may not be as shown. Not valid for current subscribers to Love Inspired Suspense books. All orders subject to approval. Credit or debit balances in a customer's account(s) may be offset by any other outstanding balance owed by or to the customer. Please allow 4 to 6 weeks for delivery. Offer available while quantities last.

Your Privacy—Your information is being collected by Harlequin Enterprises ULC, operating as Harlequin Reader Service. For a complete summary of the information we collect, how we use this information and to whom it is disclosed, please visit our privacy notice located at corporate.harlequin.com/privacy-notice. From time to time we may also exchange your personal information with reputable third parties. If you wish to opt out of this sharing of your personal information, please visit readerservice.com/consumerschoice or call 1-800-873-8635. **Notice to California Residents**—Under California law, you have specific rights to control and access your data. For more information on these rights and how to exercise them, visit corporate.harlequin.com/california-privacy.

LIS21R2

#403 THE WRONG COWBOY
The Cowboys of Garrison, Texas
by Sasha Summers
Everyone knows Crawleys and Briscoes don't get along.
When horse whisperer Mabel Briscoe helps Jensen Crawley's
daughter overcome her fear of animals, Mabel and Jensen
are the talk of the town. What happens when they fall for each
other unexpectedly?

#404 WORTH THE RISK
Butterfly Harbor Stories • by Anna J. Stewart
Cautious Alethea Costas is still grieving the loss of her best
friend when a wrong turn throws her into the arms of
Declan Cartwright—a daredevil race car driver who could
possibly help her embrace life.

#405 A RANCHER'S PROMISE
Bachelor Cowboys • by Lisa Childs
Rancher Jake Haven has always done the responsible thing.
Now that means raising his orphaned nephews. When his ex
Katie O'Brien-Morris returns home with her young son, can he
let past wants distract him from family needs?

#406 A NEW YEAR'S EVE PROPOSAL
Cupid's Crossing • by Kim Findlay
Architect Trevor Emerson doesn't trust anyone after an
accident at his last job site...which makes it tough to renovate
a local mill with Andie Kozak! As a woman, the contractor has
been questioned too often. Can working together change them
both?

Visit
ReaderService.com
Today!

As a valued member of the Harlequin Reader Service, you'll find these benefits and more at ReaderService.com:

- Try 2 free books from any series
- Access risk-free special offers
- View your account history & manage payments
- Browse the latest Bonus Bucks catalog

Don't miss out!

If you want to stay up-to-date on the latest at the Harlequin Reader Service and enjoy more content, make sure you've signed up for our monthly News & Notes email newsletter. Sign up online at ReaderService.com or by calling Customer Service at 1-800-873-8635.